"You caught the

"You know what that means," Bliss teased. "So who's measuring you for a harness? That little blonde who kept shooting daggers at me at the fund-raiser?"

"I'm, er, currently unattached," Logan said coldly.

Bliss was enjoying his discomfort too much for caution. Moving closer, she dragged a finger along his strong jawline.

His eyes were hot. Hers sizzled. His mouth twisted in a sensuous line. She licked her dry lips.

"Don't play this game," Logan warned. But he was pulling her closer.

Bliss felt her bones melt and her belly heat as his gaze devoured her. What she felt was want—pure, primal, simple female desire for a dangerous man. She wanted to move closer, to melt against him, to find out if it was still as good as it used to be.... But did she dare?

Dear Reader,

Happy New Year! We look forward to bringing you another year of captivating, deeply satisfying romances that will surely melt your heart!

January's THAT SPECIAL WOMAN! title revisits the Window Rock community for the next installment of Cheryl Reavis's FAMILY BLESSINGS miniseries. *Tenderly* is about a vulnerable young woman's quest to uncover her heritage— and the once-in-a-lifetime love she discovers with a brave Navajo police officer. Don't miss this warm, wonderful story!

It's a case of unrequited love—or is it?—in *The Nine-Month Marriage,* the first story in Christine Rimmer's delightful new series, CONVENIENTLY YOURS. This starry-eyed heroine can't believe her ears when the man she worships proposes a marriage—even if it's just for their baby's sake. And the red-hot passion continues when a life-threatening crisis brings a tempestuous couple together in *Little Boy Blue* by Suzannah Davis—book three in the SWITCHED AT BIRTH miniseries.

Also this month, fate reunites a family in *A Daddy for Devin* by Jennifer Mikels. And an unlikely duo find solace in each other's arms when they are snowbound together, but a secret threatens to drive them apart in *Her Child's Father* by Christine Flynn. We finish off the month with a poignant story about a heroine who falls in love with her ex-groom's brother, but her child's paternity could jeopardize their happiness in *Brother of the Groom* by Judith Yates.

I hope this New Year brings you much health and happiness! Enjoy this book and all our books to come!

Sincerely,

Tara Gavin
Senior Editor and Editorial Coordinator

Please address questions and book requests to:
Silhouette Reader Service
U.S.: 3010 Walden Ave., P.O. Box 1325, Buffalo, NY 14269
Canadian: P.O. Box 609, Fort Erie, Ont. L2A 5X3

SUZANNAH DAVIS

LITTLE BOY BLUE

Silhouette®

SPECIAL ▼ EDITION®

Published by Silhouette Books

America's Publisher of Contemporary Romance

SILHOUETTE BOOKS

ISBN 0-373-24149-6

LITTLE BOY BLUE

Printed in U.S.A.

SUZANNAH DAVIS

Award-winning author Suzannah Davis is a Louisiana native who loves small-town life, daffodils and writing stories full of love and laughter. A firm believer in happy endings, she has three children.

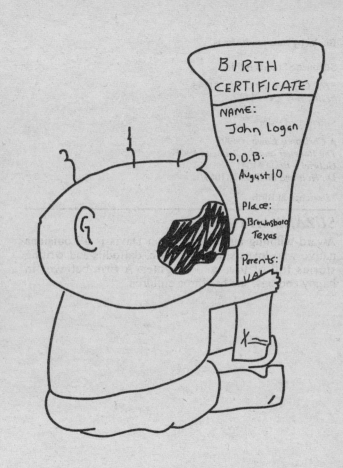

Prologue

"Jack, are you coming in?"

"Be right there, darlin'."

With a grin of satisfaction, "Black Jack" Campbell propped his bare heels on the stucco wall forming the balcony railing of the luxurious Acapulco villa and hung up the telephone. From this cliff top vantage, the Pacific Ocean spread out before him like a shimmering tapestry, the tangerine orb of the setting sun just touching the purple water on the horizon and limning the sky with hues of magenta and gold. The soft sounds of a woman moving around inside the suite, doing whatever soft feminine things women liked to do before a night on the town, including humming snatches of an old Spanish love song, made his grin under his grizzled mustache grow even bigger and his groin tighten in anticipation.

He reached for the cigarette still smouldering in the

ashtray and took another drag. Life was good, even for a sixty-five-year-old oilman who'd been around the block a few too many times. But by damn, for a man who'd lived hard, worked hard, and built Campbell Drilling from the ground up into a million-dollar company folks respected, it felt good to take a few days off every once in a while for a little pampering.

Of course, seemed whenever he sneaked off for a little adult R & R with a sassy lady, a crisis of some kind inevitably erupted, and this time was no exception.

Kids. Jack shook his head. The years had turned his black hair nearly silver, but he'd earned every gray hair, and his locks were still thick. In only a pair of khaki shorts, his tanned chest bare, it was clear to anyone looking that his six-foot-plus physique was still lean and vigorous enough to turn a head or two.

Still, he didn't raise a pair of twin sons and a foster daughter without putting some miles on himself. Jack fingered the creases beside his mustache. *Character lines,* he thought, echoing his lady's assessment. Sign of a mature man.

And speaking of maturity, he wished his own children would get their acts together. Not that he wasn't proud of them—they all were competent and established in their professions. It was their personal lives that concerned him.

Jack flicked the finished cigarette over the railing. Boys were easy. All Logan and Russ had needed was some occasional discipline to keep them in line, not that he'd had much opportunity to mold Logan when he'd gone to live with his mother after the divorce. Jack grimaced. Logan, *golden boy.* The high society life had left its mark, but his attorney son had proven more than once in court he knew how to go for the jugular, so

Jack guessed things had turned out all right on that account.

But daughters, even ones acquired by accident, well, that was something else entirely. Jack had to admit he'd been totally bamboozled more than once by the workings of his adopted daughter's mind. But this time....

Jack grinned again. Yes, sir, this time things were going to be different. All Bliss needed was a shove in the right direction. What would come of it—well, he could only wait and see.

"Jack?" The sultry voice drifted from inside the plush room. "If you don't come shower now, we're going to be late."

He stood up, easing his way through the door toward the shapely brunette in a gauzy white peignoir. His voice was suddenly husky. "Darlin', something tells me that shower might make us late anyhow."

Dark eyes flashed an invitation. "Why don't we find out?"

Chapter One

"Didn't you hear me, Logan? I think we ought to get married."

Logan Campbell's amber gaze raked the woman clinging to his tuxedo-clad arm with cool amusement. "But then I might have to pay some attention to you, Cammela."

The blonde's perfectly etched lips formed a pout as sultry as the thick New Orleans air, and the family emeralds dripping from her earlobes and circling her creamy neck winked as though mocking her ambitions. "You really are a bastard."

"You wouldn't find me nearly so interesting if I weren't."

Cammela Chastan's brown eyes flashed with thwarted temper, but she knew when to back off. "It must be tedious to be right all the time."

Her laugh was a trill of well-practiced flirtation that

rose gratingly, in Logan's estimation, above the murmur of the elite cadre of guests crowding the sprawling halls and manicured grounds of the historic St. Charles Avenue showplace known as Gaspard House. His mother's annual September fund-raiser for the New Orleans Symphony was again a rousing success, and he'd grown accustomed to the periodic invasion of his privacy for such a worthy cause. Valerie Gaspard Campbell was still the acknowledged queen of polite society in the Big Easy.

What was tedious was Cammela's growing possessiveness. With a sigh, Logan admitted that it was past time to disentangle himself from their liaison. While it had been pleasant—he grimaced at the pallid word—perhaps *convenient* was a more appropriate description, for passion certainly hadn't been a hallmark of their relationship, it was time to move on, just as he'd moved on with every relationship during his thirty-five years of bachelorhood.

It was a state of affairs that suited him despite the fact that according to friends and family, the blue blood in Cammela's veins made them perfect for each other. Her perfect and artfully streaked blond hair, perfect aristocratic profile, perfect family connections and perfect Bryn Mawr education all added up to the perfect mate for a man still on the rise. The problem was that perfection was stifling, and Cammela, for all her assets, had begun to bore him—not that Logan ever let matters of the heart rule him. In fact, there were many among his acquaintances, especially the feminine half, who'd be quick to say that Logan Campbell didn't have a heart, which was one reason it had been so easy for him to break so many so often.

After tonight, it was clear that he'd have to bring

things to a refined and cultivated end. It shouldn't be hard. After all, he'd been honest with Cammela from the beginning, and she had only to look at her predecessors to know that he wasn't the marrying kind. He wondered briefly why women always thought they could change a man just because they got a notion to build a nest. Of course, knowing Cammela as he did, it was as much as his ability to provide a gold-plated nest as any real feeling for him on her part that interested her. So he didn't even have to feel guilty on that account. Not that he would have, at any rate.

Logan snagged two flutes of champagne from a passing waiter and handed one to his companion, showing a pair of dimples that had enflamed more than one feminine imagination. "Being right has its compensations."

"Such as a one-point-two-million-dollar settlement against Merchant Petroleum?" a familiar voice said from behind him.

The swarthy man whose large hand clapped Logan's shoulder in congratulation bore the stamp of old Louisiana Creole blood in his dark hair and eyes. Though his evening wear was custom-made, he wore it awkwardly, a consideration that no one noticed because of his easy friendliness and volubility.

"Hello, Remy," Logan said to Remy Hebert, a long-time friend and the owner of his own very successful public relations firm.

"Heartiest felicitations, my man. Heard the Golden Boy wowed 'em again."

Logan concealed a grimace. "Thanks. Just doing my job."

"Golden Boy" was an old sobriquet from his youthful heyday on the tennis circuit, a name he'd never liked. With his sandy hair and golden brown eyes, the moniker had fit, but never suited him personally, and it irritated him that the nickname stuck.

Maybe it was because his father had never truly approved of his son's "pretty-boy" sport. "Black Jack" Campbell had been a football buff himself, overtly disappointed that neither of his twin sons had pursued the game. Logan's auburn-headed brother, Russ, had never had the opportunity for organized sports, growing up from pillar to post, following the wildcatter's life all over the world with their dad after Jack and Valerie split when the brothers were barely nine. Even though Logan had been a champion on the amateur circuit, even having the opportunity to go pro, Jack's not-so-unspoken disapproval made Logan choose law school instead— not that Jack had understood that choice, either. Sometimes Logan thought he'd spent his whole life vying for Jack's approval.

With an inward scowl, Logan thrust the thought aside. He was what he was because of his upbringing, and he gave thanks that he'd had the more settled existence, the best schools in New Orleans, rubbing elbows with the moneyed and powerful echelons. At the edict of divorced parents, the brothers had traded out, Russ spending the summers with their mom so that she could try to knock off some of her wilder child's rough edges—and generally failing, Logan spending his summers on a rough-and-ready run with Jack. All in all, the system had never worked worth a damn. Maybe that was why he and Russ had never really gotten along and still didn't.

Logan pushed aside the edgy feeling thinking about his family always evoked as Remy grinned at Cammela.

"You're looking exceptionally beautiful tonight, Cammie. This outlaw treating you right?"

"Logan is a dog when it comes to women, didn't you know?" she answered, her smile suddenly brittle.

"Ouch." Remy's eyes gleamed with appreciation as he took in her slender curves under her slinky designer gown. "Maybe you should spend some time with a man who'll appreciate you, *chère*."

"Maybe you're right." Cammela's glance toward Logan was defiant, as she transferred her hand to Remy's arm. "I'd love to dance."

"My pleasure." Remy lifted an eyebrow, silently asking the question, one male to the other.

Logan deftly relieved Cammela of her glass and made a sweeping gesture. "Enjoy yourselves." If Cammela had expected an argument, some sort of male territorial thing, Logan thought wryly, she was going to be disappointed. In fact, as far as he was concerned, if Remy was interested, all the better.

The woman's lips tightened as she turned away with Remy. Logan gave silent thanks and made a mental note to send her roses the next day. No one could say he didn't know how to break off a relationship with class.

Logan mingled with the elegant crowd, wending his way with a word here, a small joke there, doing his part as host and generally hiding his growing ennui. The crystal chandelier in the marble-floored foyer glimmered on the city's most elite citizens, but somehow they all seemed bloodless caricatures, people bound by the hallmarks of the society in which they moved. And while Logan acknowledged that he was a part of that society and depended on the business and social contacts such events as this one brought, there were few here—other than Remy—he really cared to know.

In fact, at this moment, he'd much rather be in his office poring over the latest information his private in-

vestigator had unearthed in regard to an old grudge his
father was determined to see revenged. Jack had made
it a priority, and that challenge was good enough to fire
Logan up for the fight. Yes, sir, if Thomas Barnette,
candidate for Texas state senate, thought that the Campbells were ever going to let bygones be bygones over a
pile of money they'd lost because of Tom's insurance
scheme a decade ago, then he had another think coming.
The powerful Texas Lattimer family had also been a
patsy to Barnette's shenanigans, and Ben Lattimer and
his son, Jake, weren't the kind of cowboys to forget a
grudge, either. Logan had seen them not a month ago
when Jake had married a Dallas cop by the name of
Shelby Hartman.

Funny thing. A few weeks ago Jake Lattimer had
been all set to wed another woman and was left standing
at the altar when his then-fiancée had eloped with another man—a man who'd turned out to be Jake's
long-lost identical twin brother, Texas Ranger Zach
Rawlings. Even now, Logan wasn't sure how things had
been settled, but everything had appeared pretty cordial
at the reception at the Lazy L Ranch. Zach even ended
up as Jake's best man. Logan didn't know if he would
have had the magnanimity for such a gesture, but he
supposed it took all kinds.

At any rate, Ben Lattimer, Jake's adoptive father, had
raised several interesting questions—not only about
Tom Barnette but about the night the twins were
born—and Zach Rawlings had even steered a Dallas
reporter onto the case. Laura Ramirez was a spitfire with
a reputation for integrity and tenacity, and Logan could
feel it in his gut that things were coming to a head.

Now as he made small talk with a silver-haired couple whose net worth rivaled the Rockefellers', he let his

mind wander pleasantly over the ramifications of exposing Barnette for the liar and fraud he was. Yes, sir, there were some things in life more satisfying than money.

"Excuse me, sir." A liveried butler with a harried expression bent to whisper in Logan's ear.

"What is it, Dalton?"

The servant looked flustered. "A small, er, altercation at the entrance. You'd best come."

Logan excused himself, a frown marring his brow. They had plenty of staff to handle every emergency, so what did they need him for?

Stepping around a group of simpering debutantes, Logan strode toward the Malliard-carved walnut archway delineating the front entrance, one of Gaspard House's most historic architectural details. A cluster of bodies milled under the arch, mostly wait staff in various attitudes of confusion, and Logan's scowl darkened. His family had paid good money so that this kind of thing would be avoided. The group parted and Logan felt a jolt like a punch in his imported silk cummerbund.

The woman was tall, only a couple of inches less than Logan's six-foot frame, and curvaceous in a way, under her faded blue jeans, that brought forth terms like Amazon and Valkyrie. A sheer waterfall of shimmering platinum blond hair—an unlikely mix of gold and silver that could never have come from a bottle—fell to her waist. She wore a chambray shirt with the arms torn out, and a large hand-worked silver belt buckle and dangling earrings that reflected the argent strands in her straight hair. There was a frayed hole in one knee of her jeans, and she sported a custom-made pair of Rocketbuster boots covered with red and green chili peppers.

Her face was the kind that haunted men's fantasies, the cheekbones high, an unusual, slightly arched, no-nonsense nose, the mouth lush and peachy. But it was her expression that startled and intrigued, at once cocky and mocking, and as she stepped through the door—sauntering inside as if she were stepping onto her own private yacht—every woman present paled in comparison.

"I don't care if you're the Queen of Sheba, Charlie," she told the majordomo in a musical voice that had charmed South American headhunters and cowed the most chauvinistic men. "I was invited to this shindig, and I've got the invitation to prove it."

In one fell swoop, Logan's boredom vaporized, his blood pressure skyrocketed, and passions he didn't even know he'd suppressed boiled over like molten lava.

Damn it all. *Bliss.*

The butler's hiss of protest was no more than the buzz of an irritating insect, dismissed the moment Bliss Abernathy looked up and met a pair of hostile, lion-tawny eyes.

Oh, Lord. Here we go again.

Tossing her mane of hair over her shoulder, she kept her smile insolent. Ignoring the flustered servant, she used her best hip-swiveling saunter to approach Logan Campbell. Her sapphire eyes shone with mocking humor, and her voice took on an intimate huskiness that was almost a purr, guaranteed to get a certain man's goat.

"You're a hard man to get an appointment with, Counselor." His jaw tautened.

"Bliss. This is an unexpected...pleasure."

Her gurgle of laughter told him what she thought of

that lie. Flicking a finger over his satin-edged lapel, she murmured, "Still slick as goose grease, too."

"Charming, as always, especially when you crash a party." With a nod, he dismissed the relieved butler, then his glance flicked over her and his lips twisted. "Don't you own a dress?"

She shrugged, tilting her head only slightly to meet his antagonistic gaze. "I figured Campbell Drilling's more than sizable donation would get me through the door no matter what I wore. I've never been the sequins and pearls type, have I?"

"Mud and sweet crude," he muttered.

Her laugh exploded in pure delight. "So the Golden Boy hasn't forgotten his roots. Russ will be so proud." She stroked a finger down his lean cheek. "By the way, it's good to see you, too, amigo."

Logan's reaction was snake-fast, his fingers clamping on her wrist. For a fraction of a second, they were immobile, two wills battling as golden brown eyes warred with blue. Bliss prayed that he couldn't feel the way her pulse thrummed erratically beneath his touch. Damn the man. That would be the ultimate humiliation.

But she hadn't grown up around men in a thousand rough honky-tonks in a hundred different countries around countless wildcat rigs—not looking the way she did, anyway—without learning a thing or two about protecting herself. She'd found out a long time ago, it was all a matter of attitude. If you showed an ounce of weakness, then it was all over.

She didn't intend to show Logan Campbell she had any weakness where he was concerned. Not if she had to swallow strychnine or dance naked in St. Pete's nave. Because if he guessed she had any vulnerabilities, then she might not be able to get exactly what she wanted from him. And she was too tired and too soul-weary to waste any time being anything less than ruthless when it came to getting what she wanted.

Bliss gauged Logan, assessing him. Not much had changed in the eighteen months since their paths had last crossed. He was suave, charismatic, too good-looking for his own good, even though his features were saved from mere prettiness by a strong nose and square chin he shared with his brother. The tiny space between his perfect front teeth gave him just the right touch of little-boy charm. His physique was lean, without the bulk she was accustomed to in oil-field workers, but panther graceful and just as inherently dangerous.

And no man had a right to look as good as he did in a tuxedo.

They'd never been friends, not like she and Russ were, not since the day her father, Chuck Abernathy, had died in an oil rig accident. That day, Jack Campbell had taken a sobbing and devastated nine-year-old orphan into his brawny arms and promised her he'd never leave, that she, the daughter of his partner, would always be a part of his family, which included inheriting almost fourteen-year-old twin brothers.

While she and Russ Campbell had been buddies or soul mates, hanging around the drilling sites together long before tragedy made them unofficial siblings, Logan had always made her feel the outsider. That, taken with his and Russ's unrelenting rivalry and antagonism, had been enough for Bliss to choose sides early on. She'd made Russ her brother in spirit, and her own fierce protectiveness had clearly placed Logan in the enemy camp. They'd rubbed each other the wrong way from the day Bliss had salted his bunk with itching powder. The feud hadn't abated even though with adulthood, the rules had changed to something more nervy and dangerous and, at times, explosive.

So she wasn't exactly thrilled that she'd had to beard the lion in his own den, but that wasn't going to stop her. After all, it was Jack's idea. *You're a big girl. Take care of it.* No, sir. And she hadn't flown the company jet all the way in from Alamagordo just to let a shiny society shindig put a damper on her determination.

"Where's your mom?" she asked brightly. "I want to say hello."

With a practiced move, she twisted free of Logan's grip. "And I'm starved. You got some eats in this joint?"

Before Logan had a chance to react, she was striding toward the high-ceilinged dining room, liking the way he was forced to trail in her wake. She attracted a considerable amount of rather shocked, covert attention, but she held her head up with her usual aplomb. If there was one thing she was accustomed to, it was creating a stir.

She'd been to Gaspard House many times with Russ and Jack, always as a visitor, but she hadn't forgotten her way around or a detail of the elegant interior. The first time she'd seen the place, she thought she'd stepped into Cinderella's castle, but she knew now that no fairy-tale edifice could rival the sheer history and elegance of the home. She noted a few decorative changes Valerie had made, and the flower arrangements and potted palms imported for tonight's festivities added a touch of the exotic, but nothing could disguise the fact that despite its historic importance, this was a home, a place of permanence and stability for one lucky family. Bliss stifled a sigh of envy, then resolutely picked up a buffet plate.

"God, I'm glad your mother leans toward real food," she said, piling spicy chicken and Andouille sausage jambalaya onto the delicate china plate. Candles blazed in the elaborate sterling epergnes on each end of the long, linen-covered table, and a sparkling ice sculpture of a tower of musical instruments rose from the center. "I can't stand those Scarlett O'Hara I-can't-eat-barbecue-because-Ashley-won't-think-I'm-a-lady types, can you?"

"Never gave it much thought," Logan replied, offering her a napkin as she shoveled rice into her mouth.

She let her gaze drift over the assorted females daintily nibbling petit fours and watercress sandwiches with their tiny sips of champagne. "Pains in the butt."

"Your way with words never ceases to amaze me."

"I can curse in over twenty languages. Wanna sample?"

"Spare me—or at least my mother's guests," Logan warned. She grinned and stepped up to a smiling African-American man in impeccable white livery who was shucking fresh oysters iced down in a real pirogue.

"Ten to one, no one would understand anyway."

Bliss accepted the plate of succulent shellfish with a grateful nod, then dragged one plump morsel through a dollop of horseradish-rich cocktail sauce with a tiny fork and gulped it down. She closed her eyes in ecstasy at the salty bite. "God in heaven. Why did I stay away from this town so long?"

Logan was watching her, his expression closed so that she couldn't tell if the gleam in his eye was disdain or admiration. "I see you're still a woman of considerable...appetites."

The innuendo wasn't lost on her, and she let her smile

turn sultry, sexy, challenging. "Only one way for you to find out for sure, amigo."

His jaw hardened. "I've had just about enough—"

"Bliss!" A dark-haired woman in a long green satin gown flew across the room and hurled herself into Bliss's arms. "Goodness! Did you just drop out of the sky, darling?"

"You could say that."

Laughing, gulping, wiping her mouth, Bliss set aside her plate and hugged Valerie Gaspard Campbell, returning the busses on each cheek with real affection. "You look terrific, Val!"

"And you kissed the Blarney stone when you were just a wee young 'un."

"No, it's true. You just keep getting younger."

Valerie's dark eyes and petite figure would have been the envy of many a younger woman, much less one who boasted thirty-five-year-old twin sons. Her vivacious personality and quintessential talents as a hostess also hid a mind as incisive as a razor and a go-for-the-jugular business instinct that had made her a force to be reckoned with during her reign as CEO of the multifaceted Gaspard Enterprises. Now that Logan had taken over the reins, she was allowing herself more leisure, but that didn't mean she was one to let grass grow under her feet—as the success of this evening's fund-raiser could attest.

"It's kind of you to say so," Valerie replied, patting her dark chignon with a beautiful woman's complacency. "I just returned from a little vacation."

"Well, wherever you went, you ought to bottle it. Hey, I brought something for you." Bending from her superior height, Bliss kissed Valerie's cheek again. "That's from Jack."

A slight blush rose under Valerie's olive complexion at the mention of her ex-husband. "How is the old scoundrel?"

"Raising hell, as usual. I left him and Russ down in Alamagordo. They were talking about going over the border, maybe prospecting some leases around the Big Bend area."

"That Jack! Always looking for the pot of gold at the end of the rainbow."

"And finding it, mostly. Lucky for Campbell Drilling, right, Logan?" Bliss goaded.

"Dad's always had the devil's own luck," he agreed grudgingly. "I'm surprised he could get along without his company pilot, though."

"I'm allowed some time off." Bliss didn't like the defensive edge that colored her voice and forced a smile to disguise it.

She'd earned her pilot's license at sixteen and had been ferrying Campbell Drilling's crew since then. At thirty, she knew she'd clocked more hours in the air than most commercial pilots her age, and she'd sure come through more close calls, thanks to Jack's and Russ's penchants for picking the world's trouble spots to hunt for crude. It was enough to give a girl gray hair. Maybe she ought to check out Valerie's vacation spot.

"I, for one, totally agree," Valerie said, linking her arm through Bliss's. The forties rhythms from the big band sound of a popular city dance orchestra boogied through the room. The crush was almost stifling, but everyone was smiling—except Logan Campbell. "Those two slave drivers never know when to quit, do they? So, Bliss, what brings you to New Orleans, and how long can you stay?"

Bliss glanced at Logan. "That all depends."

"You'll stay here, of course," Valerie insisted.

"Uh, no. I couldn't impose." Bliss shook her head. "I booked a suite at the Royal Orleans...nightlife, the Quarter, you know."

"Absolutely not. I will not have a member of the family staying in a hotel when we have dozens of perfectly good rooms—"

"Mother, if Bliss prefers her privacy—" Logan interjected.

"I never said I *preferred*," she said, taking a perverse delight to thwarting him. It was an ongoing game between them, and sometimes her impulsiveness pushed her to actions that fit in the old-fashioned term cut off her nose to spite her face diction. She wondered if she'd just pulled another boner.

"That's settled, then."

"Mother, if Bliss has plans—"

Bliss cocked a belligerent hand on a shapely hip covered by skintight denim. "Look, don't try to tell me what I can and cannot do, buster."

Valerie drew a long-suffering breath. "That's enough, children. No squabbling, do you hear? It's my night, and I want you both on your best behavior for once."

Suitably chastened, they both nodded, two mouths tight, two sets of eyes shooting lethal daggers.

Valerie patted Bliss's hand approvingly and gave Logan a look that surely made him feel ten again. "That's better. Now, Bliss, tell us. To what do we owe the pleasure of your company?"

Bliss took a deep breath. "Well, I guess you could say that I'm throwing my own retirement party."

Valerie and Logan spoke together. "What!"

Bliss nodded, shaking her fair hair over her shoulders

in an undulating wave. "I'm getting out of Campbell Drilling."

Valerie looked puzzled. "But—"

Logan's expression was harder to read. "Does Dad know?"

She gave him a disgusted look. "Of course he knows. Who do you think sent me?"

"He sent you?"

Bliss spoke slowly, as if to a dim-witted child. "I'm cashing out, partner."

"But you—"

"That's right. I'm taking Dad's part of Campbell Drilling with me." She gave Logan a bland smile. "The only question left is whether I want cashiers' checks or cash."

Chapter Two

Mercenary witch.

Whack!

Logan's racket slammed into the yellow tennis ball with a solid thud. The ball careened across the red clay court, landed one-quarter inch inside the green-painted baseline, bounced and came to rest against the chain-link fence separating the courts from meticulously designed and scrupulously manicured Gaspard House's gardens.

The automatic ball server gave an explosive whoosh and launched another volley over the net at high velocity.

Spoiled ingrate.

Whack! Logan hit the ball hard enough to dislodge the cover, his muscles bunching satisfyingly under the sultry New Orleans dawn. It was barely six o'clock, but the promise of the day's heat was already making itself felt, and Logan's regulation white tennis shorts and knit shirt were soaked with perspiration. The last of the season's magnolias gave off a citrus-smelling aroma that mingled with the muddy scent of the Mississippi River, which curved around the city. From the interior of the house, a well-ordered whisper of workers discreetly removed all evidence of last night's fund-raiser, packing crystal stemware, taking down flower arrangements and boxing leftovers to be delivered to nursing homes and food kitchens, and removing the puddled remains of ice sculptures melted to unrecognizable lumps.

Disloyal hellion.

Whack! He wished some flunky would pack up Bliss Abernathy and ship her right back where she came from, too.

She had a hell of a nerve showing up with such outlandish demands. Her share of the partnership—what a load of garbage. Didn't she have the vaguest idea how these things were supposed to be handled? You just didn't pull the financial rug out of a multimillion-dollar operation without at least considering the ramifications for all concerned! And there were bound to be ripples that Logan hadn't even thought of yet—stock options, cash payouts, equipment sell-offs. Why, there might even be a nasty run on Campbell Drilling stock if their investors got nervous, even layoffs. It didn't bear thinking about.

Whack! This was just another example of how Jack Campbell had spoiled his foster daughter. What Bliss wanted, Bliss got. Selfish to the bone. She and Russ had always been the chosen ones, living their lives in perfect freedom, no accountability, no ties, no responsibility. Maybe Jack was finally reaping what he'd sown.

Well, Logan knew what responsibility was. He had

taken over the reins of Gaspard Enterprises early because of family duty and blood bonds. He'd always known it would be his legacy to watch over. From the time he'd played under Grandpère Gaspard's office desk, he'd been fascinated and awed by the workings of power he hadn't been old enough to understand. He swore. Maybe he ought to simply let Jack have his way, give Bliss what she wanted and let the chips fall where they may. But dammit, someone had to be sensible, rational, responsible. He guessed that someone was him—again.

Panting with effort, Logan smashed another ball, laying into it with all his frustration, his deep grunt of effort hanging in the thick air. The ball went out of control, landing well out of bounds. He made a sound of disgust. That's what happened when you forgot control. Well, he wasn't out of control. And if Bliss thought for one minute she was going to manipulate—

"What's the matter? Afraid of a little human competition?"

Bliss's distinctive husky voice broke Logan's concentration, startling him so he half-turned, then awkwardly dodged the next explosively launched ball to avoid being coldcocked. Cursing under his breath, he stepped out of the flight path and gave Bliss a resentful glare.

She met his gaze brazenly, her chin going up to reveal the long tanned line of her graceful throat. Her turquoise tank top didn't attempt to hide the fact that she wore no bra, and he could see the outline of her nipples through the soft, ribbed cotton that cupped her full breasts. She had on tennis shoes and a pair of cutoffs so short he could see where the curve of her buttocks topped her slender, well-muscled thighs. The only thing restrained about her was her hair, pulled in a low ponytail. She was blatant, flaunting her feminine sexuality with no thought to consequences—or maybe too much calculated thought. He didn't really know which—just that the sight of her set his teeth on edge.

The ball server kept up its rhythm, depositing balls in the court behind Logan. He ignored them. "You got a point, Bliss?"

She smiled, a slow cat's smile that lowered her eyelids and fanned shadows of her thick lashes across her high cheekbones. "Just an observation." She gestured at the server, chugging to an automatic stop as the ball basket finally emptied. "Is this the best you can do these days, Golden Boy? Robots instead of real people?"

"Don't start something you can't finish, Baby Sister," he retaliated, calling her by own despised nickname. He scooped up a towel to wipe his sweaty face.

"Afraid I'll beat you?"

He gave a little jerk of surprise. "You want to play me?"

She sauntered to the basket of rackets by the fence and selected one, shrugging. "Why not? You aren't too chicken to take on a mere woman, are you?"

"Do the words hopelessly outclassed mean anything to you?"

She stiffened and her sapphire eyes got hot. "If I'm willing to take a licking, what's it to you?"

Logan wondered if he'd pushed a button of some kind to warrant her response. Still, if she were fool enough to open herself to this kind of humiliation, then he was more than willing to take her down a notch or two. "Suit yourself. You can serve first."

"Oh, no," she said, too sweetly. "I wouldn't want

to be accused of taking advantage of being the weaker sex. After you."

Shaking his head, Logan wondered at her mood. But then he'd never been able to read Bliss, not like other women. She was a foreign creature, outside his experience. He'd call her a changeling if he believed in such things. He'd never liked the feeling that no matter what he did, she was silently laughing at him. Like now. And he couldn't do a damned thing about it.

"This is ridiculous," he muttered, moving the server and kicking several balls to clear the court. "I've got to get to court and—"

"An easy transition—tennis to jury room." Smirking slightly, Bliss took up her position on the other side of the net, balancing easily on the balls of her feet. "Just part of one big game to you, right?"

His mouth hardened. Stuffing one ball into the pocket of his shorts, he lifted another in his left hand. "As usual, you don't know what you're talking about. Ready?"

"When you are, amigo."

Patience vanished in a resentful flash. He'd thought about cutting her a little slack, letting them have a game of sorts, but she was already whipping him with that sharp tongue of hers just for sport, and he'd had enough. He'd blast her with some aces and lay this farce to rest in short order.

He stretched, tossed the ball and delivered it at lightning speed directly to the baseline. Bliss didn't even move, made no effort whatsoever to return it.

"Nice shot," she said easily, then moved to the opposite side of the court to receive the next serve.

Puzzled, he frowned. He didn't like her coolness.

That serve would have rattled the most experienced player. Gritting his teeth, he served again.

This time, her racket connected, sending the ball back so he had to return. He won the point, but her smile was serene. It made him nervous.

She took her position. "So, when can I expect to see my money?"

Bliss returned his next serve, and they exchanged volleys. Logan was forced to admit he'd underestimated her. She won the point. He looked at her hard and replied, "These things take time."

"That's no answer."

"I've got to consult with Dad."

"He'll tell you to give me what's mine."

The next few exchanges weren't exactly even, but Bliss gave him more competition than he'd expected. It both surprised and infuriated him. A damned ringer, that's what she was. She'd been coached...by an expert.

"There are issues here he's not aware of," he said, panting.

"Sure."

Her next shot took him. He wasn't exactly a chauvinist, but to have a female—this particular female—matching him at his own game was galling in the extreme.

"You've been taking lessons," he said.

Bliss shrugged. He wondered if she was really as unconcerned under that dewy, exhilarated expression as she looked. "Just a pickup game or two with François."

Logan's eyes narrowed. "François?"

"Villos."

Shock reverberated through him. The Venezuelan player was the number-one seed in the tennis world. And also the biggest playboy. Logan's gut clenched. So she was seeing a high-rolling jet-setter with a reputation for partying in all the hottest spots from Rio to Bali and always having the most beautiful women in his bed. It only confirmed what he'd suspected about her life-style. Logan told himself grimly that Bliss's private life didn't concern him.

He strode toward the baseline. "Forty all."

Bliss lifted her ponytail, arching her neck sensuously in an effort to cool her sweat-dewed skin. "This is boring. Calf rope—I give."

"Huh?" He felt stupefied at her unexpected and completely unwanted capitulation.

She walked off the court with that hip-swaying swagger that was bound to inflame males from two to ninety-two and stuck her racket in the basket.

"Talk to Jack, Logan. I'm not a patient woman."

"You've got a lot of nerve, Bliss."

She smiled. "Glad you noticed. So don't buck me on this, amigo. I want my grubstake and I want it now."

"No matter what the cost? Where's your loyalty, *querida?*"

She shrugged again. "You can make it painless. That's what they pay you for, right? So make yourself useful for a change." Her eyes darkened. "And, Logan? If you know what's good for you, you'll realize this is one game that you can't win."

Bliss didn't like the way her hands were trembling. Even a cool shower hadn't done much to settle her nerves after her early morning tennis game with Logan. How could she have been so stupid? Antagonizing him was going to get her nowhere. It just seemed she couldn't help herself. But then that was nothing new.

Dressed in a fresh—although well-washed—T-shirt

and shorts, she paused on the landing of the upper hall, inspecting her reflection in the gilt mirror centered over the eighteenth-century mahogany console. Her hair was still damp, and she frowned at the color that still stained her cheeks. She had to get hold of herself. Any evidence that Logan could get to her was ammunition she couldn't afford to give him.

Her stomach rumbled in hunger, and she caught the drift of muted conversation coming from the downstairs sunroom where the family normally shared its informal meals. Still, she hesitated, taking a deep breath and letting her gaze wander over the collection of silver-framed photographs littering the console. She picked up one showing two adolescent boys lolling on a pier by the ocean, the auburn-headed one grinning from ear to ear, the blond one's expression too serious and melancholy for one so young. The picture had evidently been taken during one of the twins' all-too-infrequent truces.

From a distance that seemed only yesterday, she heard the frequently remembered, heated words again.

"Dummy."

"Don't call him that!"

"Cool it, Baby Sister," Russ Campbell said, rubbing at a russet-colored cowlick. "He don't bother me none."

"He can't talk to you that way!" Ten-year-old Bliss threw her pencil on the rickety table that doubled as school desk and dining table in the shabby trailer Campbell Drilling had set up at the newest drilling site. A pile of unfinished workbooks and school texts gave mute testimony to the last-ditch effort Bliss was making to help Russ pass the spring semester's home schooling program.

It wasn't that he wasn't bright. In fact, Russ was

downright brilliant when it came to wellheads and machinery and male blarney. But, to Bliss's frustration, he couldn't be bothered to apply that brilliance to something as boring as schoolwork. While Bliss sailed more than four grade levels ahead of her age group, Russ had to be dragged to meet the basic requirements. Only his dad's promise to withhold the privilege of going up on the next rig provided any motivation. And just when Bliss had finally gotten him to buckle down, Logan came by to antagonize him and spoil everything!

She glared at Logan. Despite the fact that he was just like Russ, all knobby adolescent knees and elbows, he seemed to her like a young god—golden and privileged, dressed not in the worn jeans she and Russ favored, but starched khakis and soft colorful designer knit shirts that only emphasized the two different worlds they came from.

She loathed him with all of her being, more than the rattler Russ had killed under the flatbed trailer just that morning. Logan had come again, and her beloved foster brother, her companion, her other self, was leaving to spend the summer with his mother in New Orleans. The months stretched like an eternity of—she dared say it to herself because Jack used the swear words—pure damn hell on earth.

"I can say what I want to," Logan had said, sneering, lounging against the scarred plastic-topped cabinet that formed the minuscule kitchen inside the trailer. The space was littered with an empty carton of milk, used cereal bowls and an assortment of fruit in a red plastic French fry basket lifted from a local diner. Logan's expression turned mean. "Especially if it's true. A dummy who lives in a dump."

Bliss bolted from the chair. "Take it back!"

Logan's lip curled. "Who's gonna make me?"

"Bliss, take it easy." In an unusual move, Russ made an attempt to diffuse the growing tension. But Bliss was too raw, too heavy with foreboding and hatred to be placated.

She plucked an apple out of the basket and hurled it at Logan's fair head. "You damned...poop head!"

He ducked, hooting. "You long-legged giraffe! You can't even swear!"

His barb at her unusual height pricked her most vulnerable point. With the feral scream of an enraged cat, Bliss hurled the rest of the fruit basket at him, then launched herself. The barrage of apples, oranges and bananas distracted Logan for the instant it took her to tackle him. They tumbled into the narrow aisle. Logan rolled on the grimy tile, protecting his head with his arms, but she was all over him, coltish arms and legs digging into him while she pummeled him with a banana.

"Bliss, stop it!" Russ wrestled with her from behind.

"Damn! Get her off of me!" Logan shouted, ducking and dodging. "You crazy little..."

"What the hell is going on here?" The roar came from the burly mustached man filling the open doorway. His broad shoulders blocked the light and cast shadows that only accentuated the fury in his expression. "You damn kids! Can't I leave you alone for a minute?"

In a stride, Jack Campbell reached the fracas, shoved Russ aside, then clutched a still-struggling Bliss around her middle and hauled her off his other son. She screeched her fury, arms and legs kicking like an insect thrown on its back, fingers curled into claws as she tried to reach her tormentor. Frustrated, she hurled the blackened and smashed banana, just as he lurched to his feet.

It smacked the middle of his impeccable royal blue shirt, leaving a white ooze.

Jack held Bliss against his bulk and gave her a shake. "Settle down, Baby Sister. Right now, you hear?"

"He...he—" She was so angry the sobs caught in her throat, but she wouldn't cry. Not in front of *him*. A little niggling fear tickled her spine. Jack had promised he'd never send her away, but she'd gone after Jack's blood relation, his son. What if Jack thought that was unforgivable? Fear turned her blood to ice, and her hatred for Logan Campbell multiplied a hundredfold.

Logan wiped the smear of banana from his shirtfront, the anger in his expression shared equally between the goo and the alien creature still snarling at him. "Hell, she's nuts! I didn't do anything to the bit—"

Russ shoved Logan hard. "Don't you call her that, you bas—!"

"That's enough!" Jack's roar filled the trailer and he set Bliss on her feet. "I won't tolerate that kind of language from any of you! Now I don't care who started this, but it's over as of now. Bliss, Logan—shake hands."

Bliss looked at her foster father in horror. "I won't!"

Jack's dark brows drew together in a ferocious scowl. "You'll do as you're told. You, too, Logan."

Bliss trembled, anger warring with the love and respect she bore Jack Campbell. Reluctantly, her features set in stone, she offered her hand to Logan. "Sorry."

With just as much reluctance, his expression showing that he thought she was the lowest form of slime on the face of the earth, Logan touched her hand, releasing it in the barest of split seconds. "Yeah. Sorry."

"That's better." Jack's face relaxed and an approving half smile lit his handsome features. "Lord, I don't know what I did to deserve a trio of fair-haired hooligans like you three, but you're going to make me old before my time. Now, let's try to keep the peace around here for more than five minutes, okay?''

The fact that he didn't appear to be too mad anymore made all three of them breathe a sigh of relief.

"Sure thing, Dad," Russ agreed cheerfully, his usual devil-may-care attitude in place. Then his grin widened, and he strove to restrain a laugh but couldn't. "Gosh, you should have seen 'em.''

Jack's grin erupted and his big chest began to shake. "Both of 'em hell on wheels. God, I'm doomed." And his guffaws joined his auburn-haired son's.

Only Bliss and Logan were silent, and the heated light as they met each other's eyes had said clearer than any words that it wasn't over yet.

The hand holding the silver picture frame trembled again and brought Bliss back to the present. She set the frame on the console in disgust. She wasn't a child any longer to be intimidated by Logan Campbell. Neither was she at the mercy of her fiery temper. Her request was simply business, and as long as she stayed in control, Logan would have no choice but to play the game her way. After all, she was well within her rights as her father's heir, and she had Jack's approval.

Squaring her shoulders, she headed for the sunroom.

"Bliss, *chére!*" Valerie looked up from the morning paper with a welcoming smile. "Come join us."

Bliss hesitated only momentarily. Logan, looking every inch the picture of the successful attorney in an impeccably tailored blue pin-striped suit, sat at the head of the antique gateleg table. Any other woman would say that with his sandy hair and handsome features, he was downright mouth-watering. Ignoring a faint sense of breathlessness, Bliss congratulated herself for not being like other women. Logan's challenging look was all it took to make her saunter to Valerie's side and drop a kiss on her upturned cheek.

"Good morning." Outside the mullioned windows, the gardens were a lush expanse of old oaks, azaleas and curving beds edged with tufted monkey grass and filled with colorful red and orange impatiens. "It's a lovely day, isn't it?"

"Perfect, now that the benefit is over," Valerie said with a laugh. She hardly looked as though she'd had a late night, clad in a floating silk caftan, her dark hair piled in a chic knot atop her head. Deftly, she poured twin streams of hot coffee and milk from sterling pots into a wide earthenware cup and passed the steaming café au lait to Bliss along with a basket of fresh, crisp-crusted baguettes. "You must be starved. I'll have Sophie fix you an omelet."

"That would be great," Bliss replied, sinking into the chair and reaching for a plate of butter pats in the form of scallops.

"I see you didn't fill up on last night's buffet," Logan said, pushing back his own empty plate.

"I can't stand those girls who pretend to eat like birds," Valerie said easily.

Bliss refused to let Logan bait her. She merely shrugged. "I'm a big girl. It takes a lot to keep me going."

"So I imagine," Logan murmured.

"What I can't imagine," Valerie said, sipping her coffee, "is your retiring from Campbell Drilling. Not that you haven't earned your time off, not with the way Jack's kept your nose to the grindstone all these years at his beck and call. But if you're not flying, what are you going to do?''

Bliss stiffened. How could she answer without having Logan sneer at her little ambitions? Because it was a certainty he wouldn't understand. No, he already had everything she wanted—the home, the family, the roots she'd lacked nearly all her life. How could she reveal that in the past year she'd realized that being footloose and fancy-free was the last thing she wanted out of her life? She'd seen the world, from high-class to the lowest of the low, and the world no longer held promises that beckoned to her. What she really wanted was just to stop.

Stop.

She wanted permanence. A home. Sure, she and Russ shared a disreputable trailer they hauled from site to site and an ill-tempered, ugly mutt named Gusher, but the trailer was only a place to store some clothes and a few mementos, not a real home. What would it be like to stay in one place more than a month or two at a time? To find a place of her own and plant roots. And flowers. To have lasting friends and neighbors who wouldn't mind loaning her a cup of sugar or sharing a glass of iced tea along with the latest gossip on a summer's afternoon? Perhaps even to find Mr. Right, a solid kind of guy who didn't want to roam the world, who'd take pride in his yard and barbecue on Saturday nights and give her a couple of kids to love and raise. Heck, she'd even join the PTA and coach Little League. After all the years of rootlessness, that was her idea of heaven on earth.

And she'd figured out how to do it. With her start-up money, she was going to open her own charter service. It wouldn't be hard to find an airfield within a competitive market, buy a couple of planes, hire another pilot or two. Sure, she would continue to work, but at the end of the day, she'd know that she was going home to her own place, not some godforsaken hole-in-the-wall in the middle of nowhere with no one special waiting for her.

She loved Jack and she loved Russ, but their blood was infused with a wanderlust that had evaporated from hers over the years. Their dreams were no longer hers—if they ever had been—and she'd finally faced that fact. What was surprising was that when she'd gathered the courage to tell Jack, instead of reacting with one of his world-famous outbursts, he'd been understanding, even supportive. It had been rather mystifying, but surely that was just another sign that she was making the right decision. After all, at thirty, she was entitled to carve out the kind of life she wanted, but that didn't mean she was going to let Logan laugh at her dreams.

With a casual shrug, Bliss carefully buttered a piece of French bread. "Can't say for sure, Val. I've worked hard, and I want to play for a while. You know me. Just like the song, I've got friends in low places. Some in Vail, the Derrick Club in Tulsa, and there's this group in Chamonix I like to hang around with." She shot Logan a glance under her lashes. "And lately I've had an interest in following the professional tennis tour."

Logan scraped back his chair. "I've got to get to the office. I've got a mid-morning appointment with that reporter we met at the Lattimer reception. Remember? She did that great story on the Odessa Blowout and Russ and Dad about five or six years back. She's going to help dig up some dirt on Tom Barnette."

"Oh, Logan." Valerie's perfectly arched brows drew

together in a worried furrow. "You're not still pursuing that, are you?"

"I promised Dad."

"You know your father can be as wrongheaded as they come."

Logan shrugged. "Don't worry yet, Mother. Nothing may come of it."

"Well, you have a nice day, *chér,*" Valerie said, lifting her face as Logan gave her a goodbye kiss. "Slay a dragon for me."

"Of course, Mother." He nodded. "Bliss."

"Yeah, bring its head home on a pike, will you?" Her tone was faintly mocking.

Logan's mouth flattened. Without another word, he strode out of the room. Within minutes, the roar of an automobile's powerful engine sounded from the drive. Valerie set her cup on her saucer, then sighed as she eyed Bliss. "I had hoped—"

"What, Val?"

"That you and Logan might have buried the hatchet after all these years. You want him to help you get this business worked out, don't you, Bliss?"

"Well, of course." Bliss shifted in her chair, puzzled and uncomfortable.

Valerie's look was pointed. "Then, *chére,* I'd advise you to remember the old saying. You can catch more flies with honey than vinegar."

"I'm terribly sorry, Logan, but I can't make it." Laura Ramirez clutched the cordless telephone receiver in one hand and pressed two fingers to the bridge of her nose. "I intended to catch the early flight to New Orleans to meet with you, but I've spent the night in the emergency room with my son."

"No problem, Laura. I understand," Logan Campbell said over the long-distance line. "Is he all right?"

"Yes, for the moment. Some sort of violent gastric upset."

Laura tried to calm her shattered nerves. She was pale and shaky. It looked like she hastily threw on a pair of jeans and a top. She wasn't wearing any makeup, and her hair was a disheveled mess—totally unlike her usual professional appearance. As a crack investigative reporter—who just happened to have sultry Hispanic looks and a curvaceous figure—she had to be careful about her image. But at three o'clock in the morning with an ill child, that had been the least of her concerns.

Now, at mid-morning and finally home again, she stood in the doorway of her son's room in her modest Dallas ranch house, checking her son for the umpteenth time. Five-year-old J.R.—or Rufio, as he was called because of his mahogany locks—lay curled in a ball on his Dallas Cowboy sheets, sleeping restlessly.

"The doctors couldn't really put their finger on it, but at least he's stopped being sick," she told Logan wearily. It was times like this when being a single parent really took its toll, when she needed someone strong to lean on and Rufio needed a father. With an ironic sigh, she focused on the man on the other end of the wire and put aside useless regrets. "I'm going to have to find a new doctor, a specialist maybe. They thought some more tests..." She paused.

"Well, don't you worry about a thing," Logan assured her. "We can do this anytime."

"Thanks. By the way, I've located a source in the state attorney general's office who's willing to talk to me confidentially about the Aegean Insurance investigation."

Enthusiasm infused Logan's deep voice. "That's great news. I've got some information from the private investigator I put on the case, too. If Tom Barnette was foolish enough to leave a trail, I'm sure we're going to find it. But for now, you see to your boy, okay?"

"Yes. Thanks." She leaned against the door casing. Recalling her blazing, short-lived affair with Logan's brother, Russ, Laura knew she was crazy for getting involved with the Campbells again. She was playing with fire, but there was a heck of a story here—maybe two stories—and a good reporter didn't let personal matters interfere with her work. "I'll get back with you soon. And maybe I can talk to your mother about the night Zach and Jake were born."

"I thought you had everything figured out about how the two of them came to be separated," Logan said.

"Me, too, but then I found out that Abby Rawlings gave away one of her sons because of a heart condition, but neither one of them has heart problems, so now I'm back to square one. I called that nurse who was on duty that night again, but she's gone off on one of those blue-haired-lady bus tours to the Pacific Northwest or Canada or someplace, so I'll have to wait until she gets back to question her again."

Rufio rolled over, his groan of distress twisting her heart. Zach and Jake's problems were forgotten. "Look, I need to go."

"Sure. Thanks for calling. And, Laura?"

"Yes?"

"If there's anything I or my family can do for you—anything at all—you just let me know, okay?"

"Sure thing, Logan." Her throat tightened, and she could barely get out the rest of the words. "Thanks again."

Laura punched the button to end the call, then dashed the glimmer of tears from the corners of her eyes. ''Damn, damn, damn.''

She was just feeling tired and weak and alone, she told herself firmly, but she could handle it. She had been handling it just fine for six years. Straightening her shoulders, she went to take care of her baby.

Chapter Three

"I don't care what you say. You don't look like any pilot I ever saw."

Bliss's soft gurgle of laughter hardly echoed in the plushly appointed anteroom of Gaspard Enterprises. "Well, aren't you just the sweetest thing to say so. No wonder your boss man keeps a silver-tongued devil like you around to charm the ladies."

Said boss man stopped cold in his office doorway, waylaid by the scene before him. Logan blinked, taken aback by Bliss's transformation from this morning's tomboy to femme fatale. Dressed to the nines in a sleek taupe linen vest, flowing African motif skirt, heels, hosiery and chunky gold jewelry, she sat perched on the corner of his secretary's desk, holding court among a bevy of admirers made up of most of the junior associates.

Chuck Borden, the fresh-faced kid who'd just paid

her such an inept compliment, had the dazed expression most men got when faced with Bliss Abernathy for the first time, and even Madeline Hughes, Logan's plump, efficient and long-suffering dragon lady of a secretary, looked on with amused approval totally at odds with her usual all-business demeanor. Bliss's long hair was loose, shimmering down her back in a fall that made a man ache to bury his hands in the silken mass. Her long locks undulated as she laughed, and Logan knew every man present felt the temptation. It made him furious, and he scowled as Bliss looked and caught his eye.

"Here's my partner now," she said, sliding off the corner of the desk. The flash of sleek, silken-covered thigh she revealed made Logan grit his teeth. She walked to the doorway, slipped her arm through his and gave him a bland smile. "Well, it's about time."

Something about Logan's expression must have been ferocious, because there was an immediate exodus of Bliss's admirers. Their chorus of falsely cheerful, "Well, back to work," couldn't totally disguise the fact that they were slinking off like dogs with their tails between their legs.

"Causing trouble, as usual," he muttered. In her heels, she was on eye level with him. Her eyes flashed, but he could have imagined the glimpse of resentment, so brief had it been, replaced immediately by friendly amusement.

Bliss shrugged, and the exotic musk of her perfume tickled Logan's nose. "My middle name."

Off balance, aware that Madeline was watching them with interest, irritation made his voice sharp. "What are you doing here, Bliss?"

"Taking you to lunch."

"I haven't got time—"

"Yes, you do. Doesn't he, Maddie?"

Maddie? No one called his formidable secretary that, not even him.

"Absolutely," Madeline replied, flipping through the day calendar on her pristine desktop. "Now that Ms. Ramirez has canceled, there's no reason you can't take a little time off, Mr. Campbell."

"Why do I get the feeling I'm in the middle of a conspiracy?" he growled.

"Oh, lighten up," Bliss said, laughing. "We've got business to discuss, and as two mature adults, surely we can do it over a nice lunch. I'll even buy."

"Feeling plump in the pockets, are you?"

The dig failed to hit a mark, and she smiled again, as if he were a recalcitrant little boy. "Don't be difficult, amigo."

She drew him skillfully toward the glass entrance. Gaspard Enterprises was housed in a historic five-story building on the National Register and reeked of old money, continuity and class. They headed toward the creaky but still efficient elevator that would deposit them on Canal Street. "I'll bring him back safe and sound, Maddie."

"Take your time," Madeline encouraged, waving vaguely at a stack of files nestled next to her word processor. "I never catch up, so any break I can get from my workaholic boss is fine with me."

"She can be replaced," Logan said as they stepped into the elevator and he punched the button for the ground floor.

"Yeah, in your dreams." Bliss brushed her hair over her shoulder. It was a mannerism that was beginning to drive Logan nuts. Why didn't she wear her hair in a sedate twist or pulled back like other women he knew?

It was as though everything in her life was out of control, and the wildness of her silver-gold hair was just another symptom.

Bliss gave him an arch look. "You should give Maddie a raise for putting up with you, Counselor."

"Mrs. Hughes is well compensated." The muggy south Louisiana atmosphere slapped them in their faces as they stepped onto the street. Logan felt the moisture pop out under his jacket, dampening his cotton dress shirt at the armpits.

"There's more to life than money." Automatically, Bliss turned toward the French Quarter. She looked cool despite the heat, like an ice princess untouched by climate.

"That's funny, coming from you."

Bliss's jaw hardened, and she lengthened her stride, turning the corner onto Royal Street, famous for its many antique and jewelry shops. "You're beginning to irritate me, Logan. So, where would you like to eat? Antoine's? Or there's always the Court of Two Sisters."

"It doesn't matter. This is your party."

She stopped in front of a display window showing a tray of Victorian estate jewelry and, beyond that, rows and rows of antique tables and chairs. "How gracious of you. Maybe if I feed you, you'll quit snarling at me."

"I don't snarl." He found he was speaking to himself, for she'd stepped into the cool, dimly illuminated shop, making the bell over the door tinkle. He followed her inside, shaking his head at her impulsiveness. It was just another sign of how unstable her life was. But that instability couldn't be allowed to undermine Campbell Drilling just because she'd taken a notion to retire.

He caught up with her admiring a large pine kitchen table, something out of the Texas Hill Country, he guessed. It was beaten and battered, with gouges and scorch marks and nicks marring its aged golden surface. "I said, I do not snarl. It's undignified."

"Maybe so, but you snarl all the time. At least at me." She smoothed her hand over the surface of the table. "Isn't this beautiful? Do you like it?"

"It's trash." He turned over the tag, then made a sound of disgust. "And this price is highway robbery."

"It looks like a family used it for years and years. Can you imagine all the stories it could tell?"

"You'll get a splinter every time you sit down to eat."

But she was enraptured. "Nonsense. It's got character. And history. I think I'll put a hold on it."

"This is how you plan to spend your ill-gotten gains?" His lips tightened. "At least buy something new. Get your money's worth."

The look she gave him was aghast. "But you live with beautiful old things."

"So?"

"So," she said slowly, "you're a Philistine, Logan. I just never realized it before. How disappointing."

He didn't know why the criticism rankled so much, but before he could form a retort, she was out the door again, striding up the street. He went after her, catching her by the arm.

She jerked against his grip. "Let go!"

"Now what have I done to tick you off?"

"I think it's something in the DNA," she replied with spurious sweetness. "Why don't you shut up before you do any more damage? Maybe a hunk of raw beef will improve your mood."

"I don't get you."

"No, you never have." Suddenly, her sapphire eyes

were snapping with temper. "This wasn't such a hot idea. Just tell me one thing. What did Jack say?"

The muscle in Logan's jaw throbbed as he had to admit, "I couldn't get in touch with him."

"What? Why not?"

"Because he and Russ have taken off on some damn fishing trip over the border into Chihuahua. They're supposed to be back in a couple of days."

"But he just got back from one of his jaunts," she protested.

"So what? You know Jack when he gets one of his harebrained notions. There's no stopping him."

Frustration etched her features. "Great. Just great."

"Why so impatient, Bliss?" Logan asked nastily. "François waiting for you to bankroll his next party?"

She gave him a look that could have melted steel. "I've changed my mind. You can eat dirt for lunch, Counselor, and when you're done, you can go to hell."

Honey. Yeah, right. Bliss fumed, stalking up the street in her audacious—and damned uncomfortable— stiletto heels. Try to turn on the sweetness with Logan Campbell, and all you got were insults and snide comments for your efforts. So much for Valerie's advice.

She heard Logan shout something behind her but ignored him, crossing against the heavy traffic coursing down Canal Street to a bevy of honking horns and curses. Dodging a city bus, she made a dash to catch the old-fashioned green and red streetcar making a turnaround where St. Charles Avenue crossed the city's main boulevard. Mounting the open streetcar's tall steps, she dug in her purse and shoved coins into the tinkling contraption at the driver's elbow.

Red-faced from the heat, the burly, uniformed driver

gave her a wide-eyed look of appreciation she'd seen countless times before and then a big grin. "Welcome aboard, *chére*."

"Thanks." The car was three-quarters full, a mixture of honeymoon couples and tourist families with kids headed for the zoo, business people riding out to the Garden District for their lunch hour and university students with backpacks and T-shirts from Tulane and Loyola. Grabbing a brass bar as the car jerked into motion, she swayed her way down to the end, sliding onto a slick wooden seat.

"Bliss!" Logan's fair head appeared in the streetcar's doorway just as it picked up speed. Spotting her, he took a step down the aisle. "What the hell—"

"Every rider pays, bud," the driver said.

"Huh? Oh, yeah." Logan fumbled in his pockets for change.

Bliss gritted her teeth and turned her face toward the window, inspecting the streetscape intensely. She couldn't imagine the last time Mr. Hotshot had taken the pleasant streetcar ride home to Gaspard House—too plebeian for a snotty upper-crust type, she was sure—but she certainly didn't want his company now.

Logan slid onto the seat beside her. "What the hell's the matter with you? You know you nearly got us both run down crossing against the lights?"

The brush of his muscular thigh against hers in the cramped space between the seats and the scent of his masculine skin, heated and musky, nearly overwhelmed her. Irritation at her involuntary reaction made her voice sharp.

"Who asked you to follow me? Go away, Logan." She slipped her hot shoes off and glared at him.

"I've never met a woman so unreasonable," he said, irritated.

"You don't get out much, do you?" Feeling crowded by his nearness and wilting fast in the heat despite the breezes playing through the open windows of the lurching car, she stood up, reached under her skirt and began to shimmy out of her panty hose.

"What the hell are you doing?" Logan's tone was scandalized as he grabbed her arm. Several other passengers had taken notice of Bliss's maneuverings, a couple averting their eyes but most taking in her antics with amusement. It was New Orleans, after all, and you could see anything in the Big Easy.

"Damned instrument of torture," Bliss muttered, sitting down to strip the nylons from her sweaty feet and ankles.

"Amen to that, sister." Across the aisle, a young matron holding a toddler on her lap agreed fervently.

"Ought to be outlawed," Bliss said.

"Bliss—"

Logan's warning tone was all it took. Smiling devilishly, she stood again, whirling the panty hose over her head and announcing, "I'm hereby declaring my independence from overpriced, too-hot stockings forever!"

She pitched the nylons out of the moving trolley's window. They sailed over the neutral ground and got hung in a crepe myrtle in front of a multistoried, Corinthian-columned Garden District showplace. It was just the right touch for such a stuffy antebellum edifice, she thought with satisfaction. The round of applause from the passengers and the look on Logan's face were merely an added bonus.

Logan jerked her elbow so hard she was forced to sit

again. "Will you stop it? You're making a spectacle of yourself."

"If you don't like it, then why are you still here?"

"I thought you wanted to talk."

"Not unless you're going to say what I want to hear."

His tawny eyes grew icy. "That I'm willing to dismantle the company to suit some crazy female whim? It'll be a cold day in hell."

"Then I have nothing more to say. And it's no whim, Counselor."

He heaved a long-suffering sigh that set her teeth on edge. "Look, if you'll just—damn!" He turned in the seat just as Gaspard House flashed by. "We missed our stop."

"You can still get off if you want. I'm going for lunch."

"All right, I'm going with you. You did promise to buy."

Her smile twisted. "You may not like my choice."

"I'll chance it."

Her smile grew. "That's the first sign of real humanity you've shown since I got here. Maybe there's hope for you yet."

Bliss was still smiling several minutes later as she turned from the Audubon Zoo refreshment stand and shoved a dripping chili dog into Logan's face. "Well? What are you afraid of?"

Logan gave the rapidly growing grease stains on the flimsy paper holder a dubious look. "Still quite the gourmand, I see."

"Nothing wrong with good old American cuisine." Around them, children's excited cries mingled with the muted roar of a lion and the nearby chitters and hoots from the primates exhibit. Animal musk, popcorn and the sweetness of late-blooming jasmine scented the moist air. "Here, take it."

Logan juggled the hot dog she passed him, to little avail as a spot of chili hit his pristine shirtfront and smeared his silk tie. "Hell."

"Well, the damage is done," Bliss said around a mouthful of chili dog. She chewed and swallowed with gusto, then reached up and flicked loose the knot of his tie with one finger. "Might as well enjoy it."

Shrugging, he bit into the dripping frankfurter, following Bliss as she strolled down the path between exhibits. His hot dog disappeared in three bites. He was licking from his thumb while Bliss still nibbled at the last third of her own dog.

"Now that wasn't so bad, was it?" she cooed, watching him strip loose his tie. "Could I get you another?"

"Thanks, but no thanks. I don't care to take my life in my hands more than once a day."

"That's not Russ's philosophy."

"We both know that Russ is a daredevil and a damn fool at times."

"Part of his charm. He—what's that?"

Logan had shoved the balled-up tie into his coat pocket, only to pull out a plastic bag with a cleaner's ticket stapled to it. He was frowning over what looked to be a blue-trimmed garter.

Bliss grinned, her eyes dancing with mischief as she polished off her chili dog. "Why, Logan, it appears I may have underestimated you. Or at least your taste in women."

Annoyance creased the corners of his mouth. "This is the suit I wore to Jake Lattimer's wedding."

"You caught the bride's garter?" Bliss leaned

against the fence separating them from the chimpanzee cages and hooted softly. "You know what that means. So, who's measuring you for a harness? That little blonde that kept shooting daggers at me at the fund-raiser?"

"I am, er, currently unattached," he said coldly.

"Ooh, that is encouraging."

Bliss was enjoying his discomfiture too much for caution. Besides, playing with fire was so much more exciting. Moving closer, she dragged a finger along his strong jawline, then toyed with the second button of his shirt. The jolt when she touched his hair-dusted skin went through them both with the force of a thunderclap. Her smile died as his fingers snagged her wrist in a punishing grip.

His eyes were hot. Hers sizzled.

Beneath her fingertips, his heart pounded. The pulse in her wrist raced out of control.

His mouth twisted in a sensuous line. She licked her dry lips.

"Don't play this game," Logan warned. But he was pulling her closer rather than thrusting her away, and his expression was that of a hungry man.

Dismayed, paralyzed, Bliss felt her bones melt and her belly heat as his gaze devoured her. As helpless as a mouse caught in a snake's mesmerizing trance, she realized that what she felt was want—pure, primal, female desire for a dangerous man—but even that knowledge could not free her from Logan's hypnotizing thrall. She wanted to move closer, to melt against him, to find out if it was still as good....

No, not again!

With a supreme effort, she dug in her heels, resisting him, resisting herself and the forbidden memory. Her chin came up in challenge and defiance. "Maybe this is one game where I outclass you."

The heat in his eyes turned to an Arctic chill, and he released her abruptly, contemptuously. "So go practice somewhere else."

Behind them a chimpanzee gave a shrill cry, instantly echoed in a deafening chorus by the rest of the primates populating the cages around them. Bliss made her smile tantalizing, tempting, insulting.

"Maybe I'm not the one who needs the practice. After all, we both know this isn't the first time you've made a monkey out of yourself with a woman."

Monkey didn't begin to describe it. He'd made a ham-fisted ape of himself with Bliss a long time ago, and it looked as though neither one of them had ever forgotten it.

Logan gazed out of his upstairs bedroom window into the moonlit gardens below. With a body aching with both regret and desire, sleep was beyond him, had been for hours. He was acutely aware that Bliss lay asleep in her own bed just down the hall.

Damn her. Why'd she have to come? Just to look at her stirred things up that he'd thought buried years ago. To touch her destroyed his control. To have her near raised memories best left alone. But that was beyond him, too.

It had been the summer Campbell Drilling was speculating with some old wells down in the Yucatán Peninsula, trying to eke out another couple of thousand gallons of crude with some new technology. Between tennis tournaments, Logan had gone down at Jack's orders, not unwilling to spend time with the father he felt he'd missed during his growing-up years, and to appease Jack's desire that he dirty his hands with some "real work" and learn what Campbell Drilling was about. Logan had been almost twenty-one, and the idea of spending time with his father and seeing some of the world at the same time held great appeal.

He hadn't been prepared for the changes a year had made in Bliss, though.

They'd all met him at the airport in Cancun—Jack, Russ and Bliss—then driven through the jungle to a villa on the coast. The red-tiled mansion was straight out of a movie set with its central courtyard, lush vegetation and unobtrusive staff. But Logan couldn't concentrate on the monkeys darting across the rough road, the loaded banana trees or the colorful bird life. Nor was the villa impressive enough to make him drag his eyes from the sixteen-year-old girl sitting crammed next to him in Campbell Drilling's beat-up truck.

No, one look at the new and improved Bliss—no longer the grubby and irritating tomboy of his youth, but a sapphire-eyed siren with long, tanned legs—made Logan's mouth go dry and his libido leap. To his immense frustration, however, she made it clear within minutes that for her nothing had changed. In fact, the resentment and hostility she radiated as they sat pressed thigh to thigh in the truck filled him with dismay.

Logan asked himself how he could have been so blind, so stupid. There'd been a beauty under his very nose for years, and all he'd ever done was alienate her. Now the roll of the cosmic dice and the bolt of attraction every time he looked at her slender hands or silver-gold hair said he was going to pay for his mistake with a host of sleepless nights. He made a mental count of the days until his flight home and knew he'd never survive.

His feelings might have stayed that way if he hadn't come back to the villa alone one evening.

Surrounded by stacks of flight manuals, Bliss looked up from her seat on the plush leather sofa in the spacious, Satillo-tiled main room, taking in Logan's sweat-and-oil-stained appearance.

"Hard day at the office, honey?" she purred.

The villa's open-air arrangement filled the room with cool perfumed breezes, but Logan felt his face heat. He was filthy, dead tired and sore. His hands were blistered and his knuckles scraped. For a young man generally fastidious about his appearance, it was a hell of a note. The fact that Bliss looked as cool as the proverbial cucumber in her off-the-shoulder peasant blouse and colorful skirt—and good enough to eat along with it—didn't help, either.

"Save the sarcasm, Bliss," he said. "Some of us worked for a living today."

"For a change," she murmured. "Where are Russ and Jack?"

"Checking out the action in the local cantina."

"And you weren't up to joining them?" She closed her book and made her lush mouth in to a falsely sympathetic moue. "Poor baby."

Stripping off his dirty chambray shirt, he went around the sofa to a table loaded with a tray of glasses, ice and assorted tropical juices. "My tastes in entertainment run to something a bit more high-tone."

"Yeah, I'll bet." She hooted with laughter. "I can just see you. Tea parties and ice-cold debutantes. And the most pitiful thing is, you don't even know how boring you are."

He let a swallow of cool papaya-pineapple juice slide down his parched throat, then gave her a scowl. "I guess with your vast experience and scintillating social life, you're in a position to judge.''

Her lower lip formed a pout. "I get around."

"Sure you do. Traipsing all over the world with those two hounds, no school, no friends. Yeah, you've got it all," Logan sneered. "Sweet sixteen and never been kissed."

"I have so!" Her defensive hackles rose instantly, making her eyes heat to indigo.

The jolt of jealously at her admission caught him off guard. He set his glass down hard on the table. "Who? Russ?"

"Russ?" She laughed and gave an offhand wave. "He only likes dark-eyed, carmine-lipped floozies."

"Then who was it?" He propped his fists on his hips belligerently. "Tell me."

Bristling, Bliss bolted to her feet, and her chin came up to meet his challenge. "None of your damn business!"

The fact that she hadn't denied his accusation about Russ gave him a sharp pain in the center of his belly. At that moment, he could have cheerfully beaten the stuffing out of his twin. A red haze clouded his brain, and he tried to shake it off, to think logically. Maybe the little hothead was bluffing. He decided to call it.

"You can't tell me because you're lying, right?" he accused. "Bet you've only played with little boys."

"Then you'd guess wrong, amigo," she snapped. Defiance radiated from her. Sauntering closer, she placed her palm against the center of his bare chest and batted her lashes in an imitation of a movie seductress. "What's the matter, Logan? Thinking about sampling the wares yourself?"

Her touch sizzled like lightning through him, and he

held himself still with the most supreme effort. "Be careful," he said through gritted teeth. "You're playing with fire, Baby Sister."

"I'm no baby—" her fingers danced like flames down to the flat corded muscles of his middle "—and I'm certainly not your sister."

He caught her hand before it could stray farther, fury gathering in his voice. "I'm well aware of that."

She laughed again, a sultry, female taunt well beyond her years. "Don't waste your time, amigo. I've got better things to do than dally with a spoiled golden boy."

Logan's fingers tightened on her wrist. He was gratified to find that her pulse was pounding under her skin. She wasn't nearly as cool as she was trying to make out, and confidence thundered through his blood. "Your trouble is, you don't recognize a real man when you see one. Maybe you'd like to do a little sampling of your own?"

The pressure of his hand tugging her closer made her eyes go wide with panic. "Take your hands off me!"

"Oh, no." His eyes glinted. "You've played your hold card and come up empty. It's time for a little lesson in reality."

Digging his fingers into her hair, he jerked her against him and covered her mouth with his. She mewled a protest, but he slanted his mouth over hers and molded her slender form against his length. He wasn't a green boy, had kissed countless girls, and he knew the instant she melted and resistance faded. His satisfaction at her response lasted a mere instant, replaced by a jolt of pure sensation that sent him reeling, as much a victim of his impulsive experiment as Bliss herself.

Sweet. She was incredibly sweet. She tasted of honey and innocence, and when he stroked his tongue over the seam of her lips, she trembled violently and opened for him. With a groan, he deepened the kiss, sampling all the inner mysteries of her mouth, taking everything she could give until his knees buckled and they fell together onto the sofa.

She wrapped her arms around his neck, holding him close, and the feel of her slim body trapped beneath his drove Logan to the brink of control. They seemed to fit with a rightness that couldn't be denied. He slipped a hand under her skirt and smoothed his palm against her silken thigh, and his heart thundered so hard he feared it would beat right out of his chest.

Desperate for oxygen, he lifted his head, almost smiling at the way their breaths came in matching gusts. Her mouth was soft and swollen, moist from his kisses, and her eyes were dazed. She was adorable, irresistible, and he felt just as blown away as she looked.

"You—you're full of surprises," he murmured unsteadily.

"Don't." Her hands framed his face. "Don't talk. Don't ruin it."

He couldn't resist her urging—didn't want to—and he kissed her again, exploring in a more leisurely fashion, feeling his body change, harden, as desire grew. As he grazed along her jawbone, then trailed heated kisses down her neck to the gentle swell of her bosom spilling over the elastic neck of her blouse, he knew he was treading on dangerous ground. But Bliss was Eve incarnate to him, giving, taking—as wild and uncontrolled as ever, impulsive and inquisitive, her tongue on the curl of his ear, her hands eagerly trailing over the hard planes of his chest and shoulders.

Logan realized he was in big trouble. Her response, so unquestioning in its innocence, so demanding in its

womanly instincts, was leading them to a conclusion he
wasn't sure either of them was ready for. Instinct
screamed at him to follow his needs, but conscience and
responsibility reined him in.

Shuddering painfully, he lifted himself away from
her, resting on his elbows. He was exquisitely aware of
his thigh pressed against hers through the gauzy skirt,
the fact that her long legs twined with his would be a
man's most erotic dream, but the discipline he'd learned
over the years on the courts, in the classroom, in Grandpère Gaspard's office, made him swallow hard and pull
away.

She murmured in protest, her hands restless on his
shoulders. "Logan…"

"We've got to stop."

Eyelids slumberous and heavy with desire lifted
slowly. "Why?"

"We—you aren't ready for this."

Awareness came slowly into her expression, followed
by the red rush of acute embarrassment. "Oh…oh!"

She stirred against him, and he immediately let her
up, but when she would have moved away, he caught
her shoulders, holding her close as if to calm a skittish
filly. He was charmed by her unexpected shyness, feeling manly, older, protective.

"Shh," he soothed, his lips against her golden hair.
"*Querida,* it's okay."

"Don't make fun of me," she said, struggling.
"I—you…oh, hell!"

Tenderness filled him. He lifted her face, brushing a
light kiss across her trembling lips. "Don't think I don't
want you, but let's take it slow, okay?"

She blinked, comprehension coming slowly through

the haze of chagrin and still-smoldering passion clouding her eyes. "You mean that?"

"With all my heart."

Wonder filled her expression, made her eyes soft again. "Oh, Logan…"

A raucous shout and the sound of truck doors slamming announced the arrival of Russ and Jack. Bliss and Logan pulled apart, straightening clothes. Of one mind, they both knew what they were feeling was too new to be scrutinized, so when the others entered the house, Logan was pouring another drink, and Bliss was hiding her flushed face behind a flight manual.

After that, it was easy to be together. After all, no one expected two kids who'd been at each other's throats for half a lifetime to have any other kind of interest. So when they spent time on the beach or found an out-of-the-way spot in the gardens or a swing big enough for two on the veranda, no one was aware of the stolen kisses and sweet caresses that passed between them. Or so Logan thought.

After a week of secret moments, a wonderful time with his Bliss that had Logan in a perpetual haze that alternated between tenderness and desire, Logan was certain he was falling in love. Somehow, thinking about tomorrow wasn't a priority, not when he could have her in his arms, her sweet mouth against his. Things would happen as they should, when they should—it was only a matter of time.

He let himself into his room late one night after leaving Bliss at her door, only to come up short when he realized the dark figure sitting smoking in the corner was his father.

"Dad?"

"What the hell do you think you're playing at, boy?" Jack's voice was rough with anger.

"What do you mean?" Logan snapped on a bedside light.

"Do you think I'm blind? You and Bliss." Jack ground out his cigarette and rose to his full intimidating height. "It's got to stop."

Logan refused to meet his father's dark-eyed gaze, but his chin went stubborn. "I think that's between Bliss and myself."

Jack was across the room, spinning Logan around with a rough hand on the shoulder. "The hell it is! She's too damn young, and you know it."

"We're in love." There, he'd said it, Logan thought defiantly, so it must be true. He tried to bury the twinge of guilt at the stark truthfulness of his father's statement.

Jack's mouth under his mustache hardened, and his tone held no pity. "You'll both get over it. I want you to pack your bags. You're leaving tomorrow."

"What? But, Dad—"

"You heard me. Break it off with Bliss, and do it so she won't pine for you, do you hear? She's got a lot more growing up to do before she can deal with the likes of a pretty boy like you."

"Dammit, no!" Fury rose in Logan like a flood tide, compounded with frustration and rejection and resentment. "It's not right. You can't force us—"

Jack twisted a burly fist in Logan's shirt collar and jerked hard. "You're still not too old for me to beat the living tar out of you, boy, but I thought you had better sense than to buck me. Think about your choices, Logan. You're a man, but Bliss is still a child, and one I'm responsible for. Am I making myself clear?"

For a long instant, Logan's tawny eyes warred with

his father's dark brown ones, then his gaze dropped away. "Perfectly," he mumbled.

He'd done as his father wanted. The next day, he'd told Bliss that he was going and that he hoped she hadn't taken anything that had happened between them too seriously. After all, it was just a summer fling, and they'd both had fun. He'd been grateful when the hurt in her sapphire eyes was replaced with rage. It had almost made it easier to laugh off everything and board the plane to the States.

Almost.

Now, leaving his memories behind, Logan dropped the curtain of his bedroom window and turned from the moonlit scene below. Yes, he'd broken Bliss's heart when she was young—though not intentionally. At the same time, he'd broken his own. They'd both been kids, after all. All these years, he'd thought Jack was right, that they'd both gotten over it. Surely their return to their cat-and-dog relationship had proven that.

Now he wasn't so sure. There was unfinished business between him and Bliss, things that both of them needed to complete for their own peace of mind. Normally, he'd be the first to take the step, accomplish that goal, get on with things. Only now, doubts assailed him.

Pacing the dark room, Logan prepared for a long sleepless night, wondering if it wasn't safer for all concerned this time to just let sleeping dogs lie.

Chapter Four

"Close it down, my man. Looks like you could stand to work off some frustration."

Logan glanced up from the latest Campbell Drilling spreadsheet to find Remy Hebert lounging in his office doorway, a gym bag slung over one burly shoulder, his suit coat tucked under the other arm. He glanced at his watch and swore when he saw that it was long after quitting time.

"Hell, I'm sorry, Remy. I didn't mean to keep you waiting."

Remy's eyes crinkled at the corners in his usual good humor. "That's what you always say. And from the look on your ugly puss, I say it must be woman trouble."

"After a fashion."

"So what else is new?" Remy's grin was the devil's

own. "By the way, Cammela and I are getting along like a house on fire. Thanks."

"Don't mention it," Logan returned sourly, loosening the knot of his silk tie. "If I had good sense, I'd swear off females for good."

"Womankind's loss," Remy replied airily. "But enough chitchat. We've got a date with some free weights."

"I'll be with you in a minute." Logan searched through the printout, couldn't find the figures he wanted and slapped the buzzer on his desk intercom. "Mrs. Hughes—"

Madeline Hughes had already anticipated him and bustled past Remy with a courteous nod, then dumped an armload of financial documents in the center of Logan's desk. "I think you'll find everything in order, Mr. Campbell. If that's all, I'll be going."

"Of course, Mrs. Hughes. Sorry to have delayed you. If this wasn't important—"

She nodded, poised and efficient in her tailored suit even at this late hour. "No problem, but I would like to miss the last of the Friday night traffic."

"Go ahead, I'll finish up here." An absent look came over his features as he began to peruse the new paperwork. "And thank you, Mrs. Hughes."

"Mr. Campbell?" Madeline paused beside Remy, her mouth flattening into a suddenly determined line.

Logan looked up, distracted. "Yes?"

She took a deep breath. "I've worked here six years now. Don't you think it's about time you started calling me Madeline?"

Astonished, Logan's jaw dropped. It had never occurred to him that his all-too-efficient secretary might wish a more informal relationship. Was he that stiff and

uptight? Stuck in a personal rut that stagnated relationships? Maybe Bliss was right about him. The thought
was daunting. Madeline looked a bit nonplussed when
he walked to her side and laid a hand on her shoulder.

"You're absolutely right, Madeline. Or do you prefer
Maddie?"

She gulped. "Maddie's fine, sir."

"And it'd better be Logan from now on, too." He
gave her the megawatt smile that had charmed women
since he was two. "Now you get on home. I know your
husband's going to have my hide for keeping you late
again."

Madeline beamed. "No, he never minds the over-
time. I'll see you Monday. Don't let him work too late,
Mr. Hebert."

"I'll try," Remy said without much conviction. She
bustled out to her desk and picked up her purse. Remy
cocked a crooked eyebrow at Logan. "Now, that was
something."

"What?" Logan asked suspiciously.

"Mr. Straight-and-Narrow loosening up. What's
come over you?"

"Give me a break, Remy," Logan said irritably.
"I'm not that bad. Am I?"

"Let's just say that you give new definition to the
word *staid.*"

"Just because a man takes his responsibilities seriously—" The buzz of the phone cut off his complaint.

"Don't answer it," Remy ordered as Logan's hand
automatically moved toward the receiver. "Time to
play."

Logan hesitated, the temptation to throw obligations
out the window warring with his long-standing habit of
always being available for work-related duties. The

choice was taken from him as Madeline scooped the phone up in the outer office, spoke softly into it, then called through the doorway.

"Line one, Mr. Camp—Logan. It's your brother."

Logan grimaced at Remy. "Sorry. Gotta take this one."

"Yeah." With a resigned shake of his dark head, Remy threw himself into a lounge chair and stretched out his legs in preparation for a long wait.

Logan picked up the phone. "Russ? Where the hell are you?"

"Chihuahua city." Russ's robust Texas drawl vibrated over the long-distance line. "Let me tell you, the Mexican hospitality around here is great."

"I thought you and Dad were fishing."

Russ laughed, and Logan could picture him rubbing the auburn curls at the nape of his neck in a habitual gesture.

"Yeah, we're on a fishing expedition, all right. For oil leases. You know Dad. He and Señor Garcia have been talking turkey for days."

Logan frowned. "And you've just been cooling your heels?"

"Hey," Russ protested, "you and Dad are the brains of the outfit. I'm just the leg man. And Señor Garcia's got this daughter..."

"Let me guess. Black eyes, sultry looks—I don't want to hear it."

"You need to lighten up, brother of mine. So, how are you and Bliss getting along?"

"How do you think?" Logan returned. "That woman's got more prickles than a pine burr."

Across the room, Remy's expression perked with mischievous interest. Logan sent him a quelling glare.

"Listen, buddy," Russ said, his voice a protective growl, "that little girl's as sweet as honey. Anybody'll tell you that. If the two of you are having trouble, it must be because you're being your usual egotistic self—"

"I said I don't want to hear it," Logan interrupted. Something deep and unnameable but green-eyed ate at his belly and made his words sharp. The last thing he wanted from Russ was advice on how to handle Bliss Abernathy. "Put Dad on."

"Yeah, sure, he's right here." Russ's tone was surly. "But if you mess with Baby Sister, you're going to have to answer to me."

Exasperated, Logan gritted his teeth. "Just let me talk to Dad, will you?"

There was the rattle of the phone exchanging hands, and then Jack Campbell's familiar smoke-roughened voice came on the line. "God almighty! You boys having a fistfight long distance again?"

Logan's jaw tightened. "Hello, Dad."

"What the hell's so important you had to track me down on vacation?" Jack demanded.

Logan scowled. "Don't try to pull that on me. Russ already explained you're using the Campbell blarney on poor, unsuspecting Señor Garcia."

Jack gave a mollified chuckle. "A businessman's gotta do what he can, son. So, what's up?"

"A number of things, starting with a witness my private investigator located who's willing to testify in court she saw Tom Barnette destroying documents relating to Aegean Insurance."

"What! Hell, that's great! We're going to get that SOB yet!" The size of Jack's grin could almost be heard over the phone. "About time you came up with something."

Logan grimaced. Just once, he wished his father would show a bit of approval for something he'd accomplished. A "well done, son" would have gone a long way toward healing some of the bruised places in their relationship, but after all these years Logan had learned not to expect paternal warmth from his dad.

He went on, all business. "That's not all. I've got an investigative reporter looking into things in Dallas, and she's got a line on someone inside the state attorney general's office who'll keep us informed of the investigation."

"Now we're cooking. You'd best put this woman on the payroll."

"She's in it for the story. I've promised her an exclusive."

"How'd you hook up with her?"

Logan rubbed his jaw, scraping his palm over his late-day stubble. "Actually, we've already had some dealings. Remember Laura Ramirez, the reporter who wrote the story about the Odessa Blowout? Well, I finally met her at Jake Lattimer's wedding."

Jack's guffaw blasted through the receiver. "You mean Jake actually got himself hitched this time?"

"Yeah. Shelby's a real stunner. Plus she's a gun-carryin' cop."

"Now that sounds more like the kind of gal Jake should have. Always thought Georgia was a mite too soft and sweet for the likes of him."

"Well, that new twin brother of his thinks she hung the moon," Logan replied.

Remy moved restlessly in his chair, then got up and went to the concealed bar in the mahogany credenza behind Logan's desk and began rummaging. He lifted a bottle of aged Scotch and two glasses. Logan nodded as he continued to speak to Jack. "They were all there, Zach with Georgia, Jake and Shelby, just as chummy as they could be, with old Ben grinning at them like a Cheshire cat."

"Always thought highly of Jake," Jack commented. "Damn fine football player. What's this Zach fellow like?"

His father's perennial penchant for football over tennis set Logan's teeth on edge, but he kept his voice steady. "The spitting image of Jake, right down to the curve of their mustaches. It's like seeing double. I didn't talk to Zach long, but I liked him. Laura's also working on a story about how the two of them were separated at birth and then found each other again."

"Heck of a thing, that's for sure," Jack said.

"Seems Laura had it all figured out, how the birth mother gave one boy away due to health problems, but that theory fizzled, so she's starting from scratch again. In fact, she wanted to talk to Mother to see if she remembered anything."

"Hell, son!" Jack's chuckle was rueful. "Your mama's still mad at me for stranding her in that little boonie of a town to have you boys. The nurses had her so doped up she was cussing me like a sailor. Flat made me blush."

"That'll be the day," Logan replied.

"So, is Ben with us on this Tom Barnette thing?" Jack asked.

"So he says, but I don't think he's got much enthusiasm for it," Logan replied.

"We'll take care of it then. I know I can count on you, Logan."

"Depend on it, Dad." Logan accepted the glass Remy held out to him, took a sip and grimaced at the burn of the Scotch. Yes, he'd see Tom Barnette taken down if it was the last thing he did. Jack was relying on him and that hadn't happened too often in Logan's life.

"So," Jack continued, a strangely innocent tone coming over his gravelly voice, "anything else going on?"

"As if you don't know," Logan growled. "What's this business with Bliss?"

"Oh, she's just on a tear."

"You mean her wanting out of Campbell Drilling is just some sort of feminine whim?"

"With Bliss, who knows?"

"Well," Logan said slowly, "this isn't the kind of thing we can take lightly. Chuck Abernathy's thirty-three percent is a hunk of money."

"You saying she isn't entitled?"

Logan blew out an exasperated breath. "Of course not. But with the life-style you and Russ have taught her, she'll blow off a nest egg inside six months."

"You underestimate her."

"No, I know her only too well," Logan snapped. "But the fact of the matter is we can't just plunk cash down on the barrel head, or had you considered that?"

"Look, just find a way to pay her off if that's what it takes," Jack ordered brusquely. "If that's what she wants—"

"Are you nuts?"

"Don't you back talk to me," the older man retorted, his voice heating like coals in a campfire.

"For God's sake, Dad!" Logan downed another swig of Scotch, praying for fortitude and patience. "Have you got any idea the effort this is going to take? Not to mention the price Campbell Drilling will pay!''

"So find a solution. It's what the company's paying you for, isn't it?"

"I've got more than Campbell Drilling on my plate at the moment," Logan replied coldly.

There was a moment's deadly silence from the other end of the line. "That's one of the things I've always found disconcerting about you, Logan," Jack said, his tone as icy as his son's. "That you'd choose business over family."

"Maybe some of us aren't as blind as others," Logan replied.

"What's that supposed to mean?"

"That you can stick your head in the sand all day long, but it's not going to change the fact that giving Bliss her way—as usual—could cost us the whole damn company."

"Is that what this is all about—your resentment of Bliss?"

Logan felt himself flush. "I don't know what you're talking about."

"The hell you don't. You've been mad at her since the day I took her in."

"And you're obviously losing all grasp on reality, Jack," Logan responded.

"Listen here, boy, I don't take that kind of sass off anybody!" Jack's voice rose to a roar in the receiver. "I don't want any excuses. Figure out something—stall Bliss until she changes her mind, talk her into some sort of installment plan, something. And I don't want to hear from either of you again until you've come up with a deal we can all live with, is that clear?"

"Dad—" Logan looked at the buzzing receiver in

his hand, then let loose a string of curses that startled even Remy.

"Trouble, bro?" Logan's friend asked cautiously.

Logan drained the last of his Scotch in one swallow, then held out his glass. "Pour me another, pal. Looks like the only way I'm going figure a way out of this mess is to get rip-roaring drunk."

"Here." Laura Ramirez pushed a full-grown ficus tree into Zach Rawlings's arms.

"Good God, Laura!" Handsome, hard-featured and a masculine hunk at his broad-shouldered, six-foot-plus best in a striped Western shirt, Zach staggered under the weight of the potted plant. The smile under his dark mustache was frankly incredulous. "What is this, *Day of the Triffids?*"

Laura grinned, making her oversize gold hoop earrings swing against her olive-skinned cheeks. A royal blue jumpsuit graced her curvy, petite form. "I figured no new house can really be called a home until you've got a plant to kill."

"It's beautiful. Thank you," Georgia Rawlings said. With a smile, she ushered Laura inside the modest suburban split-level house. Other guests meandered through the spacious, Southwestern-decorated living room and kitchen, sampling guacamole and melon balls and helping themselves to long-neck beers from a cooler on the clay-tiled kitchen floor. "Put it in the foyer, Zach."

"Will do, sunshine." Muttering about hernia repair, Zach lugged the plant away.

Georgia touched Laura's arm. "I'm so glad you could come."

She smiled. "Listen, I never miss a Friday night out

if I don't have to, especially when it's my best friend's housewarming."

"I take it J.R.'s better?" Georgia guided Laura toward the kitchen bar where a man with looks identical to her husband's wearing another pearl-studded Western shirt was loading a plate for a striking, angular-faced blonde.

"I left him playing hide-and-seek with the baby-sitter—and winning." Laura smiled a greeting at Jake Lattimer and his new wife, Shelby. "You'd never even know he'd been under the weather. Kids—who can figure them?"

"Well, I'm glad he's all right," Georgia said warmly. "That little hombre is a darling."

"Easy for you to say." Laura laughed with a shake of her head. "We'll go in for some additional tests in a few weeks, but I'm betting he just had a twenty-four-hour bug or something. And I'm glad I could come tonight. You've got a great place here."

"That's what I've been telling her," Shelby Lattimer said. She looked better dressed in jeans and T-shirt than any of the more lavishly attired women milling around the house. "I wish I had Georgia's way with decorating. You've really put the woman's touch around here already."

"It's coming along," Georgia agreed, shoving back a lock of strawberry blond hair. "I still can't believe it's ours. It was a stroke of luck it came on the market at the right price, and it's so much closer to the girls' school where I'm teaching than Zach's old apartment. Plus the rates were right and—well, I guess it was just meant to be."

"And how does the cowboy cop feel, being a solid,

upright citizen, complete with mortgage?'' Jake asked with a broad grin.

"I'll never be the same again," Zach quipped, coming to join the group.

Georgia slipped under his arm and gave him an affectionate squeeze, smiling to several other guests who passed through the kitchen to offer congratulations and graze on her tasty refreshments. "Good thing, too, I'd say."

"Lord, the mush in here is a foot deep," Laura teased. She slanted a glance at Jake and Shelby. "So, how's the other set of newlyweds?"

"Don't ask," Zach interrupted, handing his twin a beer from the cooler. "Let's just say that the only snapshots they took in Paris were of the inside of the hotel room."

"Punch your brother for me, will you, Jake?" Shelby asked mildly.

"Uh-uh. Been there, done that." Jake chucked his bride under her square chin. "Besides, you're the tough cop on this block."

"Not anymore."

"What's this?" Zach demanded.

"I've resigned from the force," Shelby explained. "I've been thinking seriously about finishing up my family counseling degree." There was a chorus of approval, and Shelby blushed faintly. "Well, it's something I've wanted to do, and even a rancher's wife has to stay busy."

"And out of trouble," Zach said.

Shelby's look was arch. "Well, I never said that...."

"Speaking of trouble," Laura said, eyeing Jake carefully, "the grapevine says our mutual friend Tom Barnette is up to his eyeballs in it."

The rancher scowled. "You'd never know it by his TV and newspaper ads, would you? He's coming across pure as the driven snow, and I can tell you, it's put Pop's nose out of joint."

"Has your dad heard anything?"

"No, not directly," Jake said, shaking his dark head. "He's not in that loop. Maybe Logan Campbell—"

"Yes, I'm in touch with him," Laura replied hastily, then turned a speculative gaze at Zach. She'd always been able to count on him as an inside source during her days on the crime beat. "The Texas Rangers wouldn't like to add anything at this point about a certain state senatorial candidate, would they?"

Zach's expression was purposefully bland. "You know better than that, Laura. All investigations are totally confidential."

"Then you do know something."

Zach turned aside and rummaged in a basket on the counter. "Nothing I'm prepared to comment on."

"Rats." Laura grimaced. "Just my luck to find an honest cop."

"Could we drop it, pal?" Zach asked easily. "Besides, I've got something here Jake should be interested in."

But Laura wasn't so easily deterred. "I could ask Georgia to wring it out of you, you know."

Georgia's laugh was sultry. "Now that might be interesting. And fun."

"You reporters are like pit bulls," Shelby complained. "Let the boy do his job."

"Oh, all right, seeing as how I'm outnumbered." Laura's grin proved there were no hard feelings. She punched Zach in the chest with her forefinger. "If something were to break, though, would you maybe give me a ten-second head start on the competition?"

Zach grinned. "Maybe."

Jake shoved a platter of tortilla chips and spicy salsa toward Laura. "Looks like you'll have to be satisfied with that." He ignored Laura's good-natured grumbling, his attention suddenly riveted on the time-worn pile of snapshots Zach was spreading on the counter. "What the hell's this?"

"Found 'em when I was packing up to move." Zach pushed a single photo toward his brother. "I don't have many pictures of Mom, but this one's pretty good."

Jake's features tensed, and he took the proffered snapshot gingerly, as if it were a rattlesnake. He looked at the faded faces for a long moment, Shelby leaning over his shoulder to take a peek for herself.

"She was pretty, wasn't she?" he finally said.

"And not an unkind bone in her body," his twin added softly. They both stared at the soft-eyed blonde who was their birth mother.

"Who are these other folks?" Jake asked.

"That's Grampa and Gramma Pickett." Zach pointed. "Must have been Mother's Day. See the corsages?"

Jake frowned at the silver-haired man in the picture who held the two women's elbows in a lock grip. "He looks, er, a formidable individual."

"I already told you he was a hellfire-and-brimstone preacher from the old school," Zach replied. "I never knew him as anything but gray-haired, but Mom told me as a youth he had a copper-penny head, and the temper to go with it. He lost the color, but kept the temper, the best I recall."

"And Abby had to deal with it. No wonder she

agreed to marry Dwayne," Jake said, referring to the man Zach had believed to be his natural father. Only recently Zach had learned that he and his brother had been sired by someone totally different, a mystery biological father whose identity Abby Pickett Rawlings had never revealed to anyone. As the twin who'd been given up for adoption—admittedly to a wonderful Texas family—Jake still had issues about those circumstances that remained unsettled. He looked at his brother. "Would you mind if I kept this one?"

"We'll have them all copied," Georgia suggested. "It's your legacy, too, after all."

"When the time comes and I complete my article, I'd like permission to use one of these, too," Laura said. "If that would be all right."

Jake looked at Shelby, then at Laura and gave a shrug. "Sure. After all this time, I don't see what difference it could make. Could I see the rest of them?"

Four heads bent over the pile of photos, and Laura retreated discreetly from what had suddenly become a private family matter. Grabbing a beer, she wandered into the living room, nodding to several acquaintances, but her instincts were on red alert. No matter what, this whole affair had her reporter's antennae quivering. Despite the fact that she was playing with fire dealing with the Campbells again, despite the fact that Tom Barnette's alleged infractions might come to nothing, despite the fact that Abby Pickett Rawlings's secret might never be revealed, she knew she had to keep digging.

She looked—and felt—like something the cat dragged in. It didn't matter.

Humming under her breath, filled with an excited euphoria that probably had something to do with the fact she'd gotten no sleep at all, Bliss let herself into the well-appointed kitchen at Gaspard House. The clock over the stove said it was just past noon, too late for breakfast, but surely she could rustle up a snack for herself, even though the staff was off on Saturdays. Then a shower and a long nap and time to contemplate everything she'd learned—gosh, life was good.

Grinning, she twisted her hair around a fist and secured it haphazardly on the top of her head with a pewter clip. Her slacks and red cotton sweater looked as though they'd been slept in—which they hadn't—and she couldn't wait to strip and get naked between the sheets for a long snooze. But first to feed the inner woman. She opened the stainless steel door of the double refrigerator and peered in.

"Just where the hell have you been?"

Logan's harsh demand made Bliss jump, and she nearly dropped a jar of black Italian olives. She pivoted on her heel, jar clutched in her hand, to find him glaring at her from the kitchen archway. As usual, his pressed khakis and knit shirt were impeccable, all the more reason for her to feel grungy and inadequate, but at least his sandy hair looked as though he'd been running his fingers through it. That small sign that all was not right with Logan Campbell gave Bliss a jolt of satisfaction, made her straighten her spine and flash him her blandest, most infuriating smile.

"I didn't know that I was accountable to you, amigo."

"Mother was worried when you didn't come in." Logan's jaw was taut with irritation. "As a guest in someone's home, I'd expect more consideration."

There it was again, that condescension, that looking-down-his-nose attitude that said she was nothing more than a piece of white trash, a guttersnipe who'd never learned the most basic manners. And, because way down in her deepest heart there was the tiniest belief that there was some truth to that assessment, his attitude enraged her.

"I left a note saying not to expect me," she said, her voice like ice. "Didn't you find it?"

"That's not the point," Logan said. Shoving his hands into his pockets, he advanced on her, his tawny eyes angry. "People—that is, Mother was concerned."

"Then I'll apologize." Bliss smacked the olive jar on the counter. "Where is she?"

Logan caught her arm as she strode by, swinging her to a halt. "She's resting now. Don't disturb her." His fingers tightened on her arm. "But you might do me the courtesy of telling me where you've been."

Her mouth flattened mulishly. "If you must know, I flew to Miami with…a few friends."

Logan's features hardened. It was absolutely clear to Bliss that he'd again drawn the worst possible conclusion about her sojourn.

Well, let him, damn him! Let him think she'd gone partying with the lowest lowlife, that she'd been out on a drunken orgy, that she'd committed some heinous crime. If he didn't have any greater trust in her than that, so be it.

She'd never tell him in a million years that she'd spent the night as copilot—a freebie, at that—for Buzz Anderson, a longtime pal who owned his own charter service and wasn't averse to letting her pump him for information about running such a business herself. She'd come back to New Orleans filled with ideas and enthusiasm, and now this jerk was treating her like some sort of criminal.

She glowered at Logan and added. "Not that it's any of your business what I do or where I go."

"It is if I'm responsible for you."

She saw red. "Responsible! Look, bud, I'm full grown and I don't need—"

"And it is since I finally spoke with Jack and maybe we can really talk business now. Or are you having so much fun you've forgotten the reason for your little visit to our fair city?"

"I haven't forgotten that I think you're the most obnoxious person I've ever known, Golden Boy," she said, sneering. "Now let go of me."

"Don't you care what Jack had to say?"

Rage made her ears ring, but she stood her ground. "So tell me."

Resentment curled Logan's lips. "Anything Baby Sister wants, she gets."

She tilted her chin defiantly. "Works for me."

"So between you and Jack Campbell, you're going to drive Campbell Drilling straight into bankruptcy. Is that what you want?"

She hesitated, then narrowed her eyes in suspicion. "I don't believe you."

"Why should I lie?"

"I think you've got such a chip on your shoulder you'd do anything to thwart me—just for fun." She pierced him with a hot blue glare that brought back memories of young love, hot jungle nights and betrayal. "As I recall, you're just that kind of guy."

She'd hit a button. With an oath, Logan shoved her against the refrigerator, his face an ominous scowl. "Back off, Bliss. You don't have the faintest notion who I am."

Nose to nose, she breathed defiance at him. "I remember."

"Is that what this is all about?" His eyes were heated, his features taut. "Grow up. Get over it."

Her soft, surprising laugh was rife with mockery. "No, you misunderstand. I'm grateful that I learned an early lesson about men I'll never forget. Quite possibly you've shaped my whole personality."

His hands were on her shoulders, pressing her against the cool steel, her palms braced against the muscular planes of his chest. Somewhere in the silent house a telephone rang. They both ignored it. "Damn you," he muttered.

"Yes, indeed." Her smile was feline. "*Now* you can feel responsible."

"It's just a game to you, isn't it?" His voice was harsh as flint on steel. "Well, maybe two can still play."

Bending, he swept his mouth along the satiny curve of her neck. Bliss felt the burn of his lips on her skin like a skittering of electricity that jolted through her entire body. She gasped in outrage, in surprise, in shocked pleasure, and he pressed a sizzling kiss in the tender hollow behind her ear, sending shivers and shock waves straight to her core.

Fear coursed through her, icing her veins, and she struggled against him. "Stop it. What do you think you're doing?"

Logan pulled away, staring into her startled eyes. His fingers flexed on her shoulders. He reached up and released her hair clip, letting her blond hair fall loose and free down her back. His eyes darkened at the sight, and the intention Bliss read in their depths made panic rise like a flood tide.

"Don't you dare," she whispered, shaking in every fiber. "Don't you dare."

He didn't seem to hear her warning, bending closer, his gaze locked on her mouth. Bliss held her breath.

"Logan!" Valerie stood in the kitchen doorway, her dark eyes wide, her face white. "Dear God—Logan!"

Logan pulled away, and Bliss slumped against the refrigerator door, her knees like jelly.

"Mother," Logan began. But Valerie had taken a step, staggering so she almost fell, and whatever explanation he'd meant to make was lost as he leaped to her side, taking her elbow and guiding her to a kitchen chair. "Mom, what is it?"

Valerie looked at him with eyes as scared and wounded as a child's, and Bliss felt her heart sink with a terrible premonition.

"That was Russ," Valerie said, choking. "Your father—dear God, Logan! Jack's had a heart attack!"

Chapter Five

The roar of the twin turboprops of Campbell Drilling's six-seater Beechcraft filled the cockpit. Sitting in the copilot's seat, Logan was glad for the noise that made the stony silence that had hovered between him and Bliss since they'd taken off from the New Orleans airport less noticeable. They flew into the setting sun, and he looked away from the glare, between wisps of clouds, at the rugged west Texas terrain flashing beneath them. To the southeast, an ominous purple band of thunderheads, which Bliss had changed course to avoid, rose from the horizon.

Damn it all. Logan cursed himself roundly. With the news of Jack's attack, he and Bliss had both reacted in typical fashion, ending up in a shouting match when he'd insisted on accompanying her in the company plane to Chihuahua. After their confrontation, Bliss hadn't been willing to give him the time of day, much

less a lift to Mexico. Only Valerie's tears and pleading
had settled them down long enough to form a temporary
truce. Despite their antagonism, it made sense for them
to go to Jack's side together, but it didn't make it any
easier.

Logan realized it was all his fault, of course.

Why didn't he have sense enough to keep his damn
hands off her? he asked himself, feeling the familiar
surge of irritation and frustration that dealing with Bliss
inevitably produced. Whatever tenuous status quo their
sparring and bickering had given them, he'd nearly destroyed that artificial wall when he'd touched her. If
there was ever a woman who was wrong for him, it was
Bliss Abernathy. Why, then, couldn't he forget his fas-
cination with the hellcat? He gave himself a little inter-
nal shake at his foolishness, supremely conscious of the
woman at his side expertly piloting the aircraft.

For once, she had her hair pulled back in a sedate,
businesslike French braid, and she'd changed her rumpled clothes for the royal blue zippered jumpsuit with
the orange Campbell Drilling logo over the left breast.
It was the same logo that graced the outside of the white
and blue plane. It didn't help that the garment fit her
like a second skin, and the zipper that ran from collarbone to navel was enough to tempt any man. A folded
blue bandanna circled her forehead, and her eyes were
hidden behind gold-rimmed aviator sunglasses.

Logan felt that it was just as well he couldn't see her
eyes, considering there was always the possibility that
looks could kill.

It was hard to know what she was really feeling, now.
After all, Jack was as much—more—of a father to her
as to Logan. After the first moment's shock and angry
reaction to his plans to accompany her to his father's

side, she'd been icily collected. He could only guess that she felt the same incredulity that hammered at his consciousness.

This can't be happening. Black Jack Campbell was invincible. A larger-than-life figure who'd played the role of warrior king, shaping and forging paths that had made his children what they were. The possibility that mortality had finally caught up with him seemed an incongruity not to be reckoned with.

Dammit, Dad, don't you die on me, Logan thought angrily. Not with harsh words hanging between them, not with unfinished business dividing father and son. Logan's fists clenched. A raw ache burned in his gut. As usual, Russ, the chosen son, was the one who was at Jack's side and Logan's fear and love for his father churned in his belly with equal parts of resentment and anger.

"How much longer?" he demanded suddenly.

Hands playing lightly on the controls, Bliss barely spared him a glance. "An hour or a little better. We just crossed the Pecos River into Big Bend country, but I wanted to avoid that line of weather. We should be across the border by dark."

Logan grunted an acknowledgment, letting his gaze drift over her grim features. It occurred to him with a sense of shocked wonder that it was the first time he'd ever seen her when she was less than stunning. But it appeared her late night partying and the stress of the situation had caught up with her, making her lovely mouth droop with fatigue and painting faint blue circles beneath her sunglasses. Finding out that the goddess was human after all tugged at a part of him he'd rather not confess existed where Bliss was concerned, the part that found her feminine frailty appealing, the masculine instinct that wanted to protect her.

He stifled a mirthless grin. The last thing a hellcat like Bliss needed was protection, especially from him. She'd scratch his eyes out if he so much as hinted at any weakness in her character. Despite the signs of strain, she was all business, perfectly at home in her job, her strength and competence apparent in every movement, every adjustment she made to the controls.

A sudden burst of turbulence caught the plane, pushing it up, then dipping it downward in a belly-clenching drop. Logan caught his breath as Bliss brought the craft under control. He'd flown in the company plane—small enough for short, off-the-beaten-path runways, big enough to transfer critical pieces of oilfield equipment when necessary—but usually in the passenger seats. His toes curled in his tennis shoes and the sweat popped out under his arms at the sudden wind shear. Being right where the action was going on was disconcerting, but he'd be damned if he'd show Bliss he was nervous.

"You buckled in?" she asked.

"Yeah."

"We might run into some more of that."

He grimaced. "Great."

"You aren't going to throw up, are you?"

"Hell, no."

"There's some motion sickness tablets in the—"

"I'm all right," Logan said. "You just pay attention to what you're doing."

Her mouth compressed. "Look, amigo, I don't need advice from the likes of you, so—"

A jolt like the blow of a giant fist rocked the plane. Immediately, it careened to starboard, and Bliss broke off as she struggled with the bucking aircraft.

Logan gripped his seat as the world tilted on its axis. "What was that?"

As if in answer, small plumes of acrid smoke drifted from the overhead vent and from underneath the instrument panel.

"Damn. Lightning hit us." Bliss tore off her sunglasses. "Hit the radio with a Mayday. We're going down."

"What!"

"The radio, dammit!" Small beads of sweat appeared on her upper lip as she wrestled with the control stick. The nose of the plane dipped, and they plummeted toward the Texas desert.

With his stomach lodged somewhere in the back of his throat, Logan flipped the switch and grabbed the mike. A shaft of flame spurted from the overhead vent. "It's dead," he announced.

"Electrical fire," she muttered. "My instruments are gone. Hold on. This is going to be rough."

Logan had never experienced anything so soul-terrifying as those minutes falling toward the earth. Mountains rose in ragged peaks below them, spreading out between the desert flats, and he was certain Bliss would never be able to negotiate between the rocky red summits. Smoke filled the cockpit, and he coughed harshly, the air suddenly too hot and thick to breathe. Bliss had pulled on an oxygen mask, and he searched for his own, sliding it over his nose gratefully. Then they were leveling out, rushing down a canyon across a sandy expanse studded with mesquite and cactus.

Struggling with controls gone sluggish, Bliss slapped at instruments that might or might not respond, her eyes tearing against the gray-black smoke. "Hang on," she repeated hoarsely.

The sand looked flat and relatively even, and Logan had sudden hope of a safe landing, but just as she touched the wheels down, a deep arroyo sprang up before them. Panic settled in Logan's chest. If they slammed nose-first into that crevasse—

Bliss pulled up on the controls with all her might, lifting the nose slightly, no sign of panic in her steady actions, only the most intense concentration Logan had ever seen. Then they were over the obstacle and the wheels bumped...bumped, slamming his head against something so hard that he saw stars and black space.

Somehow they were down, the landing gear slewing on the sand and scrub separating razorback mountain ranges, the plane careening madly, dragging a wing. He had visions of the aircraft cartwheeling, but miraculously, they slowed, then jolted to a precarious stop, resting on a crumpled wing. Snapped to reality, Logan felt something wet on his face, but Bliss was already stripping off the oxygen mask, fumbling with buckles, unstrapping herself. He followed suit.

"The fire extinguisher—"

"Forget it!" he snapped, tumbling free of his seat and dragging at her arm. "We've got to get the hell out of here!"

The stair door was halfway sprung from the impact, and for a horrified instant, Logan feared they were trapped inside with the smoke curling around them, obliterating all vision. Then the latch gave, and the doorway with its built-in steps opened outward, at a crazy angle, to be sure, but still revealing an escape route to open sky. The fresh air fanned the flames and smoke, and superheated air rushed from the passenger compartment.

He reached for Bliss. "Come on!"

"Wait."

Before he could protest, she disappeared into the inky smoke. Petrified, he roared her name. "Bliss!"

He was about to plunge into the blackness after her when she reappeared, choking and gasping, dragging the straps of a blue duffel bag. Furious and frightened at the thought of what could have happened to this foolish, headstrong woman—what might still happen to the both of them—he grabbed her arm and shoved her bodily from the plane, then jumped.

It was a longer fall than he'd anticipated, and the impact on the sand took his breath for an instant. Sprawled beside him, Bliss groaned softly. Gasping, Logan rolled to his feet, clasped her around the waist and hauled her away from the smoking wreck as fast as his feet could carry them.

"Let go," she gasped. She favored her right leg and clutched the duffel as if their lives depended on it. "I can do it—"

"Shut up and run, dammit!"

They weren't a hundred yards from the aircraft when it exploded. The blast threw them headfirst into the lee of a mesquite bush. Bruised and scratched, tasting sand and blood, his ears ringing, Logan threw himself over Bliss, covering her as flaming debris rained down around them.

An eternity later, Logan raised his head for a cautious look. The plane was a flaming pile of metal, the bold Campbell Drilling logo on the side blistering into sooty obliteration. There was a curious split in what was left of the tail. He thought they were at a safe enough distance, so when Bliss moved beneath him, he rolled to a sitting position, his hand on her arm to balance her.

"You okay?" he demanded harshly. Smoke still

burned at the back of his throat, making his voice as raspy as his dad's. He blinked, brushing wetness from his forehead with the back of his hand. He was vaguely surprised to see crimson.

She sat up, brushing sand from her jumpsuit with trembling hands. "Yeah, I think. Wrenched my knee when you pushed me." Her words were shaky, and as she sat straighter her eyes went wide at the sight of the wreckage. There was a scratch on her cheekbone, and her mouth wobbled. "Oh, gee," Bliss mourned softly, her sapphire eyes wide with grief, "and she was such a sweet bird, too."

"Is that all you can say?" Out of nowhere, his anger came roaring back. He was sprawled on the hot sand, his hands locked around her forearms to shake her senseless as he shouted. "Woman, you're a lunatic! What in the hell were you thinking, going back in like that? What was so important, anyway, your makeup bag? If you ever do that to me again—"

"It's the survival pack," she said, glaring at him. "And from the looks of things, we're going to need it."

He wasn't in the mood to be pacified by logic. "You could have been killed! I swear, Bliss—"

A muffled pop as something inside the wreck exploded made them jump and turned them as one toward the plane again.

And then, to Logan's total astonishment, the hellcat beside him burst into tears.

She didn't know why she was crying. All she knew was that somehow she was in Logan's arms, her face pressed into his chest, and for the moment it was the most comforting place in the universe and she never wanted to leave.

"Shh, honey, it's okay." Logan's voice was gruff, but his hand as he smoothed the loose tendrils of hair from her hot face was tender. "We're safe. It's going to be all right."

"I'm sorry," she murmured over and over, shaking her head.

"You did fine. It's okay. Just reaction." His tone was soothing, the hand he slid over her back warm and consoling.

Bliss snuggled closer, every instinct longing to bury her tumbled, garbled, terrified self in Logan's strength. His shirt was damp with sweat and her tears. She could smell the scent of his skin and the faint pungent tang of his soap. She was embarrassed at this show of feminine histrionics, but to be held felt so *good...*

Reaction, that's all it was, just as he'd said. They'd both been through something totally harrowing, so it was natural to gravitate toward each other for solace, but in the depths of her heart, she knew it was foolish, dangerous. With a supreme effort, she drew a deep breath to still her racing heart and tried for some semblance of composure.

Reluctantly, she pushed out of his embrace, swiping at her damp cheeks with the back of her hand. She pulled off her bandanna, dabbed at her eyes and shoved it into her pocket. "Here you are bleeding, and I'm blubbering like a baby. I'm sorry. Let me see what I can do."

"I'm all right."

She snorted, inspecting his bloodstained face. Scarlet all but obscured the right side of his head. The deep gouge running from his sandy eyebrow to his hairline still oozed blood.

"Right. You look like a stuck pig." She unzipped

the duffel and dug for the first aid kit. "You must have taken quite a wallop."

Logan fingered his forehead gingerly, almost in surprise. "I don't remember."

Bliss ripped into a package of alcohol swabs, then grimaced as she came up on her knees, breathing through her mouth at the stab of pain from her right knee.

"What is it?" Logan demanded. The acrid odor of smoke scented the parched desert air and mingled with a hint of ozone from the rumbling thunderheads to the south. The sun hovered on the western horizon, and spiny yucca, creosote bushes and prickly pears cast long, eerie shadows, making Bliss feel as though she'd stepped through the door into an alien land.

"Nothing," she denied, ignoring the pain. "Hold still, this is going to sting." Catching his chin in one hand, she began to clean the wound.

Logan jumped and mouthed a string of extremely colorful expletives.

"Not bad for a city boy," Bliss complimented, working swiftly.

"Yeah, I'm a man of many talents," he replied, gritting his teeth. "Although I haven't had your opportunities for a foreign education in four-letter words. What the devil's taking so long?"

"Relax." She frowned and chewed her lower lip. "It's not as bad as it looks, but it could use a few stitches."

"Just tape it up."

"It'll scar and spoil your pretty face."

His mouth twisted. "Save it, okay? What other choice have we got, anyway? Unless you're willing to do the stitching?"

"My skills don't extend that far," she said hastily. "Let me get a couple of butterfly bandages on it. Are you dizzy? Seeing double?"

"Don't be such a mother hen," he growled, batting her hand away as she applied the last adhesive strip. "I said I'm okay."

The adrenaline surge of their close call was receding, and she still felt chagrined at her crying jag, so Bliss took refuge in the familiar—irritation and anger. "Look, buster, we're stuck out here, and I don't want you playing hero and making things worse, okay? Now, how do you feel?"

Logan's face was more or less clean, so his glare of resentment was easy to read. "I've got a King Kong-size headache, and I feel like I'm going to be sick. Satisfied?"

"As long as you do it over there where I can't see."

"I'll try to oblige." He rolled to his feet, and it was clear he was making an effort not to stagger. Automatically, she struggled up to steady him, wincing at the pain in her knee, but he shook off her hand angrily. "And you can stow the sarcasm, okay? We're in a hell of a fix, or hadn't you noticed? God, woman! We were both nearly killed!"

In an instant, the sting of tears was back, and her throat clogged so she could only whisper, "I know. It's my fault."

Logan scowled, startled. "What?"

She turned away, her movements uncharacteristically awkward. "My fault. Maybe I shouldn't have flown. I was too upset and worried about Jack. And I haven't had any sleep." She hit her palm against her forehead. "Stupid, stupid. I must have made some mistake."

"It was a lightning strike!" He sounded mystified.

"It shouldn't have done that kind of damage."

Logan grabbed her shoulder and swung her around, frowning into her face. "So this time it did. You can't blame yourself."

She tossed her head, swallowing hard. "So who made the decision to go north around the storm front? I guess I should have gone south over the Gulf. No, it's my responsibility."

"It was a freak accident, came out of nowhere! You couldn't have anticipated it. Just look at the damn tail!" He hauled her around to face the wreckage. "There's a crack in it the size of the Mississippi!"

"But—"

"I won't hear any more of this, do you understand?" he growled, his fingers tightening on her shoulders. "You were magnificent! You got us down, and we walked away from it."

"Ran," she revised, the corners of her lips twisting.

"I stand corrected." The tension in his face relaxed, and he almost smiled. "At any rate, ma'am, I am both indebted and in awe. You saved our lives."

The respect in his expression was unexpected, and the touch of his hands made her feel flustered. *Reaction,* she reminded herself, struggling to think straight.

"For the moment, anyway," she said, slipping from his grasp. "The question is, what's our next step?"

"Better try to take our bearings," he responded. "And that was quick thinking, getting the survival gear, even if you did scare the bejesus out of me. First off—dare I hope there's water in there?"

"We'll see how much."

For the next few minutes they explored the survival kit, revealing emergency rations, compass, flashlight, flares, knife, a high-tech, paper-thin metallic survival blanket, the first aid kit and four quarts of water.

Logan shook his head in dismay. "Damn. This isn't good. We need a gallon a day each in the desert."

"It might be enough," Bliss hazarded, a frown pleating her brow at the array spread out on the sandy ground. "If we stay with the wreck and conserve our strength..."

Logan sat on his haunches and looked at her as if she'd just grown two heads. "Are you nuts? We're not staying here."

"It's standard procedure," she began.

"Dammit, no." Logan rose to his feet and shoved a hand through his sandy, sweat-streaked hair. The bandage on his forehead gave him the air of a bandit. "Dad's condition wasn't stable. We just can't sit around here until someone comes to rescue us—if they do. It might be too late."

A spurt of alarm had her on her feet as well. Although dusk was approaching, the temperature still hovered in the nineties, and sweat dripped down her spine and stained her underarms. "Logan, be reasonable. We can't just head out into the desert. That would be suicide."

"The way I see it, we don't have much choice."

Her lips compressed. "For a city boy, you're making an awfully big leap of faith."

"Am I?" His tawny eyes narrowed. "Tell me, do you know where we are?"

She hesitated. "Not exactly. North of the national park, at least. And I'm fairly certain we crossed a north-south highway sometime back, but this is pretty empty country, and I changed course to avoid that weather...."

"Right." His mouth flattened into a grim line. "So we were off course to start with, we weren't able to radio our position, and the flight plan you filed is virtually useless to anyone who'll be looking for us. Not that anyone will be for at least several more hours, because we're not even overdue yet."

"Someone might spot the wreckage from the air."

"That's a long shot, and you know it."

"No," she said shaking her head. "The smoke—"

"Won't be visible after dark. And that's not going to be long from now." He gestured at the bands of tangerine and violet beginning to stain the peaks poking up along the western horizon. Daylight lasted a long time in this part of the country, but when night fell, it came in a hurry.

Bliss thought desperately. "There's still the transmitter."

He made a disgusted sound and jabbed a finger toward what was left of the plane. "Are you kidding? What are the odds the emergency locator transmitter survived that last blast?"

"Not very good," she admitted.

"Bingo. And even if it's still functioning, it'll take Russ some time to figure out what's happened and alert the authorities. In the meantime, we could be using the cover of night to make some miles toward that highway. All we have to do is go east."

"That's crazy." She limped toward the gear and began packing it. "We haven't got any idea how far away that could be. We could get out there and get stranded while meantime the county search and rescue locates the plane—then where would we be?"

"So we'll leave them a note. Pile rocks in an arrow to show the direction we've gone. We can't just sit here."

"I can. And you're making an emotional decision

because you're afraid Jack's going to die with Russ at his side instead of you," she accused hotly. "This isn't some sort of kid's game you're talking about, you know."

His features hardened into stone. "Keep your nose out of my relationship with my father."

"He's my father, too!" she shouted, shoving the last of the gear in the duffel and standing to face him. "Almost, anyway. I'm just as worried about him as you are. But getting ourselves killed out in the desert isn't going to help him."

"I'm willing to accept the risks," he responded, his fists clenching. The look he shot her dared her to argue, said he'd gladly send her merrily to hell if she tried. "So take it or leave it, Bliss. I'm going whether you do or not."

Shock made her blink. "You'd leave me here?"

He turned from her hurt expression, scrubbing his palms down his face. "Hell, it might be the best plan anyway," he muttered. "Double our chances. Whichever one of us got help first, we could send a rescue party back."

"No." Despite the heat, she shivered.

"Think about it. That knee of yours—"

"It's okay," she said quickly.

"The hell it is."

Before she could react, he shoved her on the sand and began rolling up the leg of her jumpsuit. What he saw made him curse again. "Dammit, Bliss! It's already swelling. Why didn't you say something?"

His fingers examined the puffy flesh around her knee-cap, making her wince even though his touch was gentle. She barely suppressed a groan. "It's nothing, really," she panted.

"I did this to you. Honey, I'm sorry."

She shrugged. "Small price to pay for saving my behind. I probably would have tried to put out the fire."

"Yeah, you and Russ—courageous fools," he said, digging in the duffel. He retrieved an elastic bandage from the first aid kit and began wrapping her knee. "Here, this should help."

The touch of his hands on the inside of her leg gave her a quivery sensation in her middle. "I can do it," she said hastily.

Annoyance tightened his mouth. "For once, will you shut up and let me help? I've had some training."

"Yeah?" Her tone was skeptical. "Where? Handing out Band-Aids to the beautiful babes at the Racquet Club?"

He tied the ends of the bandage neatly, his scowl deepening. "You never let up, do you?" He grabbed a bottle of water and passed it to her. "Here, drink some of this."

Bliss couldn't contain her surprise. "Shouldn't we be trying to conserve it?"

"The point is to stay hydrated, even if you run out of water tomorrow. Otherwise you get fuzzy-headed and start making bad judgments, making a bad situation even worse." He nodded as she took a long swallow, then took the bottle and drank.

Seeing his lips on the rim of the bottle where hers had rested produced that quivery feeling again. Bliss decided she was already on the point of making some serious errors in judgment where Logan was concerned. The attraction that wouldn't let up, the history between them—it all added up to a disaster much bigger than any plane crash. And his practical knowledge and coolness under pressure impressed her despite herself. Her knee was already beginning to feel better. She had better get a grip before things got out of hand.

Steeling herself, she forced casualness into her tone. "So, how come you know all this stuff?"

He capped the bottle, not meeting her eyes. "Picked it up here and there."

"No, really. Tell me."

He gave her a resentful, challenging look. "I was an Eagle Scout, okay? And I've backpacked into the wilderness a time or two—Tetons, Appalachia, Alaska."

She'd had no idea. But it only reinforced her conception of him—golden boy, Mr. Success, like a modern-day James Bond, at home wherever he went, never at a loss. It was hard to compete with someone so clearly superior.

Carefully, she began rolling down her pants leg. "Eagle, huh? Is there anything you ever did in your whole life that wasn't absolutely perfect?"

He frowned. "I'm as human as they come, Bliss."

"It never seemed that way to me."

From out of nowhere, his grin flashed, dazzling her, as brilliant as the sun just setting on the horizon. "You think I'm perfect, huh? That's very encouraging."

"Don't get the big head," she snapped. "Overconfidence can lead to those bad judgments you were talking about, and we're not out of this yet."

His expression sobered as he helped her to her feet. "Yeah, I know. Which is why I think we ought to think seriously about splitting up. You're obviously reluctant to make the trek—"

"No!" The thought of being left behind produced a jolt of panic.

"I'll rig some sort of shelter for you and make a

signal fire before I go." He picked up the duffel. "We can divide the gear and—"

"I said no." Her voice rose. "What do I have to do to get you to listen to me, hit you over the head with a two-by-four?"

He sighed, then said gently, "You'll only slow me down."

She swallowed hard, a knot of abandonment clogging her throat. "I won't, I promise. But I'm not staying here alone. I know you don't like me, but I can't believe you'd do this."

He turned to look at her, suddenly aware of the stricken expression on her face. Indecision warred behind his golden brown eyes, then he laid an arm around her stiff shoulders. "It has nothing to do with the way I feel about you. But we've got to be practical."

"But you're the one with the head injury. How practical will it be if you pass out two miles down the trail?" Her lips felt frozen, but she forced steadiness into her voice. "No deal, amigo. Stay or go, we're together."

Seeing the determination in her expression, Logan's arm tightened around her, and then he surprised her completely by pressing a kiss to her forehead. "All right, honey. Together it is. I just hope you've got your walking shoes on."

She stuck out a foot, displaying a sturdy leather flight boot. "I'll bet you a hundred bucks I do better than you."

"You could be right." He scowled at his athletic shoes. "These aren't going to be much help if—when—we run into the worst of the desert critters out there."

"The worst?"

"Rattlesnakes. They hunt at night."

Bliss swallowed. "Oh, God."

"At least we'll have a full moon. The September one is supposed to be the brightest of the year. That ought to help."

"Yeah, I'll try to remember that while I'm listening for that warning rattle," she said uneasily.

"I never said this wouldn't be hard. You can still back out."

She straightened. "You're not going to get shut of me that easily, Logan Campbell."

He gave her shoulders a squeeze. "That's my girl."

"So we go together?" Bliss was chagrined to find that relief made her words wobble. It was all she could do not to lean into him.

Logan looked toward the east, his eyes narrowed as dusk swept toward them like a black wave. "As I said, what other choice have we got?"

Chapter Six

"There's no other choice. We've got to assume the worst."

"Oh, Russell, no."

Leaning against the nurse's station, Russ Campbell gripped the phone hard as his mother's moan of distress drifted over the crackling long-distance line. The late-night routine of the Chihuahua Medical Center flowed around him, the white-uniformed nurses murmuring in Spanish, the odor of antiseptic, the beep of monitors coming from the cardiac ward where his father lay, finally resting more comfortably.

Russ steeled himself. God, he hated hospitals. Had since he was a kid and had spent so much time being poked and prodded and stuck with needles. The sights and smells made him break out in a cold sweat. Only the fact that it was his dad—that it was Black Jack Campbell himself—in that hospital bed hooked up to

all those wires and tubes made it possible for Russ to
even pass through the doors.

And now this. Dammit all to hell!

"We've got to face it, Mom," Russ said, rubbing his
grainy eyes.

It was well after midnight, and he had gotten only
snatches of sleep since Jack's collapse during Señor
Garcia's fiesta in the Campbells' honor. He felt a sympathetic hand on his arm and looked into Manuella Garcia's dark eyes. Precocious daughter of his host, she'd
stayed at his side throughout the hospital vigil. Giving
her fingers a fraternal pat, he smiled and indicated with
a nod of his auburn-tinted head for her to take her seat
again on the waiting room bench.

As Manuella dutifully followed his directions, he
hoped he hadn't given her the wrong idea with his attentions. She was a sweet señorita, but rather insipid,
especially compared to the still-vivid memory of another black-eyed girl and an unforgettable six weeks of
heaven and hell....

Caught unaware by the direction of his thoughts, he
shook off the fancy as the perambulations of a stressed-
out mind and focused on what he was saying to Valerie.

"They're eight hours overdue. No matter what, Bliss
wouldn't leave us hanging all this time, not if there was
any way on earth she could contact us. Something's
happened."

"They—Bliss, Logan—they're down, then."

Russ's throat tightened in rage and terror and help-
lessness as he tried not to think about the unthinkable.

Bliss. Logan. Oh, God.

"Maybe they just had engine trouble and had to make
an emergency landing," he said, trying to sound hope-

ful, "but the fact that we've heard nothing over the radio…"

He heard Valerie take a shaky breath at the implication, but then she rallied like the trooper she'd always been. "All right," she said, "just tell me what to do."

"Dad's stable enough to move to Dallas by Medevac in the morning. I hate to ask, but could you come and oversee that?"

"Your father and I have had our differences, but of course I can," Valerie agreed. Russ could almost see her calculating the logistics of getting to Mexico with her former CEO's expertise. He had no doubt she'd be there before dawn. She continued, "And meantime, you'll…"

"Fly to San Antonio to head up the search operations," Russ replied. "That was the last radio contact we had from them. I'll notify the proper authorities and call in all the favors I can—friends, competitors, anyone with a plane or a chopper. It's a damned huge amount of territory to cover between here and there, and mighty rough country. We'll have to rely on volunteers."

"Call Jake Lattimer," Valerie suggested. "He still flies a helicopter. I know he'll help."

"Good idea."

The Lattimers of the Lazy L had always been good friends as well as occasional business partners. In fact, Russ knew that, at Jack's behest, Logan had been in contact with them about that Barnette business. But Jack certainly wasn't in any condition to worry about old grudges at the moment, and as for Logan…

Russ shoved a hand through his hair, an identical gesture he'd shared with his twin since they were kids. "Look, Mom, don't worry. They're all right. I'd know if Logan was…if he…"

Russ grimaced. Okay, so it was a twin thing, and maybe meaningless to anyone who hadn't shared a womb with a sibling. And all right, he and Logan had butted heads—and sometimes knuckles and bloody noses—since the day they were hatched, but there was a *connection*, and his instincts said it hadn't been broken. Yet. Russ couldn't express the certainty he felt in his gut any better than that.

"He's okay," he repeated.

"I pray you're right," Valerie said, choking. Then her voice became stronger. "I've got calls to make. Don't worry, I'll take care of your father."

"Good."

"And, Russell?"

"Yes, Mom?"

"Find them."

Russ's jaw flexed. "I will, Mom. I promise."

He hung up the phone, only to meet Manuella's hopeful, love-struck gaze. He found himself wishing heartily that she would just go home. Because he had a lot to do, and nursing the ego of a sultry señorita with a crush on him wasn't high on his agenda. No, when it came down to it, what mattered most was family, and his needed his undivided attention at the moment.

He thought about Bliss's smile and Logan's hard-headedness, and tried to fight off the all-encompassing dread that formed a knot in his chest. They had to be all right. *They had to.*

"Logan," he muttered, "I told you if you messed with Baby Sister you'd have to answer to me. Don't make me whip your butt."

"I don't like the looks of this."

"What?" Her groggy voice shrill with sudden alarm,

Bliss lurched to a reeling stop, forcing Logan to sidestep her to keep from plowing into her from behind. "Is it a snake? Where?"

He caught her arms to steady them both on the uneven ground of the dry wash. They'd been walking for hours in the moonlight, following a circuitous path between the dagger blades of lechuguilla and the flat needle-studded pads of prickly pear cacti when they'd come across the wide ditch. Since it led generally east and its floor had been scoured clean of the worst of the desert's more venomous vegetation, it had seemed logical to descend the sloping walls of the wash to follow the easier path. Now Logan was beginning to have the uneasy sensation that he'd made a miscalculation.

"No rattler, but—"

Something small skittered through the clumps of grass to the right of them, and Bliss jumped and pointed. "There. What was that?"

"Jackrabbit. Or maybe a kangaroo rat. Lighten up, Bliss," he groused. "Anything out here is more scared of you than you are of it."

She twisted free of his grasp and, although the moonlight filtering through the rapidly clouding sky was fitful, he was sure the look she shot him was laden with resentment. "Easy for you to say. You're not the one blazing the trail."

"You volunteered," he reminded her. "Said your footwear was more protection than mine. And I did cut you a shillelagh."

She waved the bent and mutated club he'd hacked out of a dead mesquite bush. "Much good it'll do me when I step on the Godzilla of rattlers."

"As much racket as you're making, no self-respecting snake would come near you, so relax."

"If you think you can do better, be my guest!"

"I'm not complaining, for crying out loud!"

In fact, despite a bum knee, she'd been doing a hell of a job, setting a pace that he knew was costing her while he carried their supplies, handles of the duffel bag strung over his arms like a backpack. But he also knew that despite the relative coolness of the night, her stamina was waning, as evidenced by her increasing irritability. Of course, with her astringent tongue, sometimes it was hard to tell. But they couldn't afford to stop, so if his goading her kept her going, all the better. Besides, there was a new worry to consider.

"We've got to find a place to climb out of this hole," he said, scanning the dark shadows of the mini cliffs rising on either side of them.

She turned to stare at him. "Are you loco? I'm damned tired of dodging rock nettles and every other kind of booby-trapped plant. I've got needles in places I don't want to mention. Besides, we've made twice the time—"

Logan gave her a shove. "The subject isn't open for discussion. Get moving. It's going to rain."

"So? What's wrong with cooling things off?"

As if in answer, a rumble of thunder vibrated through the air. Logan glanced over his shoulder just as a darker-than-night cloud obscured the moon. Stars disappeared, to be replaced by the ever-closer flashes of lightning. Logan stifled a curse as Bliss balked.

"Haven't you ever heard of a flash flood?" he demanded roughly, giving her another push. "If it's raining upstream—" His tennis shoes squished on a tiny trickle of moisture dampening the stream bed, a harbinger of greater, more deadly things to come. He didn't bother to stifle his curse. "Dammit, I said *move!*"

Despite her fatigue, she caught the urgency in his tone. "All right, I'm going. You don't have to shout."

A crack of electricity and a nearly simultaneous clap of thunder prevented any answer. Grabbing her arm, Logan supported her, and they ran awkwardly together toward the sandy slope. The light they'd enjoyed was gone, and the mesquite bushes struggling for life on the side of the crevice made specterlike shadows, a confusion of images that made it difficult—impossible—to judge where their easiest ascent lay. Logan went with gut instinct, chose a hearty mesquite as a step stool and shoved Bliss upward.

"Climb," he ordered tersely.

This time she didn't argue.

Though the incline was only ten to twelve feet high, by the time they'd scrambled and slithered up the rocky, sandy, unstable face of the cliff and tumbled over the top, they were both filthy, scratched, winded and drenched in sweat. But Logan wasn't satisfied. With the thunder coming in great, deafening reverberations and lightning sizzling over their heads, he put an arm around Bliss's waist and hauled her through the scrub away from the edge.

"Wait," she gasped. "I've got to catch...my breath."

"In a minute."

Large drops of rain plopped into the dry earth, scenting the air with precious moisture. The drops became a flurry, then a shower, then a raging downpour as the skies let loose their watery burden amid the furies of an all-out electrical storm. Logan blinked against the water streaming down his face. In the millisecond-long flash of a lightning strike, he saw a rocky outcropping jutting from the slope of a small dune and instantly changed direction. It wasn't much shelter, but it was better than nothing.

They fell into the small haven with gasps of gratitude, their ears ringing, half-blinded by the driving rain. Logan shoved Bliss as far under the overhang as possible, slid off the duffel and delved into it.

"Stay here," he ordered.

"Logan!" Bliss spluttered, wiping her eyes, obviously mystified that he'd brave the elements for some mysterious purpose.

Within the space of half a dozen thunderclaps, he was back, crawling into the cramped space with her, sluicing water from his hair and face. A fine mist of rain could still reach them, but at least it wasn't the driving, blinding downpour drenching the open desert.

"What the hell did you do?" she demanded, crossing her arms over her chest. The rapid drop in temperature, coupled with the wind and moisture, made her shiver visibly.

Logan wrung water out of the hem of his shirt. "Pegged out the survival blanket. If we're lucky, it'll catch us some drinking water. Maybe. If it doesn't blow away. If it doesn't split open."

Bliss wiped her face with her fingertips, tugging the wet tendrils of hair that had escaped her braid. "Pretty quick thinking for a city boy."

For once, her tone lacked her usual acerbic quality, and Logan had the feeling that she meant the compliment sincerely. It gave him a strange inner quiver to think that Bliss might admire him for something. He was so accustomed to her dismissing him as a soft-palmed playboy, a whiz in the corporate world but generally useless otherwise, that he savored the feeling.

"I guess even tennis bums have their moments," he said.

"On occasion." He could hear the smile in her voice, then the puzzlement. "Why did you ever quit it, anyway? You could have gone pro, from what I heard."

Logan remembered the dilemma, the conflict he'd felt. How the lure of the pro circuit was so sweet he could almost taste it, how desperately he'd wanted to give it a try, just to see if he was made of the right stuff, just to see for himself, for no one else...

"It was kid's stuff," he said gruffly, using Jack's unfeeling words. "And I had obligations. Grandpère Gaspard was dying, and Mother needed help at the helm of the family business. Then there was Dad and Campbell Drilling to consider."

"So you gave up your dream to take on someone else's load," she said softly.

He shook his damp head. "No, just exchanged it for something with more future to it. And I haven't been disappointed. Much as you like to sneer, I've found success, money, power."

"But at what cost?"

"I'm not complaining about the trade-off."

"Maybe you should. Seems to me you spend all your time working—and maybe not for anything you really believe in or want."

The tenor of the conversation was beginning to irritate him more than his soaked clothes, more than the sand grinding into his skin or the dripping mist blowing across his face. How dare she question his decisions? "Lay off, Bliss," he growled. "What I believe in is taking responsibility, and you're in no position to judge my choices, anyway."

Shifting uncomfortably, she hugged herself against

the raindrops blowing into their meager shelter, and her tone turned mulish. "All I meant was, sometimes you have to do something just for yourself."

"Is that what you're doing?" he demanded harshly. "Leaving the company, taking what you can get, and to hell with the consequences?"

"It's not like that."

"Then tell me what it is like," he demanded.

She hesitated, as if she were about to confess something important, but then the belligerence in his words turned her stubborn. In the off-and-on flash of lightning, Logan could see her tucking her wet hair behind her ears, shaking her head. "You wouldn't understand."

Disapproval, disappointment—it was hard to tell which—made his mouth hard. "I understand that loyalty appears to mean nothing to you."

"Now who's making judgments?" she snapped. "Oh, just forget it!" She scooted against the sandy rock face, drawing her legs up, but couldn't stifle a gasp or control a wince of pain.

Sudden concern made him scowl. "How's that knee holding up?"

"What do you care?"

The petulance of her retort almost changed his scowl into a smile. God, how was it that two supposed adults always ended up in childish bickering? They were ridiculous, the two of them, and if they didn't stop, it might get them killed.

"It's important to know whether you're going to be able to keep up or not," he said.

She shrugged, nursing the knee. "I'll live."

"That's the idea."

They were silent a long moment, each weighing their chances, neither willing to voice the fears inherent in the path they'd chosen. Another thunderbolt over their heads made Bliss cringe.

"Yeah, but who'd have guessed Mother Nature would complicate matters with a free-for-all like this?" she quipped. Logan could hear the delicate chatter of her teeth. It seemed unthinkable that the fearless Bliss he'd always known could be afraid of a little thunder and lightning, but then that wasn't the worst of their problems, and they both knew it.

"Not unusual this time of the year," he said, glad to change the subject. It seemed simpler, less painful, to ignore any further discussion of choices and dreams. "Feeds the wildflowers. You cold?"

"Uh...a little." She gave a rueful chuckle. "I'm wet down to my panties."

The image of her underthings—wet and clinging to her curves—gave him a start that warmed him in places better left unconsidered. "Come here, then," he said gruffly.

He slung an arm around her shoulders and dragged her next to him, their backs against the rough, rocky wall of the outcropping, their sides pressed as close together as wet clothes would allow.

"Let go!" Bliss pushed at him. "I can take care of myself."

"Why do you have to fight me tooth and nail about everything?" he asked. "If we share a little body warmth, we'll both be better off."

"You just want an excuse to cop a feel," she spluttered.

He gave a derisive snort. "In your dreams. I'd rather curl up with one of those prickly pears than a vinegary old maid like you. But if we don't work together, we're going to be in a heap more trouble than we're already in. Even you can see that."

"I'm not an old maid."

"Well, don't take it personally," he goaded. He took advantage of her ire to inch her closer, his arm heavy about her shoulders. "Maybe you can convince François to make an honest woman of you when we get back."

She sucked in a breath that heaved with indignation. "You leave François out of this."

"Gladly. If you'll hold that acid tongue of yours long enough to admit I'm right."

"That'll be the day."

He gave a long-suffering sigh. "Look, Bliss. Your teeth are chattering so hard they can hear them in Albuquerque. And this hasn't got anything to do with the man-woman thing. It's pure survival. So don't be a dunderhead."

She drew a breath to blast him, then slowly let it out, considering. Her words were sullen but resigned. "You're right. Sorry, I'm wasted, not thinking straight."

"Understandable."

"But you understand I'm not enjoying this?"

"The feeling's mutual, Baby Sister." He called her by the hated nickname to make his point.

She relaxed against him, and the scent of her damp hair wafted to his nostrils, tantalizing and floral and feminine. "As long as we're clear," she muttered.

"Sure." The word was barely a croak as he fought all the feelings he'd so recently denied. Wretched and dirty, she was still the most desirable woman he'd ever known. Hastily, he shifted that knowledge to the deepest depths of his brain and slammed the door on it.

"Dunderhead, huh?" she mumbled. "You city boys are something...."

Logan couldn't repress a grin. As always, when the storm passed with Bliss, you never knew what to expect, and sometimes it was her wry sense of humor. He rubbed his palm up and down her arm, using friction on the damp fabric of her jumpsuit to warm her. "Better?"

"Umm." Her answer was little more than a hard shudder.

He could feel her shivering, and increased his efforts, soothing the gooseflesh raising bumps on her skin. "Better try to enjoy it while you can. You'll be praying for coolness when the sun comes up."

"We'll have to find a place to hole up, won't we?"

"An oasis with palm trees and scantily clad serving maids comes to mind."

Her snort was faintly derisive, faintly amused. "Typical male. How about an RV with air-conditioning and indoor plumbing?"

Logan laughed. "And I thought I was the practical one." She shuddered and snuggled against his shoulder, stifling a yawn. He tilted his chin so that he sheltered her from the worst of the spray still drifting into their sanctuary. "Poor baby. You're miserable, aren't you?"

"Yeah."

"And beat."

"I could use forty winks," she admitted. "My brain is mush."

"Then take a nap. I'll wake you when the storm passes. It shouldn't be long, and I guess we both deserve a rest."

"I'll just close my eyes for a minute," she mumbled against his shoulder.

She was asleep before her next breath. Somehow, the trust of that reached down and touched Logan in a secret place. Awake, she might scratch and spit at him, but somehow her acceptance of his protection said more than all their bickering. Logan settled as comfortably as he could against the rock face and stretched out his legs. His muscles ached, but it was pleasant to hold an armful of sleeping female.

Pleasant, hell! He grimaced. It was downright heaven.

Their bodies were warming where they touched, and her curves pressed against him, teasing him with the images of what lay beneath her sodden jumpsuit. Her hand lay relaxed against his chest—long, competent fingers, delicate wrist. He wondered what her pulse would taste like if he pressed his mouth there.

His fingers, as he continued to stroke her arm, brushed the fullness of her breast, nicely rounded under the blue cloth, and Logan drew a shaky breath as his body hardened.

Okay, so he was a liar. Maybe he'd insisted she let him hold her so that he *could* cop a feel. Maybe after all these years, it took more self-control than even Logan Campbell possessed to deny himself the opportunity of seeing if she still felt as good as he remembered.

The sobering truth was that she felt even better.

But he couldn't do a damn thing about it. No, she'd made it abundantly clear she'd neither forgotten nor forgiven. So he sat there with his body aching, knowing he'd lost whatever chance he might have had with Bliss Abernathy years ago. The loss, the ache—it turned an armful of heaven into pure torture, living hell. And somehow, as the ache built, it was easier to blame her than himself, to let anger mask the frustration he felt. It was the only way he could stay sane.

When the downpour abated half an hour later and the lightning moved into the distance, Logan breathed silent thanks, then disentangled himself and shook Bliss roughly awake. "Rise and shine, lazybones. We've got to haul butt."

"What?" She shook her head, groggy, and tried to burrow a hole in the indentation where he'd been sitting, curling into a sleepy ball. "Buzz off."

"Dammit, I said get up!" This time he wasn't even remotely courteous, dragging her arm and shaking her hard. "Get your fanny out here. I caught enough water to give us both a good drink."

More awake now, she shook off his hand and gave him a resentful, almost hurt look, then crawled from beneath the overhang. "I'm coming. You don't have to be so damn cranky."

The moon, low on the horizon, was still bright enough to illuminate the silver puddle of water in the center of the pegged-out survival blanket. Bliss's sleepy-eyed, tousled appearance did nothing to bank Logan's irritation, nor his arousal. The fury he felt at himself was directed at her.

"You haven't seen cranky, lady," he admonished. "Someone's got to take charge. Our lives are on the line, and we've only got an hour or so before dawn to make more tracks and find shelter. Now drink so we can get moving, or I'll leave you where you sit."

His attack, coming so unexpectedly on the heels of a balmful sleep, produced a baffled, answering anger. "What the hell is your problem now?"

He couldn't answer honestly, so he took refuge in goading her, rationalizing that it would pay off in extra ground covered if she was in a temper. "I just haven't got time to mollycoddle a helpless female. Now drink."

"Helpless? Damn you, Logan." She shoved cupped hands into the precious liquid and drank, her eyes burning blue and resentful in the moonlight.

The smell of moisture scented the air, but the dry desert floor had already absorbed most of the downpour. She sat on her heels as Logan drained what was left of the water, jerked up the blanket and replaced it in the duffel.

"All right, let's go," he said gruffly, regretting his harshness, regretting nearly fifteen years of animosity. But old habits were hard to break. Evidently, Bliss felt so, too.

Standing, she grabbed up her club, her voice so venomous he was afraid for a moment that she intended to use the shillelagh on him.

"I'm with you, amigo, whether you like it or not. But just to be clear, I wish I were anywhere but here with you. Without a doubt, Logan Campbell," she said, "you are the biggest pain in the butt I've ever run across."

He was a slave driver, that's all there was to it. A malicious, sadistic slave driver.

Weary beyond belief, Bliss glared at the back of Logan's fair head and limped after him through the desert scrub. She hoped the knot he'd taken on his noggin was giving him bloody hell. It was the least he deserved.

The moon had set and the barest streak of gray just limned the horizon. Rocky crags cast darker shadows on either side of them, but the flats stretched out ahead in what seemed an endless plain. Logan had taken the lead, evidently oblivious to any potential meetings with snakes, and had kept up a killing pace since the thunderstorm. They'd spooked a lone mule deer and a couple of jackrabbits, but she was too tired to even worry about such critters. She'd be damned, however, if she'd let herself lag behind or give him any reason to criticize her.

Anything you can do, I can do better.... Out of the blue, the old *Annie Get Your Gun* tune began to warble in her brain, provoking a dry grin. Yeah, that had become their anthem, their years-old conflict a raging competition.

For Jack's affection. For Russ's attention. To prove who was superior. For someone to finally come out on top. To settle old scores.

And she was so damned tired of it all.

Bliss blinked at the sudden sharp prickle of tears behind her eyes. They said that your first love was the hardest to get over, and she guessed the old saw was truer than most. At sixteen, she'd lost her heart for a brief span to Logan, and he'd spurned her and used her and crushed everything she'd held dear under his ruthless heel. It was obvious that nothing about him had changed and that the sweet, innocent feelings she'd cherished had been nothing more than illusions.

But they were illusions that, once shattered, had made it difficult for her to trust any other man. Oh, she'd certainly had her share of suitors, but she was most comfortable as one of the boys in the all-male world of oil drilling. Relationships were fraught with danger, and she'd been wary of any man who wanted more than just friendship, and most of them wanted much more from a woman with her looks. In an odd way, her aloofness only made her more desirable in masculine eyes. She was cynical enough to recognize that, to play them like fish on a hook and then move on.

There had been one or two men with whom she'd

had serious emotional involvements, but nothing had come of it, and she was astute enough to know that it had been her fault. But if her wariness was a character flaw that kept her from taking romantic risks, then she could only blame Logan, who'd dashed her innocence against the rocks of his ego and left her floundering so long ago.

Stop it, she told herself fiercely, rubbing her eyes. With an effort, she shook off the regretful musings. She had a lot to offer a man, but her nomadic life hadn't lent itself to a stable relationship. Maybe once she was settled, had started her business and planted permanent roots, things could be different. It was just that she hadn't spent this much time near Logan in years, and all the old feelings were bubbling to the surface. She wouldn't allow such feminine weakness to undermine her determination. *Anything you can do, I can do better....*

Only she was nearing the end of her rope both physically and mentally, and if they didn't find a place to rest soon, all of her good intentions were likely to go up in smoke.

"The sun's coming up," she remarked hopefully.

"I'm not blind." Logan's tone was surly.

The sweat dripped at her temples. "We need some shade."

"You want me to twitch my nose and conjure up a silken tent for milady?"

The nastiness in his sneer raised her hackles. "We've got to go to ground soon, that's all."

"We can get another couple of miles in before things heat up."

"That's pure stupidity," she snapped. "Drink some water, Logan, your judgment's going."

He rounded on her, his expression furious in the dimness. "Look, I'm making the calls here, understood?"

"Then find us a place to rest," she shouted. "Or neither one of us is going to see Jack alive again. What are you trying to prove, anyway?"

"Nothing you'd understand," he muttered.

"I understand better than you think." Bliss tossed the ragged tendrils of her braid out of her eyes. "But you can't outdo Russ if you go and get us both killed."

"You don't know what you're talking about. Russ has nothing to do with anything."

"Only that you've been competing with him for your dad's approval for as long as I've known you."

Logan stiffened as if she'd slipped a stiletto between his ribs. "Damn you, Bliss. You're not family, remember? You've got no right—"

He'd returned the dagger blow with shattering force, and she caught her breath with a pained gasp. No, she wasn't blood family, but Jack had promised she'd always be a part of the Campbell clan. "I've got as much right as you," she said shakily.

"Maybe you have," he admitted, surprising her. His voice held a wealth of bitterness. "More, in fact. After all, you and Russ are the favorites, the chosen ones."

"I think I was one of those obligations you like to talk about so much, at least at first," she said bluntly. "But as for Russ—my God, Logan! How many times have I heard Jack say he took Russ because he didn't want him growing up a sissy?"

"What?" The word was a startled bark.

She nodded. "Jack was afraid Valerie would coddle him too much because he'd been sick as a baby, and he knew you had the backbone to come out okay."

"That SOB!" Logan cursed and kicked the earth,

sending a shower of sand flying. "Why the hell didn't he ever say that to me?"

Somehow the agony filtered through the anger, and Bliss felt a sudden spurt of compassion for the little boy who'd felt cheated of his father's love. "Maybe you can ask him that when we get home," she said softly. Then her mouth twisted. "But don't think I feel sorry for you, Logan Campbell. You had Valerie. There are some of us who'd have given anything to have a mother like her."

He looked at her strangely. "God knows I'm not complaining."

Bliss felt suddenly exposed, as if she'd revealed too much. She didn't want to give Logan any more emotional ammunition against her, so she sent him a mocking smile, fully illuminated by the first rays of the rising sun that sent insubstantial shadows fleeing and brought the desert's night specters into the light of reality.

"Oh, no?" she asked with a laugh. "Sounds to me like the spoiled rich boy whining that he didn't get everything his own way. Grow up, Logan. Nobody has it easy in this world."

"That's why we're going on while we can," he snapped. "And if you don't like it—"

"My God, what's that?" At her abrupt question, he broke off in mid-sentence. Her eyes widened incredulously. Logan turned at her pointed finger. Excitement and relief laced her voice. "It's a roof, isn't it? A house! Hallelujah!"

"Bliss, wait up!"

But she was running toward the structure coming into view, revealed by the light flowing over the distant crags, her breath ragged but her smile as big as Christmas. Clusters of orange desert marigolds swirled around her ankles, a gift of the desert after the rains, while images danced in her head like the proverbial sugar-plums.

Help. Water. Food. A telephone. Even a bathtub.

Lord be blessed, they were saved! And she wouldn't have to deal with Logan Campbell anymore, either.

She stumbled over the gentle rise and down the other side, Logan somewhere behind her, then came up short just yards from salvation. It was a house, all right, and at one time it had been a showplace, someone's grand two-storied home. Now the glassless windows shone like blind eyes, and two-thirds of the roof was gone. Evidence of fire, perhaps forty years old, well-preserved in the desert dryness, still marred the crumbling timber and adobe exterior.

Dismay and disappointment turned her relief to bitter ashes on her tongue. It was Christmas morning, but there weren't any presents. Behind her, Logan squeezed her shoulder, his grip unknowingly painful in an expression of his own frustration.

"Well," he said heavily, "looks like we're out of luck again."

Chapter Seven

"**T**urn on your television."

"What? Who—" Laura Ramirez squeezed the hand-held phone receiver against her ear and frowned. She was dressed for Sunday morning Mass, and Rufio was already waiting in the car. "Zach?"

"Flip it on, quick!" he ordered. "Channel six."

Knowing her friend never spoke with such harshness lightly, Laura felt an instant shiver of apprehension. "Yes, okay."

She crossed the modest living room and hit the TV button, twirling the dial to the proper channel.

"...missing in the south Texas Big Bend area," a well-coiffed anchorman informed her, his plastic features cast in sober lines expressly to show the seriousness of the situation. "Search parties have already been mobilized to look for a crash site. Logan Campbell, son of local area oilman John 'Black Jack' Campbell of

Campbell Drilling, and company pilot Bliss Abernathy were the only reported passengers of the Beechcraft Kingaire.''

"Oh, my God!" Laura breathed.

From the phone, Zach's voice echoed tinnily. "Thought you'd want to know about this, from what you said the other night about your working with Logan on the Barnette investigation.''

"Yes," Laura said faintly, her horrified gaze scanning the graphic of the south Texas-Mexico border area the anchorman was describing. It was an immense area. How could they expect to find anyone in such a vast and inhospitable landscape? And would there be anyone left alive when—if—they did? "How did you find out?"

"Jake's been called in to help fly some search patterns," Zach replied.

"Do they have any idea what happened?"

"*Nada.* Not a clue. Their plane just disappeared off the scope sometime yesterday evening. The word Jake got was that Jack had a heart attack in Chihuahua, and they were headed down there to be with him.''

Laura shook her head in dismay. "This just gets worse and worse." She swallowed hard and asked the other question she had to. "Where—where's the other brother?"

"Russ? Down in San Antonio, spearheading the hunt. He's the one who got Jake involved in the search.''

The TV anchorman had gone on to other news, so Laura switched off the set with a shaky hand and spoke again into the phone. "At least something's being done. Do—do they hold out much hope?"

"Who knows at this point?" Laura could almost see Zach's shrug.

"Their poor mother must be beside herself."

"Jake said she'd gone down to be with Jack."

Laura nodded in understanding. "Of course. Even divorced, as parents they'd want to be together at a time like this. Valerie's quite a lady, but I've never met Jack."

"Neither have I, but Jake likes him, calls him a man's man. Jack was quite a fan of Jake's during his football years. Evidently Jack played himself in his younger days and never lost his taste for the sport."

"Sounds like just your type, Zach," she said with a half smile.

"Yeah. I hope I get to meet him someday."

"Do you know his condition?"

"Stable enough to move to a Dallas hospital sometime today, according to Jake," he replied.

"Well, that's the one bright note in all this mess," Laura sighed. "I wish there was something I could do."

"There is, sweetheart."

"Yes?" she asked hopefully.

"Pray."

She prayed for relief.

Coming out of yet another round of fitful dozing, Bliss stifled a sigh and tried to ignore her sodden, sweaty discomfort as well as the man sleeping heavily beside her. The shade cast by a crumbling yet relatively stable corner of the abandoned homestead gave only minimal relief to the temperatures that had risen steadily since dawn and were now reaching their late afternoon peak. Her disappointment when she'd realized the house was empty and long-deserted had been palpable, but the threat of Logan's mockery had kept her dry-eyed even when she'd longed to bawl out her frustration.

PLAY...

"ROLL A DOUBLE!"

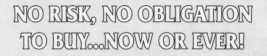

NO RISK, NO OBLIGATION TO BUY...NOW OR EVER!

GUARANTEED

PLAY "ROLL A DOUBLE" AND YOU GET FREE GIFTS! HERE'S HOW TO PLAY:

1. Peel off label from front cover. Place it in space provided at right. With a coin, carefully scratch off the silver dice. Then check the claim chart to see what we have for you – FOUR FREE BOOKS and a mystery gift – ALL YOURS! ALL FREE!

2. Send back this card and you'll receive brand-new Silhouette Special Edition® novels. These books have a cover price of $3.99 each, but they are yours to keep absolutely free.

3. There's no catch. You're under no obligation to buy anything. We charge nothing – ZERO – for your first shipment. And you don't have to make any minimum number of purchases – not even one!

4. The fact is thousands of readers enjoy receiving books by mail from the Silhouette Reader Service™. They like the convenience of home delivery...they like getting the best new novels BEFORE they're available in stores...and they love our discount prices!

5. We hope that after receiving your free books you'll want to remain a subscriber. But the choice is yours – to continue or cancel, any time at all! So why not take us up on our invitation, with no risk of any kind. You'll be glad you did!

***THIS SURPRISE MYSTERY GIFT
COULD BE YOURS <u>FREE</u> WHEN
YOU PLAY "ROLL A DOUBLE"***

"ROLL A DOUBLE!"

Place label here

SCRATCH HERE

SEE CLAIM CHART BELOW

235 CIS CDWJ
(U-SIL-SE-01/98)

YES! I have placed my label from the front cover into the space provided above and scratched off the silver dice. Please send me all the gifts for which I qualify. I understand that I am under no obligation to purchase any books, as explained on the back and on the opposite page.

NAME

ADDRESS   APT.

CITY   STATE   ZIP

CLAIM CHART

4 FREE BOOKS PLUS MYSTERY BONUS GIFT

3 FREE BOOKS PLUS BONUS GIFT

2 FREE BOOKS

CLAIM NO.37-829

The Silhouette Reader Service™ — Here's how it works:

If offer card is missing write to: Silhouette Reader Service, 3010 Walden Ave., P.O. Box 1867, Buffalo, NY 14240-1867

BUSINESS REPLY MAIL
FIRST-CLASS MAIL   PERMIT NO. 717   BUFFALO, NY

POSTAGE WILL BE PAID BY ADDRESSEE

SILHOUETTE READER SERVICE
3010 WALDEN AVE
PO BOX 1867
BUFFALO NY 14240-9952

NO POSTAGE
NECESSARY
IF MAILED
IN THE
UNITED STATES

Still, she had to take the find as a blessing in disguise, because it offered them the shelter they needed to wait out the day's blazing sun and killing temperatures. Logan had cleared the area of charred timbers and a decade's accumulation of tumbleweeds and debris to give them room to stretch out and rest. An empty window frame set in what had once been the center of the wall allowed circulation of air over their makeshift bed, but her jumpsuit clung to her sticky skin. Even after the rain, the still air tasted dusty, and the weathered and fire-cracked tile flooring on which they lay, with only the paper-thin survival blanket they shared as scant protection from the coarse ground beneath them, was worse than a bed of nails. And besides that, her knee ached like the very devil.

With another sigh, Bliss rolled on her side, trying to get comfortable. Now she had an unobstructed view of Logan's sleeping features, making things more difficult than ever. In slumber, his face with its rakish bandage looked harder, more masculine, even more enticing than when he was awake and exuding all of his not inconsiderable charm. Not that he usually wasted any of it on her, of course.

He'd stripped off his knit shirt, and her gaze drifted to the sandy curls furring his muscular chest. Tiny pearls of perspiration beaded among the hairs, clustering heaviest where they thickened and arrowed beneath his waistband. Bliss swallowed hard, her mouth dry, not only from the blasting heat, but from her temperature rising internally.

She was definitely losing it. The man was a pig. A self-centered chauvinist bully who loved trying to push her around. How could she forget it? And why did she feel an almost uncontrollable urge to press her lips to that expanse of broad chest and taste the salt of his skin?

She squeezed her eyelids closed, trying to blank out the sight of him, but his image remained impressed on her brain to tantalize her. She was nuts, she told herself, to be so physically aware of a man who did nothing but annoy her beyond endurance. Of course, she did have to give him some credit. Logan had proven he wasn't totally useless, had in fact surprised her with his knowledge and survival skills. Her newfound respect was grudging, so she kept it to herself. If he just wasn't so driven, so obsessive in his desire to find a way out of this desert on their own and reach his ailing father, then she might feel more comfortable.

Bliss still didn't know if they'd made the right decision, leaving the wreck. Not that she'd had much choice in the matter. She suppressed a tiny shudder. No, even though they got on like cats and dogs, she couldn't imagine herself staying behind alone, not for one night. Logan's company was certainly better than no company at all. She'd visited a lot of exotic places around the world, seen and done a lot of things in environments as harsh, but this was one experience she'd just as soon never have to repeat.

A trickle of moisture dripped between her breasts. With another sigh, she fumbled for the zipper of her jumpsuit and lowered it a notch, praying that the air would cool the damp cotton singlet she'd chosen in favor of a bra when she'd dressed for what should have been a short, uneventful flight. Logan stirred beside her, and her lashes fluttered open in alarm, but he was only shifting position in his sleep.

This time, the temptation to look her fill was too much to resist. She noted the fine lines at the corners of his eyes. Too many hours squinting across a tennis court, she thought sourly, refusing to admit that they gave his handsome face a ruggedness and character that had been missing in his youth. Sandy stubble roughened his lean cheeks, and her fingers curled into fists as she fought the urge to test the masculine texture. Hastily, she averted her eyes, skipping down his chest, past the bronze coins of his nipples, past the waistband of his rumpled khaki slacks to snag on the masculine bulge beneath his fly.

Vastly disturbed by the feelings curling like a hot ribbon in her belly, determined neither to acknowledge nor act on them—ever—she gulped and sat abruptly.

That's when she saw it. Multisectioned, sand-colored, scaling across Logan's upper thigh with pinchers raised and poisonous, crescent-shaped tail erect—*scorpion!*

As if sensing her horrified regard, the creature paused warily, stinging tail swinging to and fro, then changed directions and began to inch across Logan's zipper. Logan grunted in his sleep and raised a lazy hand to bat away the annoyance intruding on his rest.

Bliss pounced, catching his hand in mid-flight and slamming her other palm against his mouth. His tawny eyes flew open in confusion, then flaring anger, and he tensed for a struggle as she bent over him.

"Don't move," she whispered between her teeth. "For God's sake!" She saw the puzzlement in his eyes, the reservation, and she gulped, praying that he had enough trust in her not to question her just the once. "Scorpion," she whispered.

Bliss felt his tension increase, every muscle in his body turning to iron. She glanced at his mid-section, then sucked in a breath. The insect had already climbed over Logan's belt buckle and was tentatively testing the newest terrain before it—Logan's bare stomach.

"Don't move," Bliss repeated, so softly she wasn't even sure she said it aloud.

When Logan gave the barest of nods, she released him, moving back by increments, so slowly she was almost motionless, doing nothing to alarm or excite the intruder. While she knew that in most cases a scorpion sting wasn't life-threatening, it could be extremely painful, and their situation was precarious enough without her partner suffering a debilitating injury. With only a limited water supply, if they were delayed even a day...

The crumbling adobe wall at her back stopped her withdrawal. Eyes focused on the creature picking its way up Logan's belly, crossing the indentation of his navel like a tiny valley, she felt around her for something, anything to use—and grasped the edge of a broken clay tile. Wrenching it from the sandy floor took almost no effort, but gave her only a thin triangular-shaped piece of baked clay.

Hardly a weapon. Little if no defense. It had to do.

Smoothly, she leaned forward, placing the tile against Logan's belly into the path of the insect. She could smell the musk of Logan's sweat. He hardly seemed to be breathing. The scorpion hesitated, tiny claws tapping at yet another new texture of topography to cross. It was only inches from Bliss's fingers as she held the edge of the tile, but she couldn't stop to think about that. Her pulse slammed into her throat as she watched and prayed and mentally urged the critter to keep going, onto the tile, off Logan's vulnerable skin.

Finally, the insect reacted to her mental urgings, skittering onto the slick tile. In almost the same instant, Bliss surged to her feet. The startled creature struck, his deadly stinger missing her forefinger by a mere quarter of an inch before she slung tile and scorpion together through the open window frame.

Her legs collapsed under her, and she gulped for breath she couldn't seem to find as Logan rolled to his knees beside her.

"Are you all right?" he demanded harshly. When she couldn't answer, he grabbed her shoulders and shook her, so that she nearly banged her head against the adobe wall. "Dammit, answer me! Did it get you? Let me see. Crazy kid! I ought to—"

"Just shut up!" she panted. "You ingrate."

"It didn't sting you?"

She shook her head. A shudder of relief passed through him, transferred to her where his hands rested on her shoulders. "Thank God," he muttered raggedly. "What is it about you that just seems to attract trouble?"

"Me?" Reaction left her trembling but incensed. "It wasn't me that nasty polecat decided to take a hike across. It must have taken a shine to your cologne, city boy."

Despite himself, his lips twitched. "I'm the one who smells like a polecat. Thanks. I owe you one."

"Don't mention it." She shifted uncomfortably, and he released her. But then he pointed a forefinger at her nose.

"Just don't pull anything like that again, do you hear? I won't have you risking yourself for me."

"I know you're not worth it," she quipped, "but who else would I get to carry the luggage?"

"It's nice to know what I'm worth, I guess—what the hell are you doing?"

The exertion and the nervous tension had raised

Bliss's body temperature until she was perspiring profusely, making her so miserable she couldn't stand it another second. Dragging down the zipper of her jumpsuit to its limit, she began to struggle out of the long sleeves, peeling the synthetic fabric that was still damp from the earlier downpour away from her clammy skin.

"I'm stewing in my own juices!" she snapped, rising to shimmy out of the legs of the uniform, leaving her in a sleeveless cotton undershirt, untrimmed, French-cut panties and socks. "The fabric doesn't breathe a bit, and I don't intend to keel over from heatstroke."

Logan looked as though he'd been poleaxed. "But—" With a curse, he ran long fingers through his hair in consternation.

Too rattled and frustrated and hot to care, she laid the jumpsuit on the window frame to dry out. "Look, I'm sweltering. If the sight of the female form offends you, then turn your head. I've got to cool off. Where's the water?"

She retrieved a liter of water from the duffel and took a judicious swallow. "Here," she said, holding it out to him. "You look as though you could use some, too."

"Uh. Sure. Thanks." He was unaccountably monosyllabic as he accepted the bottle, his gaze everywhere but on her.

"I'm going to try to get some more sleep," she announced, shaking out the survival blanket with a jaundiced eye, wary of any further wildlife lurking in their haven. Then she lay down in the shadows, one knee raised, a forearm thrown over her eyes, and gave a giant sigh of relief and contentment—or at least resignation. "I'd suggest you do the same," she muttered. "Sunset's coming soon, and if we expect to cover any distance tonight…"

"Yes. You're right."

Bliss felt him settle beside her. She knew she ought to be worried about her rather immodest attire, but she was too grateful for the relative coolness of the air on her bare skin to care at this point. Besides, she was so sure that Logan had seen his share and more of feminine underthings and what lay beneath them that for him to be more than marginally impressed by her utilitarian garb would be a miracle. And after all, dire circumstances called for drastic measures.

Neither of them spoke for several long minutes. Just when Bliss was beginning to feel relaxed and drowsy enough to drift off for another catnap, Logan's deep voice wafted over her like melted honey.

"Thanks again, Bliss. That was quick thinking. I thought I was going to crawl right out of my skin when I realized what that thing was."

"You'd have done the same for me," she said, and realized it was true. She kept her arm over her eyes so that she wouldn't have to look at his bare chest.

"All the same, you're some kind of courageous lady. Hell on wheels, just like Jack always says."

"Ought to be," she muttered. "He raised me, more or less."

"Seems to me like you raised yourself, and Russ, too, going from pillar to post like you did with the drilling rigs. God knows Jack wasn't the best role model in the world."

"We did okay." She dropped her arms and her defenses, gazing at the ragged edges of the walls surrounding them.

No matter that the homestead was a ruin, it was still more than evident that at one time it had been a real home, probably filled with the laughter of children, the clank of dinnerware at big family meals. Even in this remote area, whoever had lived here had worked hard to gain more than a meager living with a few cows per square mile. She wished she could have seen the place in its glory days, the neighbors coming from miles around to spend the night at a barbecue and hoedown, the cowboys flirting with the rancher's daughters, grandparents gossiping and a fiddler playing in the barn.

Family. Roots. Ties to real friends. Despite the fact that it was long gone, the owners probably dead and buried or at least living in a retirement condo in Phoenix, she envied them with a soul-deep longing and a determination to have something like this of her own. And not in the distant future, either, but soon. Yes, indeed, if this ordeal wasn't teaching her anything else, it was to seize your dream while you could, because life was fleeting and time could run out before you knew it. The thought made her draw a shaky breath.

"Are you okay?" Logan asked roughly, coming up on one elbow with a frown on his face.

"I was just thinking about getting home." She gave a little mirthless laugh. "As if I had a genuine one to go to."

"What do you mean?"

"Look around you, Logan. Can't you see this place once was a real home? I've never had that. The best I've got is a secondhand travel trailer and a scruffy dog."

He looked at her, a puzzled pleat between his sandy brows. "You're the last person on earth I'd expect to get sentimental about such things."

"That's because you've had them all your life, and you take them for granted," she retorted, gazing at him with heat in her sapphire eyes. "Why do you think I want my inheritance so badly? I'm sick of living like a Gypsy. I want something of my own, a place I belong.''

"The hell you say." He looked stupefied.

"That's right. I'm going to start my own charter service, maybe out of Dallas or El Paso or any place I can find, and buy myself a house, and have neighbors and—oh, forget it.''

"That's why you want your share of the company? Why the hell didn't you just say so?''

She came up on her own elbow so she was facing him, glaring at him with her defensive hackles raised, already regretting what she'd revealed in a moment of weakness. "Because I knew you wouldn't understand,'' she said sullenly.

"I can understand that a whole lot better than your just up and leaving, taking everything that makes Campbell Drilling a viable entity!'' he replied. "Damnation, woman! Didn't you figure we could work something out less drastic, less traumatic—and still get you what you want? No, I guess not. Jack raised you selfish to the bone, so what you want, you just take.''

"That's not true.''

"Yeah, well, ten to one, what you've tried to do to Dad's company—the baby he cares about more than all of us rolled up together—is what brought on his heart attack.''

Her fist slammed into his breastbone. "You bastard. That's a lie. Take it back.''

"The truth too hard for you to swallow, Baby Sister?'' Logan asked, sneering, catching her fist before she could land another blow.

"Don't you dare blame me for that,'' she shouted, struggling against his grip. "We both know he smokes like a chimney, drinks like a sailor and never watches what he eats.'' Angry tears sparkled on her lashes. "The docs have been trying to tell him to slow down. Do you think I haven't tried to warn him? Damn you, Logan! I love him, too. *That's* what you can't accept.''

He jerked her closer, his face angry above hers. "You don't know a damn thing about it. You don't have any idea—''

Without warning, his mouth covered hers, as if to punish her for having the audacity to plumb secret feelings he'd rather let go unnoticed. She inhaled in shock, breathing in his breath, and he took immediate advantage, plunging his tongue into the depths of her mouth, taking possession so that she lost whatever thoughts were in her head and whimpered—in surprise, in dismay, in pleasure.

Memories swamped her. *He tastes the same,* she thought dazedly. But there was a sharper, darker undertone to the flavor that filled her mouth, a masculine demand that couldn't be denied. She was as surprised as he was when her tongue tangled with his, joining the passionate battle, meeting fire for fire, hunger for hunger.

Logan jerked, then groaned, and his hand closed over her breast, cupping the lush fullness. His thumb brushed the tip through the soft cotton undershirt, and it pebbled to turgid relief against the fabric, evoking such a powerful sensation Bliss shuddered against his lips. Without volition, her hands came up to frame his face, to touch the bandage gracing his forehead, to stroke the stubble on his jaw as she'd been longing to. Her palms tingled with the sensual roughness, a texture essentially male and mesmerizing. She feared she could lose herself entirely in the mere feel of him.

Logan shifted, forcing her against the sticky survival

blanket, his mouth feasting lustily on hers, his knee pressing her thighs open. The rasp of his dusty slacks against her bare skin sensitized every nerve ending, made her moan and press wantonly against the hardness of his aroused sex.

Just when she thought she'd never draw another breath, he tore his lips away, trailing his mouth down her slender throat in a series of heated kisses and love bites. Their gasps echoed harshly in the hot air. Nearly overcome, Bliss curled her fingers in the silky hair at his nape, hanging on for dear life.

When he roughly shoved aside the thin barrier of her garment and took her nipple into his mouth, she cried out incoherently. Never had she experienced such a surge of pleasure, such a crashing wave of sensuality that made her writhe with unfulfilled desire.

And it was Logan—that despicable, exasperating, altogether terrifying man—who had brought her to fever pitch in a matter of seconds.

It was incomprehensible.

Disastrous.

Desperately, she tried to claw her way to sanity, tugging on his hair even while his rapacious tongue did wicked things to her pliant flesh. "Logan! Oh, God, stop."

"I want you, Bliss." He raised his head to stare into her flushed, desire-softened face and groaned. "I've always wanted you."

The strength of his desire thrilled her. To see calm and competent Logan Campbell out of control—for her—was heady, indeed. But that only made his words all the more chilling.

Want. Pure animal lust, with no talk of affection, no

sentiment, nothing to honey-coat it beyond what it was. And she knew that nothing but regret could come of it.

Her fist pressed against his chest, she forced shaky words from her dry throat. "Your timing is incredible, amigo."

A frown creased his brow. "Don't tell me you don't feel it. It's been bubbling like a geyser between us for years."

"That doesn't mean we have to act on it. We're not oversexed teenagers anymore." She made a move to slide from beneath him. "And considering our circumstances, I'd rather conserve my energy for other things—like survival."

She wasn't expecting the strength in his hands as he caught her, pressed her hard against the flooring. His features were almost satanic as he grinned into her startled face, pure wicked temptation.

"Haven't you wondered, all these years?" he rasped. "What it would be like?"

"You're insane."

"If we're going to die in the desert, I'd hate like hell to know I gave up an opportunity to learn what I missed fifteen years ago."

She hesitated, her voice husky. "Are we going to die out here, Logan?"

His tawny eyes flickered within the deepening shadows of their protected corner. "Maybe."

It was odd that she found that admission less frightening than what he was doing to her. He slid one hand over the mountain of her breast, then down the valley of her stomach to lodge at the V of her thighs. "Admit it, you're curious, too."

Bliss struggled beneath his weight, more shaken than she wanted to admit even to herself. "You're loco!"

she said, her voice low and trembling. "There's too much water under that bridge for both of us. Best to leave old wounds alone."

"Did I wound you, *querida?*" he murmured.

Here was territory she would rather not travel, but the feel of his fingers against her most intimate flesh evoked a flash of honesty. Her whisper was ragged. "You know you did."

Logan's lips brushed hers. Tenderness. Contrition. "I'm sorry," he murmured. "It wasn't my choice."

"What?"

"I'd never have left you if I didn't have to," he told her.

Understanding dawned. "Jack."

He grimaced. "Dad's word is law, especially where you're concerned, always has been. He was protecting you."

"You could have found a better way to break it off," she accused shakily. "You were brutal."

"I was a green boy, and clumsy. I'm sorry," he repeated, his mouth grazing her temple.

For a moment she thought he might mean it. Then the realization of what and who he was and how he could use his charm to his own ends made her draw a ragged breath.

Oh, he was good! Ruggedly masculine and bringing her to the peak of feelings she hadn't experienced for too long. As if those two overused words could make up for what he'd done, how he'd broken her heart, all the history of animosity and hostility that had become such a part of their tattered relationship. A part within her cried out to accept the apology, to take what he offered, but her head was clearing now, and she knew better than to make that mistake—again.

"You can turn off the charm, lover boy," she said, willing coldness into her voice. "I've been there. I don't want to go back again."

"It's different now." He nibbled her jaw, his hands stroking, cajoling. "We're both experienced adults. No one has to get hurt."

She gasped and arched against his agile manipulations, hating herself for her susceptibility, hating him for taking advantage of it. "If you believe that, then you're a bigger fool than I took you for, Logan Campbell."

"Didn't you know, the Lord watches over fools?"

"I—"

"Just shut up and let me love you."

Logan's mouth covered hers again, but this time the roughness was gone, leaving only a softness and a consuming need that inflamed Bliss, banished reason and made her melt like candy against him. Coherent thought was impossible, not when she felt like this, not when she *needed*, too. Her arms slid around his bare shoulders, ignoring sticky skin and the rasp of sand, the prickle of his beard against her lips.

Suddenly nothing mattered. Not the wrong time, nor the impossible place, nor the fact that they were both certifiable. Nothing mattered but Logan, and with a little whimper of surrender she kissed him.

He made a deep, pleasured sound in his throat, his tongue searching out every drop of sweetness within the cavern of her mouth. Bliss let herself simply *feel*, and her heart pounded, a beat, beat, beat that seemed to match a sudden thunder over her head.

Logan raised his face, his eyes passion-clouded, then in an instant they cleared. With a curse he released her, scrambling to his feet, diving for the duffel bag. Dazed but alarmed by his sudden urgency, Bliss came to her knees, a hand pressed over her heart.

But it wasn't her pulse she'd heard. "A chopper," she breathed, recognizing the distinctive drone. Her heart leaped.

Pulling flares out of the bag, Logan vaulted through the window casing, heedless of the sharp edges of molding and old glass. Bliss limped after him, scanning the sunset-lit sky frantically.

"There," she said, pointing. An ebony silhouette, a black dragonfly in relief, cut across the crimson-stained horizon toward the southwest. Going away from them.

Logan ripped into the flares, igniting one after the other, the Roman candle explosions shooting into the air in sparkling arcs.

The helicopter never deviated in its course.

Both aware of the chance they'd just missed and why, they stood without speaking long after the chopper disappeared from sight, until the last faint beat of its engines faded into the desert's total silence.

"The glare's making it impossible to see."

"Umm."

"It'll be dark soon, and we're running low on fuel."

In the cockpit of the Lazy L's signature black helicopter, Jake Lattimer glanced at his wife sitting in the copilot's seat. The rugged landscape of the Texas desert flashed beneath them. "You trying to tell me something, angel?"

Shelby Lattimer threw her blond hair over her shoulder and lowered the binoculars with a sigh. "It's time to call it a day, cowboy."

"One more pass, then we'll head for Alpine," he agreed, disappointment and resignation tightening his jaw as he changed course to a northerly heading, toward the closest approximation of civilization. Finding the Campbell plane in this vast wilderness was like looking for the proverbial needle in the haystack, but there was always a chance.

Scenes of boyhood fun with the Campbell twins flitted through his mind. He'd shared a fair amount of mischief with Russ, and although he'd not been as close to Logan simply because he didn't see him as often, there was still a childhood bond that had lapped over into adult business deals. So when the call had come to help with this desperate search, Jake hadn't hesitated. It was the least he could do for old friends.

The only thing that scared him worse than not finding Logan's plane was what he might find if he did.

"Wait!" Shelby sat up suddenly, pointing. "What's that?"

Jake saw it then, the glint of the lowering sun on metal. He turned the chopper into a circular sweep, going lower on another pass. It was wreckage, all right, a blackened, twisted hulk at the end of a deep gouge cut through prickly pear and yucca.

"Can you tell—?" he asked tightly.

Shelby was peering intently through the binoculars. "Orange and blue. It's got to be them."

"I'm going down." Carefully, he set the chopper in a bare spot fifty yards from the wreck, speaking into the radio. "Control, this is Delta Five. Looks like we got it."

Russ Campbell's tension-filled voice rasped over the radio. "Affirmative, Delta Five. What's the status?"

"There's been a fire," Jake replied heavily, taking in the destruction as he unbuckled his seat belt. "Hang on while I check things out." He pulled off his headset and speared Shelby with a look. "Stay here."

She didn't argue. "Be careful."

Jake sprinted from the still-whirling chopper toward the wreckage. Shelby sat motionless, holding her breath with the crackle of the radio as her companion as he investigated—the twisted cockpit, the churned-up terrain. Then he was back, reaching for the headset.

"Control—Russ? They're not here," Jake reported in relief.

"Not there? What the hell does that mean?"

"Looks like they made it down okay before the fire broke out. Guess you can thank your damn fine pilot for that."

"Thank God." Logan's brother's words were both oath and prayer. "So where are they now?"

"Good question. My guess is they're trying to trek it out on foot."

The muffled cursing on the other end of the transmission would not have met with FAA approval. "Damnation, that sounds like some fool stunt Bliss would pull. Can you tell which way they headed?"

"That's the problem." Jake shook his head and met Shelby's eyes. Outside the cockpit, the desert was rapidly darkening. "There's been some sort of major gully washer, maybe almost a flash flood, tore everything up to hell and gone. I can't find the first track, nor any sign they left to indicate which direction they headed. And it's getting dark fast."

"They'll be trying to travel after dark," Russ speculated.

"If they're smart."

"My brother's no dummy."

Jake took no offense, knowing what Russ must be

feeling. Bliss and Logan could be injured, they were certainly lost, and who knew if they had water or not? Under those conditions, they might not be able to last another day.

"We can start looking again at first light," he assured Russ. "At least we know they're alive."

"For now." Desperation tinged Russ's voice. "But where the hell did they go?"

Chapter Eight

"Okay, which way?"

Clad in her dry jumpsuit, Bliss gave Logan a puzzled look, then shrugged. "You're the bwana on this safari. You tell me."

Dusk made his features hard to read, but then they'd had little to say to each other since the passionate encounter that had cost them a rescue. They'd eaten their rations, sipped on their rapidly diminishing water and shaken their shoes for more scorpions as the sun set and the time came to go. There didn't seem to be much point in wasting energy on anything else—like useless recriminations.

He hoisted the duffel bag, pointing at the almost indiscernible track that had once been the road running in front of the homestead. "The way I see it, this has to lead somewhere."

"Or nowhere."

She squinted in each direction. They were both equally unpromising. The overgrown pathway still showed the faint indentations of double tracks rutted at one time by the rancher's pickup trucks. One way surely had once taken the owners to civilization—however distant that might be—but the other could dead end in a barren cow pasture, for all they knew. And the decision was crucial to their survival. Unspoken between them lay the knowledge that this was the last night they'd be more or less at full strength. The desert was taking a toll, and when the water ran out...

"Either way, the walking should be a bit easier than hiking straight east through the scrub," Logan said, "especially after the moon rises."

"You want to flip a coin, or shall I?" she asked sarcastically, and instantly regretted it. Her nerves were more shot than she realized. But she'd use anything to keep Logan at a distance. Her emotional survival depended on that.

"This way." The decisiveness of a corporate CEO colored his words, leaving no room for doubt. "Northeast will still lead us to the main highway eventually. Come on. Get your butt in gear. I'm not waiting."

His tone set her teeth on edge. "Eat my dust, amigo."

Hours and miles later, Bliss wondered if she'd been premature in her assumptions. Her knee was swelling again, and with every step she took, fiery pain shot upward to her groin. Despite the drop in temperature, sweat rolled off every inch of skin, but her mouth was cotton-dry. The moon cast eerie shadows across the landscape, bouncing off the distant crags in jagged patterns, and she was having a hard time focusing, near-dizziness making her steps falter as she followed Logan's lead up the rutted track. There'd been no signs of habitation or use of the road the whole way. Though neither voiced the fear, the suspicion was growing that they'd made a crucial mistake.

Bliss glared at Logan's broad back, wondering if he was even human, for he'd kept a steady pace and rarely shot her more than a glance to see if she were still behind him. Curse the man! He was an unfeeling brute, no doubt about it. Her breathing rasped in her ears, but she'd be damned if she'd call a halt before he did.

Fatigue and dizziness had slowed her reflexes, so Bliss had to look twice to determine if the flicker and rustle of movement in the brush to her right were real or figments of her imagination.

Another damn jackrabbit. Bliss sighed. She was getting mortally tired of jumping out of her skin every time a skittish desert critter bolted. But something about the sudden silencing of the whir of insects, something instinctual that said there was something out there— something *big*—raised the hairs on the back of her neck and brought her to an uneasy halt.

Then the moon caught the gleam of tawny feline eyes and tawny fur glistening through the mass of prickly pear as the creature crouched, stalking...*her.*

Bliss's scream choked in her throat, but it was enough to catch Logan's attention. He swung around to find her standing helplessly rooted in place as the mountain lion sprang.

With a shout, Logan plunged past her, waving his arms. The big cat twisted in midair, landing on all four paws with an aggressive hiss a mere ten feet away. Logan scooped up a rock and flung it at the animal. His voice rang out on the desert air.

"Shoo! Skedaddle! Vamoose, you varmint!"

For an instant, it seemed the cat hesitated, then with a final snarl, it thought better of attacking this two-legged animal who was apparently not prey and evidently dangerous. With a fluid, shadowy movement of flesh and sinew, it turned and bounded into the scrub, barely disturbing the fronds of a clump of creosote bushes.

It had happened so fast Bliss could only blink. Her heart thudded against the wall of her chest, and her lungs were useless. Shock made her knees buckle, and she slid into a boneless heap in the middle of the sandy road.

Logan was beside her, supporting her shoulders. "Breathe," he ordered roughly. "Dammit, Bliss!"

Air rushed into her lungs in a ragged gasp, and she clung to him, shaking, inhaling gratefully. "Oh, my God."

"Hey," he said, shaking her gently, "he just thought you were a tasty deer or a fat javelina hog. No offense intended."

The vision of Logan flinging himself into the cougar's path to save her made her light-headed. The risk he'd taken floored her. "That was...quick thinking."

"Hey, he's more afraid of us—"

"Than we are of him," she finished wryly. "Now I owe you one."

His dimples flashed. "I'd say we're even."

"And I'd say I'm tired of all this wilderness stuff," she half wailed. "Your city life is beginning to have a definite appeal. I can't take any more of this."

"Sure you can. You're a tough girl."

"No, I mean it." As badly as she hated to admit it, she was wasted, didn't know if she could get to her feet again. "I can't go another step. Just let me find a place where I can wait—"

Logan's arm tightened around her. "Now you're talking crazy. You're doing great. Lord, I don't know of another female who'd have put so many miles behind her without a whimper."

"Well, I'm whimpering now." A shudder coursed through her. "My knee. I'm just holding you up. I can't—"

"Yes, you can." He rummaged in the duffel, pulled out the water bottle. "It's just the shock. Here, drink."

He held the lip of the bottle to her parched lips and she swallowed greedily, then pushed it away, shocked at her gluttony. "You next. That's all there is, isn't it?"

He didn't answer for a moment, then tilted the bottle to his mouth for a long swig. He passed it to her. "Finish it. We might as well make the best of what we've got."

Bliss shook her head vehemently, sending tendrils flying from the loose ponytail she'd fashioned. "No. You'll need it walking more than I will waiting, so—"

"Dammit, that's enough!" Suddenly his hands were hard on her shoulders and he gave her a rough shake, jerking her neck painfully. "Snap out of the self-pity, Bliss. The crash site was different, but if you think I'm leaving you alone out here and have to answer to Jack for it, then you *have* lost your ever-lovin' mind."

Her lower lip trembled, and sudden tears fogged her vision. "I'm just trying to do what's sensible. One of us has to make it."

"Uh-uh, baby." His tone was fierce, his hands hurtful. "We're in this together all the way. You aren't backing out on me now. I won't let you."

"Logan, please."

He seemed to sense her unexpected vulnerability, the sudden fragileness that made her voice quaver, and his fingers softened on her flesh.

"The case is closed, *querida*." Bending, he brushed his lips across hers, kissing her softly, beguiling and encouraging at the same time. "You won't let me down. I know that."

Her breath caught again, this time with longing and the incessant hunger that had seemed such an integral and yet sublimated part of her for so long. "Don't be nice to me," she begged. "I can't bear it."

"Why?" He kissed her again, so gently she thought her heart would burst. "Isn't it about time?"

She gulped against his mouth, that treacherous, tempting mouth surrounded by the disturbing rasp of masculine stubble. "No, it changes things. It makes me want…"

"What?"

Too much. She couldn't answer him. She couldn't tell him that his touch was dangerous, that his tenderness destroyed her. *Oh, God, I'm in love with him!*

Although her breath caught, the realization came as no real surprise. Hadn't she always felt the connection, the attraction? Of all the men she'd ever known, he was the only one who riled her beyond endurance while tugging at everything that was essentially female within her. She'd fought it—oh, how she'd fought it! But she was in love with Logan Campbell and had been since she was sixteen, perhaps even before that.

And it was total disaster.

He was everything she wasn't and longed to be— suave and cultured and deeply rooted in family—and there was no way their life-styles could ever mesh, not when he'd made it abundantly clear time and time again exactly what he thought of her. Certainly, the physical chemistry sizzled between them like nothing she'd ever known, and he was human enough to be tempted, to take whatever might come of that. But it wouldn't be for the long haul. No, he'd choose some petite blond socialite with cool blue blood in her veins to complete the Gaspard Campbell dynasty and work like the very devil at everything he tried to fulfill the responsibility of that legacy, whether it was his choice or not. Bliss knew she could never be more than a passing fancy, a moment's temptation, a small diversion for a workaholic whose life had been laid out for him the day he was born.

She could almost laugh at the irony. Under other circumstances, she would have been able to keep her illusions and her tough-girl facade intact. Yet they'd been through a lifetime together since the beginning of their ill-fated flight, and the pressure cauldron of emotions was roiling at fever pitch as they faced a life-or-death situation. That's what made her so unsteady, gave him an advantage over her and her emotions that he'd never enjoyed, she told herself.

But losing her head even now to this enticing, infuriating man was something she refused to do. The emotional risks were more devastating than facing certain death. Although, for a moment, it became clear to her that if she were going to die in the desert, in Logan's arms was the only place she wanted to be. She thrust that thought away and forced herself to pull her shaky legs beneath her.

"Feeling better?" he asked, helping her to her feet.

"No, but what's that got to do with anything?" She took a final swallow from the water bottle and shoved it into his hands. "I hope you'll remember when we're both parched skeletons in the sand that I tried to give you a break. You're going to regret this, I know.''

Logan drained the bottle, hurled it into the darkness almost as an act of defiance against their situation, and picked up the duffel. "You let me worry about that.''

"That's what I'm afraid of.'' She took a hobbling step, grimacing at her aching muscles.

"And the only thing I'm going to regret is having to put up with that sharp tongue of yours a while longer.'' Without taking her leave, he scooped an arm across her back, catching her around the waist to support her.

"I can do it,'' she protested, more than certain it was a lie.

His answer was to bend and kiss her again, hard. "For once in your life, Bliss, just shut up and lean on someone else, okay? I told you we're in this together.''

He'd taken whatever protest she'd meant to make and flung it to Kingdom Come, so she could do little else. As they stumbled up the track together, she leaned against the man she loved and thought that even in the worst situations, if you were lucky, you could always find a glimpse of heaven.

The next miles were hell.

Even with Logan's help, Bliss's strength flagged, much to her continued dismay. They went off the poorly delineated track more than once as the moon waned, and had to retrace their steps. Knowing there was no water left only made their throats that much drier. As dawn approached without any signs of civilization and their steps grew more stumbling and fatigued, neither of them could ignore that they were going to have to face another day in the desert. Maybe their last.

"Got any ideas?'' Bliss croaked. She tried not to press her weight on Logan, but he supported her stalwartly, and the feel of his hard body next to hers was both perdition and paradise.

"Keep going," he grunted. His breathing was labored, though he tried to hide it.

"For how long? The heat...we'll need shelter."

"I know. But we'd better take what advantage of the morning coolness we can, at least for a while."

She stared into his sweaty face. "We aren't going to get much farther, are we? Rest today, another night— how much farther can we go before we collapse?"

He didn't meet her eyes, and his mouth was grim but determined. "They're looking for us. I'll have the flares ready this time. We aren't beaten yet."

Her feet dragged, but she tried to force a smile. Somehow, when it came to essentials, it seemed important to say certain things. "Well, whatever happens, thanks."

"What for?"

"Getting us this far. Putting up with me all these years. I know I'm not easy to be around, that maybe I took a part of Jack that should have been yours and his." She made a helpless gesture with her free hand. "I never had a mother, and after Daddy died, I just needed him."

"I know. It's just taken a while for me to see that you needed Jack probably more than I did." He gave a papery-sounding chuckle. "See, even smart-mouthed golden boys can learn something. Never too late."

His words plucked a chord within her. It might be too late for them very soon—permanently. Dared she gather her courage and tell him that she loved him? In the hereafter, would she forever regret that she hadn't said it, no matter what the cost? She opened her mouth, but he was going on, and somehow the moment was lost.

"And I don't want to hear any more negative talk," he said, his voice a sandy rasp, but firm. "We've got lots of options. Why, you never know what might lie over the next rise, so...my God! Is that a gate?"

She looked to find a crooked barbed-wire and pole gap strung across the road a hundred feet ahead of them. In the graying light of predawn, she could just make out a faded hand-lettered sign. Keep Out!

"Logan!" She couldn't keep the excitement from her voice.

"I know. But don't get your hopes up, it could be just another abandoned spread."

"I don't believe it."

"You're right. It's a start. Come on."

Adrenaline pumping, they hurried to the gate, skirting it and plunging up the road. Bliss wondered if it was her imagination, or was the way a little smoother here, as if someone or something had trampled the undergrowth in the recent past? Then she stopped abruptly, nearly swinging Logan off balance as she clutched at his shoulder.

"That was a rooster! Did you hear it?"

His laugh was pure relief. "Damn, girl! I think you're right. Let's go!"

They were almost running, or as near to it as their weakened condition would allow. Then they saw it. Like a glorious mirage, a small clapboard ranch house with a low porch emerged from the shadows ahead. Sounds of life were just beginning to stir on the homestead—the mutter of chickens from a wire coop, the snicker of a horse in the corral, a faint lowing of cattle from a distant pen.

"Oh, thank God!" Bliss breathed, joining in Logan's relieved laughter. Their ungainly advance up the track toward the structure seemed to catch the animals' attention, increasing their early-morning restlessness. They stamped and murmured uneasily at the approach of two giddy strangers.

"God, I hope they own a coffeepot," Logan said fervently.

"It's like a miracle." Mere yards from the decrepit porch, euphoria filled her, swelled her admiration for his strength and courage. "You did it, Logan. You were right—"

The sharp crack of a gun blast rent the air over their heads, followed by another and another.

Reacting instantaneously, Logan tackled Bliss, throwing her beneath him on her stomach onto the grassless, sandy, hardpack yard with bruising strength. She was too stunned to register more than the loss of breath at the impact and Logan's colorful cursing.

"Hold your fire!" he shouted, keeping his arms over Bliss's head. "Dammit, we surrender!"

"That's what they all say, hombre," a gruff, belligerent voice announced from the porch.

Bliss raised her head just enough to see a shock of gray hair, a face like an old boot and a smoking, chrome-plated thirty-eight held by a steady hand.

"Stay right where you are," the figure ordered. "I ain't plugged me a varmint yet this morning, but the day is young."

Logan had never met a female he couldn't charm, but he had to admit that Mittie Powell might just be the exception to the rule.

"Hell, sonny!" Sitting at her oilcloth-covered

kitchen table, she snorted indelicately and poured a second cup of surprisingly good coffee into his cup from a sooty blue enamel pot. "That's a mighty tall tale— plane crashes, a sick papa, mountain lions. Sounds like bull hockey to me."

The room was a mixture of sixty years of accumulated junk, from an antique pie safe that held pastel Fiesta ware dishes to a faded Civilian Conservation Corps poster tacked over a crack in the plaster wall. A black cast-iron stove reigned in one corner, while a modern window unit air conditioner purred in the other.

"I assure you, ma'am, every word is gospel," he said. "Just look at us."

Bliss slumped on a ladder-back chair beside him, her beautiful face shadowed by fatigue. She was uncharacteristically quiet, her slender fingers laced around a chipped mug, her sapphire eyes darting to the pistol Mittie had carelessly tossed onto the corner of the table. Even the indomitable Bliss Abernathy had her limit, and being shot at by an octogenarian with an attitude was apparently it.

"Well, sonny," Mittie said, her weathered face creasing like old shoe leather, "a woman on her own can't be too careful, you know. Rustlers been slipping over the border, stealing my stock, just like the old Comanches done a hundred years ago. Flat gets my goat."

"I can imagine how frustrating that must be," Logan replied smoothly. "We're just grateful to come across your place, and doubly grateful your aim was off."

"Oh, hell! If I'd a meant to nail you, I would have." Clad in a man's plaid Western shirt and dungarees, she pushed the glass pitcher of iced water toward Bliss. "Drink some more, honey. You look flat parched."

"Thank you, ma'am," Bliss murmured.

"Oh, call me Mittie." She hawed loudly. "And you can relax. I ain't a-goin' to bite you. You two young 'uns want eggs? Fresh out of my own coop." She rose and began banging skillets and bowls, reaching for a wire basket of eggs and a crock of milk.

"That would be great," Logan replied, "but first, can we phone our people? I know we've got folks worried about us. My mother…"

Mittie paused in her bustling and tugged on an earlobe. "Well, now, sonny, there's the rub. Ain't never had phone service out in these parts, and that last blow tore down my radio antenna. Hadn't had a chance to string it up again."

The lack of technology boggled Logan for an instant, then he recovered. "All right, though we hate to impose on your hospitality, could you drive us into the nearest town? You can imagine the urgency—"

"Alpine's forty-seven miles. And I live on the longest dead-end dirt road in the state of Texas." Agile and feisty despite her years, Mittie deftly scrambled eggs in a black iron skillet, turned them onto two plates, added slabs of homemade sourdough bread and slammed the dishes in front of Bliss and Logan. "Eat up while it's hot."

Logan began to feel he was talking to a diminutive brick wall. "Uh, yes, ma'am." He picked up his fork and watched Bliss do the same. "About getting to town? The authorities—"

"Got things to do this morning." Mittie dropped the skillet into a scarred soapstone sink.

He swallowed eggs and frustration, trying to keep his tone even. "Then how about we borrow that truck of yours? I'll make it worth your while, even hire someone to drive it back out to you."

"Old Betsy?" It was hard to tell on the lined road map that was Mittie's face, but her expression might have been pure amusement. "Heck fire, sonny! She's as cantankerous as a wet hound with a nose full of nettles. You wouldn't get her ten feet by yourself. Got to baby her just so."

The president and CEO of Gaspard Enterprises wasn't accustomed to his wishes being stymied. "But—"

Mittie fisted her hands on her hips. "Look here, sonny. I can't just up and leave my stock. Chores come first on a working ranch. Besides, you two kids could use a breather. I'll carry you to town as soon as I get done. Couple of hours, maybe three, tops. In the meantime, you can catch a bath, take a little rest—"

Bliss perked up over her empty plate as if she'd just heard a celestial chorus announcing the second coming. "Bath?"

"Got spring-fed plumbing," Mittie said proudly. "Put it in myself back in fifty-six."

"That would be heavenly," Bliss breathed.

"Right through there, honey." Mittie pointed down a short hall. "Help yourself. There're some shirts and stuff hanging on the back of the door you're welcome to use."

Bliss was pushing back her chair, her tired eyes sparkling with renewed eagerness. "Thank you. You can't know—"

"Yes'm, I do." Mittie cackled again. "Got grit in every crack, ain't you? Well, go on. And you can stretch out on the guest bed when you get done. I guess sonny here can take the divan."

Much as his instincts screamed in protest against the delay, there didn't seem to be much Logan could do but fall in with his hostess's wishes—up to a point. He'd seen the ancient sofa with its protruding springs in the front room and he had no intention of subjecting himself to that torture rack. He rose and bent gallantly over Mittie's claw of a hand as if she were the Princess of Monaco.

"Your generosity and beauty are exceptional, ma'am, and since we hate to put you out any further than we have to, of course your plan sounds fine."

Bliss had paused in the hallway, watching him with narrowed eyes, while, for the first time Mittie looked flustered, a deep rose hue appearing under her darkly tanned skin.

She laughed girlishly. "Sonny, ain't you the one full of blarney!"

"I never let a charming woman go unappreciated." He smiled. "But if it's all the same with you, I'll pass on that divan and bunk with my fiancée."

"Why'd you tell her such a bald-faced lie?" Bliss asked.

Bathed, refreshed, clad only in a threadbare white man's shirt that must have belonged to Mittie's long-dead and quite burly husband, she perched on the edge of a creaky iron bedstead covered with the most meticulously stitched Wedding Ring quilt she'd ever seen. Gauzy tab curtains covered the windows, filtering the increasingly bright sunshine from outside into cool, softly washed shadows. Her glare as Logan entered the room, clean, shaved and wearing just his dusty chinos, was far from friendly.

"I've had all the roughing it I can stand," he replied, tossing a damp towel onto the back of a spool-legged rocking chair. "Don't be difficult, Bliss. I've had a hard day."

"You!" His nearness, soap-sharp and masculine, made her edgy. It took all she could do not to stare at his bare chest. Fiancée, indeed! "Of all the nerve—"

"Look, we've had a close call, but it'll be over soon." He came to the opposite side of the bed and stripped the blanket back to pristine white sheets. "Miss Mittie will be out doing her thing for who knows how long, so we might as well get some rest until she's ready to take us into town, and if these arrangements spare the good lady's sensibilities, who's going to be hurt?"

Me, her inner voice whispered. It was too close to a barely conceived dream, some fantasy of feeling and commitment that had no basis whatsoever in reality. It was hard enough to keep her feet on the ground where Logan was concerned, but his convenient lie changed her normally level head into something that could only be described as irrational, sentimental mush.

She jumped to her bare feet, disturbed, incensed, confused by the welter of emotions churning in her belly. Jerking up a plump pillow, she took a step to escape. "I've no intention of sharing a bed with a randy tomcat! You can just go to—"

He reached across the bed and threw her onto her back in the middle of it before she could blink. Pinning her with his weight, he held her wrists beside her ears, his temper plain to see in the flash of tawny eyes the same color and intensity as the wild mountain lion's.

"Dammit, woman!" he growled, his mouth inches from hers. "I've had enough. You're acting like a child, and we both know you're far from that."

The dig hurt, and her mouth wobbled. "Whatever you think, I've—I've got my sensibilities, too."

He drew a shaky breath, his eyes dropping to the betraying quiver of her lip. "Don't do that."

"Don't do what?"

"Look at me with those big, blue, kicked-kitten eyes. You're a sham, and it's damned unfair to make me feel guilty for—" He broke off, swallowing, a high color staining his cheekbones.

"For what, Logan?" she whispered.

"Making me want you."

His blunt admission thrilled her, empowered her, terrified her. "I don't intend to."

With a groan, he shifted his body closer to her, letting her feel the power of his thighs, his turgid manhood. She was naked beneath the shirt, and the rasp of the fabric against sensitive flesh made her throat catch as though she'd swallowed a goldfish.

"That's what makes it so damned difficult," he admitted raggedly. "You don't have to do a thing. All I have to do is look at you...."

Bliss shifted restlessly, suddenly burning with a fever that came from deep inside. "Logan."

His face went hard, and a muscle jumped on the side of his jaw. "It had to come to this someday."

"Yes." Helpless, breathless, she couldn't deny it.

"We have to finish it, you know that?"

Bliss shook her head weakly, her damp hair spreading out on the pillow. Every bone in her body went liquid. "It's crazy, foolish."

"I know." His eyes blazed. "We're going to do it anyway, aren't we?"

What could she say? Every fiber in her cried out for him. He was right. It would all be over soon, the ordeal that was both agony and ecstasy, and then they'd go back to their own worlds, resume the only relationship they seemed capable of. Yet here was time and opportunity to experience something unique with Logan, something she could take just for herself, something to cherish much, much later when the memory of her love grew old.

Was she selfish to want just this much? Incredibly foolish to risk her heart for even this fleeting moment? The answer didn't matter, because it had been decided a long time ago in a faraway clime by a young girl's heart.

Captured by his hands, she lifted her face, brushing his lips with her own. "Yes," she murmured, "yes, we are."

"And about damn time."

His mouth crushed hers and he pulled her to him, locking his arms around her. Hands freed, she clutched his strong neck, then allowed her fingertips to roam over the broad expanse of his shoulders, down the washboard of his rib cage. He felt wonderful—hard and muscular, his skin lightly dusted with sandy hair, his bulk and weight powerfully male and exciting.

Meanwhile, he slanted his mouth even closer, using the tip of his tongue to coach her lips to part for him, then plunging into the sweet cavern in a rapacious onslaught that made her light-headed with delight. He drank deeply of her, as if he'd consume her very soul, and Bliss quivered, her nails digging into the hard muscles of his hips.

He transferred his attentions to the side of her throat, licking and laving the satiny flesh. "God, I've wanted this."

She was melting and mindless and monosyllabic. "Yes. Yes."

Urgently, Logan raised to his elbows, his fingers fumbling on her shirt buttons. When he opened the garment fully, exposing her completely to his heated perusal, his hands were shaking.

"You're so lovely," he murmured, his voice like gravel. "I had only imagined..."

His hands were the hands of an idolatrous worshiper, a supplicant before a shrine, as they traced the rounded outline of her bosom, down to the slender indentation of her waist, then followed the womanly fullness of her hips. Wherever he touched, Bliss burned. It wasn't enough. She wanted him everywhere. Her hands slid to his nape, tugging him closer.

But instead of returning to her mouth as she so fervently hoped, he rained kisses across the V of her collarbone, across the swell of her breast and finally...finally took one pebbled nipple between his lips and suckled gently.

Bliss nearly came apart. Writhing, she moaned and clutched at his shoulders, her long legs tangling with his. A hot wire curled from her breasts down to her core, and dew formed between her legs. He was unmerciful, transferring his mouth to her other nipple, licking and nipping and sucking so that it tightened to match the other rosy bud.

There wasn't enough air in the room to breathe. What was he doing to her? It wasn't fair that he should dominate their encounter so entirely. Gasping, Bliss did her best to turn the tables, sliding her hands under his waistband, searching out the aroused masculine part of him and stroking him with velvet fingers.

He jerked at her touch, his groan one of abject surrender. "Careful—ah!"

At her unspoken urging, he helped her unfasten his fly, then kicked out of his pants. She was thrilled to find him naked beneath, and reached out for him again, in an agony to touch and explore and torment him as much as he was doing to her. But he forestalled her with a quick shake of his head, catching her wrists.

"Not so fast," he croaked. "What you do to me— I'll go off like a boy."

"Good," she panted. "I want you helpless. I want you crying for mercy."

He laughed. "Bloodthirsty wench. We'll see who calls uncle first."

Sliding down her body, he left a fiery trail of kisses in his wake, taking especial time with the flat indentation of her navel, then nuzzling the dark blond thatch at the top of her thighs.

Shocked and seduced, she bucked and arched against him, her hands still held captive. "Logan, no..."

"Yes, *querida,* yes."

He did wicked, wicked things to her then, using his lips and tongue, pushing her inexorably toward a height of passion she'd never experienced. Her gasps were painful, her skin dewy with perspiration. Eyes squeezed shut, she was barely conscious of anything but the exquisite, sizzling sensations coursing throughout every molecule. When he found the sensitive nodule of her womanhood and flicked it with his tongue, there was no going back, and with a high keening cry, she pitched headlong into an abyss filled with lightning pleasure, shuddering and sobbing and cursing him for having such power over her.

"It's all right, it's all right," he murmured, his voice strained as he came to her again, kissing her deeply, inhaling the ragged breaths of her pleasure like elixir.

"Damn you." Her face was wet. "Damn you, Logan Campbell."

"Shh." He licked the salty moisture from the corners of her eyes, soothing her, then pulled her more fully underneath him and parted her thighs.

The feel of him, hard and pulsing, probing her intimately, made her reel, sent her spiraling upward again, filled with an incredible need for him, for *this*, finally. Eager yet apprehensive, she stiffened, unsure. Feminine doubts stifled her. He'd been with many women. How would she measure up? Could she please him?

"Relax." His breath was a groan against her ear, his hands lifting her bottom. "You're so hot, so tight…"

Bliss's hands fluttered helplessly across his shoulders, seeking a bit of stability in a world gone topsy-turvy. "It…it's been a while."

Somehow, she sensed that pleased him. He pressed more forcefully, inching into the sweet wetness of her body by increments, though the effort not to sink himself in one thrust left him gasping.

"It's going to be all right," he said hoarsely. "Trust me, *querida*. I won't hurt you."

Ah, but there were no guarantees for that! She could welcome whatever physical discomfort might accompany their first joining, but what about the emotional costs? But then he was inside her fully, filling her completely, and all thoughts and reservations flew out of her head at the sheer *rightness* of it. This is where she belonged. Had always belonged.

"Logan!" Her voice was choked.

He seemed similarly overcome. "I know. I know." Lifting her thighs, he guided her legs around his lean hips, locking their bodies in the most intimate of embraces. "Come with me."

He took her on a journey she'd never imagined possible, moving slowly at first, then building the tempo into something glorious. She could do little but arch against him and hang on as passion overtook her again and again.

He was ruthless. Merciless. Bringing her to fever pitch just to watch her come apart, then catching her before she could fall to earth and rocketing her skyward again. Finally, when the world blackened and pleasure cascaded endlessly through her, he threw himself after her in his own soul-stirring release. Pressing into her with all his might, he called her name.

Afterward, for a long time, neither could move among the tumbled bedclothes. Breathing was the only object. At last, he lifted himself slightly, the slick stickiness of their heated skin parting with a slight sound. He framed her dazed face with his hands and, still joined, kissed her roughly, tenderly, thoroughly. She threaded her fingers through the sandy hair at his nape, held him still and kissed him in wonder.

Then they looked at each other. Smiled tentative smiles and said in serious, delirious, amazed unison, "Uncle."

Chapter Nine

"Won't be long now." Mittie Powell turned the ancient pickup onto the main blacktop highway and gunned the accelerator, increasing speed to a flat-out forty-five miles per hour across the hilly terrain. Hot afternoon air blew through the truck's open windows as they flew by a green highway sign announcing Alpine, Six Miles. "Damn, it's another scorcher, ain't it?"

"Yes, ma'am," Logan answered. "This is real tough country. But this sure beats walking, right, Bliss?"

He sat on the outside passenger seat, Bliss between him and Mittie on the cracked vinyl as they jounced along. A thread of Bliss's hair blew across his mouth as she nodded agreement, not trusting her answer to be heard against the roaring of the old truck's engine. Carefully, regretfully, Logan peeled the lock of hair away and tucked it behind her ear, smiling to himself when she shivered at his touch.

Inside he was still reeling. He and Bliss hadn't gotten much rest during the private respite Mittie's obligatory chores had given them, but he couldn't regret a moment of it, not when he looked at the still-soft curve of Bliss's mouth and knew he was the one who'd given her that well-kissed look. Had any woman ever responded with such ardor? The fire that had crackled between them for so long hadn't been misleading. They'd nearly burned each other up.

Arm draped along the seat back, Logan allowed his fingers to play across the curve of Bliss's shoulder under her rinsed-out jumpsuit. She stiffened, almost as if she were new to the touches lovers indulged in, then relaxed against his arm. An overwhelming possessiveness consumed him. He couldn't wait to get her out of that damned fever-inducing garment again. No matter what or who had come before, Bliss was *his* now, and he was already champing at the bit to get her alone again.

They were going to make some fine music together, he knew it in his bones. Oh, it might require a little creative coordination of their schedules, but now that he'd had her, there was nothing about this affair with Bliss he intended to give up anytime soon. And as for their next time together, he'd do it up right—penthouse suite, candlelight and champagne—and all her nonsense about taking her inheritance and leaving Campbell Drilling would go by the wayside once and for all. Even Jack couldn't argue with that.

The thought of his father made him frown, but then he determinedly thrust the worry aside. Jack Campbell was as tough as they came. He was going to be all right. He had to be. The old scoundrel was probably already up and ordering the nurses around in his usual high-handed manner. Up ahead, the low profile of the little town hove into view, brick homes against rolling hills, gas stations, grocery stores—civilization. Logan shifted on the seat, a knot of tension forming at the base of his neck. They'd know soon enough, anyway.

Logan forced his attention to Mittie's chatter. "As I said before, ma'am, we can't thank you enough."

"Glad to be of service, sonny," Mittie returned cheerfully. She wore a curly-brimmed straw cowboy hat pulled low on her steel gray curls. "Gives me a chance to pick up some supplies I've been needing. Actually, I've kinda enjoyed the conversation and company."

During the torturous hour-long drive to town Mittie had kept up a barrage of talk, probing Logan about life in New Orleans and Bliss about working in a man's world, salting the discussion with colorful stories of hers and her husband's early days in the badlands. They reached the outskirts of the dusty little town of about six thousand, a conglomeration of historic two-story adobe structures turned bed and breakfasts, fast-food joints and nondescript modern business buildings. Alpine was the seat of Brewster County and home of Sul Ross State University.

Mittie paused briefly at a stop sign, then turned up a main street that was quiet with the somnolence of midday heat. "Guess the first place to start with you folks is the sheriff's office. Reckon a lot of people been lookin' for you."

Bliss bit her lip. "Yes, ma'am, and the sooner we let the ones who care about us know we're all right, the easier I'll feel."

Mittie smacked Bliss's thigh encouragingly. "And check in on that pappy of yours, too, I know. Buck up, girl. You're a game one if I ever saw it, coming fifty miles through the backcountry if you came a foot. Everything'll be all right soon."

In short order, Mittie pulled into a parking spot in front of the castle-like courthouse, an imposing edifice made of red and white native stone and brick. She bustled them into the air-conditioned sheriff's offices as if she owned the place, hollering for someone called Raymond.

"Miss Mittie!" A startled-looking female clerk in a deputy's uniform jumped up from a receptionist's desk. Her eyes went wide at the bedraggled couple being towed along in Mittie's wake. "What can we do for you? The sheriff's busy—"

"Get that boy out here, pronto," Mittie demanded, then turned to wink at Logan. "Found me a couple of trespassers this morning think he might be interested in meeting."

Logan nearly groaned at the old woman's sense of humor and timing. It was time to get down to business, report their whereabouts, contact the FAA, call Valerie and Russ, find out about Jack's condition. Surely this burg had an airport of some sort. He'd charter a plane, get things rolling. Suddenly, he felt in his element. He reached across the desk and offered his hand to the secretary.

"Logan Campbell, miss. We've had a bit of trouble—"

A door to an inner office opened, and a swarthy deputy in a tan uniform appeared, his big voice booming. "What's the hoorah, Deborah? We've got to coordinate that search and—"

Bliss shrieked as a russet-colored head appeared behind the burly deputy. "Russ!"

She launched herself across the anteroom like a

rocket. After one startled second, Russ Campbell brushed past the deputy and met her halfway, swinging her into his arms. He was dressed in his usual uniform of faded jeans and blue and orange Campbell Drilling shirt.

"Bliss! Are you all right?"

She gulped and nodded. Russ looked up and met Logan's eyes. The sheer relief in his brother's identical tawny eyes made Logan speechless. Then Russ was on him, too, crooking an arm around his neck in a big, rough bear hug. "Logan, you SOB—"

"Good to see you, too, Russ." Logan was surprised at the huskiness of his voice.

Russ released them, stepping back to inspect them closely. "What happened? Where the hell have you been? When Jake found the crash—"

Between Bliss and Logan and Russ everything came tumbling out in a torrent of words.

"Lightning strike, electrical failure..."

"She brought us down like a pro..."

"Marched me through the wilderness like General Patton..."

"Then the water ran out..."

"There was a mountain lion!"

"Yes, Dad's okay for now. Mom moved him to Dallas..."

"She had a gun..."

During the deluge of explanations, the deputy caught Mittie Powell's eye.

"Well, Miss Mittie. Looks like we done found our missing persons."

She was grinning like a Cheshire cat. "Ain't it the truth? Too bad there ain't a reward."

Logan heard her and sent her a wide smile. "Who

says there isn't? How'd you like me to replace that ram-shackle truck of yours?''

"Old Betsy? Pshaw!" She shook her head. "We been together too long."

With a grin, the deputy clapped Russ on the back. "We'd best see about calling off those search planes."

"Damn straight." Russ drew a deep breath. "You two sure you're all right? Need to see a doc or something? What about that knot on your head, Logan?"

He'd almost forgotten it, and touched the bandage gingerly, pleased to find it wasn't too sore. "I'm okay. But Bliss hurt her knee."

"It's nothing," she said. Despite her denial, she'd braced herself on the secretary's desk as if her legs couldn't hold her up, and her mouth was suddenly tremulous. "Russ—"

"If it's about what we said last time, forget about it," he ordered brusquely. "I have."

Logan frowned, the meaning of their exchange lost to him but something feeling not right.

"You mean—" Her words wobbled to a halt.

"I mean forget it." Russ's look softened. "Darlin', I've come to take you home."

Taking everyone by surprise, hell-on-wheels Ms. Bliss Abernathy burst into tears. Logan stepped forward, but it wasn't him she reached for blindly. It wasn't his arms she stepped into with the grace of old habit. It wasn't his neck she clung to as she wept, or his lips she kissed.

Logan watched as his brother wrapped his arms around Bliss and kissed her. His gut clenched with a basic, primeval surge of jealousy and rage.

"Darlin', darlin'," Russ murmured, stroking Bliss's

supple back. "Everything's all right now. I'm here. I'm going to take care of you."

She'd been a damned fool.

With a sense of relief and despair, Bliss unlocked the door to the battered travel trailer she and Russ shared, which was currently parked within the fence-enclosed grounds of Campbell Drilling's Dallas work yard and offices. Russ followed her inside the musty trailer, cursing as a yapping, yipping raggedy gray and white rat ball of a dog sailed up the steps in his wake, nearly tripping him.

"Gusher! Shut the hell up!" Russ snapped. Outside, the first stars were doing their best to appear against the glare of city lights.

Bliss bent and scooped up the wiggling dog, allowing him to slurp her chin with his rough tongue. "He's just glad to see me."

Russ rubbed a hand through his dark auburn hair. "Yeah, well, he's a damned nuisance. Listen, are you sure you're going to be all right?"

"Sure. I'm just tired." She buried her nose in Gusher's fur. There was an ache in her chest that had nothing to do with fatigue and everything to do with her fragile emotional state. But Russ had enough on his plate, and though they'd shared nearly everything throughout their lives, her relationship—or lack of it—with Logan wasn't something she was prepared to talk about. She was glad the spat she'd had with Russ about her leaving the company the last time they had been together had been forgiven and forgotten. That was something, at least.

"I just need to clean up and get a good night's rest," she said, setting the dog on the floor and kicking a dish of dry food in his direction. Gusher happily transferred his attention to the meal. "That scene at the airport..."

Grimacing, Russ walked to the refrigerator for a beer, then reached out and flipped on the air conditioner thermostat. ";Yeah, that was quite a media circus. Sorry about that. I guess I shouldn't have been surprised, though. The rescue of the CEO of Gaspard Enterprises was bound to make news."

Bliss threw the keys on the scarred table with a sigh. The trailer had all the amenities of home, if you liked your surroundings secondhand and shabby, but it was comfortable enough for a couple of vagabonds moving from drilling site to drilling site. A cubical kitchen and banquette sitting area, a bedroom on either end for each of them, a minuscule bath—what more could you want? She looked at the frayed curtains, the out-of-date harvest gold color scheme, the threadbare Herculon sofa and battered TV in what passed as their living room, and knew she could indeed want a lot more.

The media attention their arrival in Dallas had generated had only reiterated the astronomical distance between the lives she and Logan lived. His coldness and distance toward her during the charter flight Russ arranged from Alpine and their subsequent arrival proved to her beyond a shadow of a doubt that he was already regretting what had happened between them. It had obviously meant nothing more to him than a physical release after a grueling ordeal.

The realization made her squeeze her eyes shut in pain. Not that she'd expected anything else, of course. After all, Logan was a scion of high society, a mover and a shaker whose responsibilities hounded him, while, to him at least, she was flighty, a free spirit who'd never be tame enough to commit to, much less marry and make the mother of his children. It was a reality she'd accepted going in, so if the ardor and passion of his lovemaking had raised false expectations within her, she had no one to blame but herself.

Yes, indeed, she was a fool.

"Hey, are you sure you're okay?" Russ repeated in concern.

"All those reporters' questions gave me a headache." Laura Ramirez, whom Bliss had met at the Odessa Blowout, had been especially insistent.

Russ nodded. "Yeah, I'm glad I left that to the two of you and went to the office to consult with the airport authorities. There's going to be a lot of paperwork about the crash."

"Tomorrow. I'll deal with it tomorrow," Bliss said wearily.

"Fine, darlin'. And you can see Dad at the hospital then, too. He's relieved you and Logan are okay and anxious to see you, but told me to see you got some rest first." He glanced at his watch. "You sure it's okay if I spend the night at the hotel with Mom? I figure I can help spell her with Dad. She's had to keep the vigil all by herself."

"Of course." Bliss forced a smile. "You go on, and give Jack my love. I'm heading for the shower."

"Good. I'll see you in the morning, then." Russ took a step toward the door, then paused. "One thing, Baby Sister." Unlike Logan, Russ used the moniker with affection.

"What?" she asked, searching the cabinet for headache tablets.

"What's going on with you and Logan?"

Bliss's fingers clenched on the child-proof cap of the painkillers. "I don't know what you mean."

He blew out an exasperated sigh. "I mean I could have cut the tension between you two with a knife, that's what. What happened? Did he pull something I need to beat the snot out of him for?"

"You're imagining things, Russ."

"I'm not blind—"

She whirled on him with a flash of temper. "Look, can we just forget it? I'm bushed and I'm not in the mood to discuss your brother, okay? Let's just say that we had our usual ups and downs out there and both agree we still don't like each other very much."

Russ raised his hands in surrender. "Okay, okay. Keep your shirt on. I was just checking."

Her expression softened, then she stepped up to him and placed a peck on his cheek. "Thanks, but it's okay. Now get out of here, ya big galoot. Your mom needs you."

As the door slammed behind Russ, Bliss was already unzipping the jumpsuit—which she was certain she'd never don again—and turning on the shower full blast. She stepped under the spray with a vast sense of relief. After all, it was one of the few places in the world a woman with a broken heart could cry her eyes out with no one the wiser.

He'd been a damned fool.

Logan stepped out of his morning shower, toweled off and donned a pair of dress slacks and an Egyptian cotton button-down shirt conveniently provided by the luxury hotel in which he'd booked a suite. Valerie had returned from the hospital last night nursing one of her sick headaches, and he hoped she was getting the rest she needed. It wouldn't hurt her to sleep in while the rest of them tended to Jack. In fact, it was just a bit puzzling why she was being so devoted, but then he supposed when you'd been married to a man and borne his sons, there was a connection that could never be broken, despite time, distance and divorce decrees.

Logan examined himself in the steamy mirror, decided the split on his forehead was sufficiently healed to forgo another bandage, then reached for his comb. He'd slept like the dead, only to wake in the early morning hours filled with an ache in his heart that wouldn't go away.

Damn, he was naive. One look at Bliss and Russ together yesterday, and he'd known. Forget about François. That was only a smoke screen. It was Russ she cared about. Hadn't they lived together for years in that ramshackle trailer? He'd been stupid, downright *blind*, to think it had all been innocent!

From the looks of things, they'd had a lover's quarrel—probably about Bliss's leaving the company—and she'd been either on the rebound or out to prove something only Bliss Abernathy could fathom when she'd come so willingly to Logan's bed. She'd used him, pure and simple. And he'd fallen for it, hook, line and sinker. His gut clenched.

Yes, indeed, he was a damned fool.

Logan threw down the comb with a snort of self-disgust. He certainly wasn't accustomed to having the tables turned on him in such a fashion. He had a fleeting burst of sympathy for the ladies he'd loved and left. So this was how it felt.

No, for some unknowable reason, this was worse. He felt betrayed beyond telling. She'd been so warm, so giving in his arms. Had it all been a sham, an act? It was hard to believe. And now that he'd had a taste of her, so vibrant, so full of life, how could he give her up? But she wasn't his, and had never been, he reminded himself fiercely. Maybe she was just paying him back for that time all those years ago. Who knew the workings of the female mind?

Besides, was there ever a woman more unsuitable for a man in his position? She'd drive him insane inside of a month! She'd rock his stable world, keep him off balance, destroy any semblance of refinement and order. And Lord, wouldn't it be fun?

He thrust the betraying thought aside, burying it deep. No, he'd made a mistake with Bliss, and the best thing was to put it behind him. It was clear she already had, the conniving, manipulative witch.

It wasn't as though he didn't have other things to think about. He'd already rousted Maddie Hughes from her bed this morning, had her fax him the most pressing business matters and was prepared to run Gaspard Enterprises from the suite for as long as it took. If all else failed, work was his universal panacea, and a woman was easily replaced by a man's responsibilities.

Logan opened the bathroom door, following the smell of room service coffee into the spacious and airy contemporary living area of the suite he shared with his mother, a serene oasis of chrome and steel Art Deco. He came up short at the sight of his brother drinking *his* coffee and staring at the mid-morning Dallas skyline through the wide bank of windows.

"Where the hell did you come from?" Logan went to the tray and poured himself a cup. He sipped with a grimace. It wasn't New Orleans coffee, and the lack already put him in a bad mood.

"Good morning to you, too, brother dear," Russ returned with a sardonic lift of his eyebrow. "Didn't sleep well?"

"I slept fine," Logan snapped.

Russ tossed him a copy of the *Dallas Morning News.*
"You made the front page. From wire service and staff,
Executive Has Close Call in Desert."

"Yeah, I'm a regular Indiana Jones," Logan drawled,
dismissing the article without at glance. "Have you
called the hospital?"

"Just came from there." Russ drained the cup and
set it carelessly on an ebony end table. His frayed jeans,
faded chambray shirt and auburn-headed roughneck demeanor made him look totally out of place in the luxurious setting. "Dad had a restless night, probably reaction to you and Bliss being found, but I left him
sleeping. We probably ought to show up for the doc's
rounds, hear what he has to say."

"I'm planning on it. You don't have to tell me where
my duty lies."

"God Almighty, you're touchy." Russ narrowed a
glare at his brother. "I'll put it down to your ordeal."

"Don't do me any favors, Russ." Logan couldn't
contain the belligerence in his tone. When he looked at
Russ, he thought of Bliss and him together, and something hot and withering burned in his belly.

Russ bristled at his brother's tone. "All right, if
you're taking the gloves off, I'd like to know a few
things—"

A sharp, imperative rap at the door cut him off. With
a grimace of annoyance, Logan went to the door. The
man who faced him when he opened it was such a total
surprise, Logan could only blink in stupefaction.

"Logan, my boy! Hope you don't mind me dropping
in like this." Candidate for state senator Thomas H.
Barnette clapped Logan's shoulder genially and stepped
inside the suite. "Just have a minute, you know. Mak-

ing a campaign speech up the street in a few minutes. Couldn't resist the opportunity to come by and congratulate you on your near escape. Read all about it in the paper. Hell of a thing, that. Damn. If it isn't Russ!''

Dapper and trim in a spanking-new three-piece suit, sandy-gray hair styled to perfection, Tom Barnette crossed the room with his hand outstretched, his dimpled grin wide and a charming sparkle in his blue eyes. ''It's good to see you, too, son!''

''Mr. Barnette.'' Russ could do nothing but take the proffered hand.

''Tom. You boys have known me long enough not to stand on formalities.''

Logan recovered sufficiently to shut the door. ''This is rather an unexpected surprise, Mr. Barnette.''

''Spur of the moment thing.'' Tom ignored Logan's continued formality and stiff demeanor. ''I wanted to check up on Jack, too. Heard he's a bit under the weather.''

''He's recovering nicely, thank you.'' Logan's tawny eyes took on a predatory gleam. ''Do you have something else on your mind, Barnette?''

''Just touching base with old friends.'' Tom's smile was ingratiating, but the look in his eyes challenged. ''Hope I can count on your support for my campaign.''

''I don't vote in the state of Texas,'' Logan replied coldly.

''But Campbell Drilling wields a heap of influence, and I would certainly welcome the endorsement.''

Logan was dumbfounded, then his jaw clenched. ''I think you know the answer to that.''

Tom managed to look hurt. ''You're not still blaming me for that bit of trouble we had, are you? Hell, Jack knows I took quite a loss on that deal, too.''

"I guess that's a matter of opinion."

Tom's expression lost its geniality, became as hard and calculating as Logan's. "So that's the way the wind blows, is it? And I'm right in assuming I've got you to thank for that private investigator snooping into my business?"

"I don't know what you're talking about," Logan lied blandly.

Tom snorted with disbelief. "Yeah, right. Well, bring 'em on, son. I've got nothing to hide, and you'll be the one who ends up with egg on your face, especially after I slap you with a defamation of character suit."

Logan picked up the gauntlet, his smile becoming feral. "I'd welcome the opportunity to clear the air in a court of law."

Tom glanced at Russ. "You feel the same?"

Logan's twin shrugged. "I stand with the family."

"I see." Tom's eyes blazed with thwarted temper, but he held himself in check. "I'll see myself out, then. Just remember, boys, when you kick over a hornet's nest, you might not like what comes out."

The door slammed behind him, echoing loudly in the suite.

With a muttered curse, Logan went to the coffeepot. "Can you believe the man's nerve? Lay off or else! That'll be the damned day!"

Russ looked thoughtful. "After all this time, what's the point, Logan? Everything's been written off long ago."

"It's a matter of principle. No one gets the best of the Campbells."

"Geez, you and Dad and all that stuff about honor. Despite that sophisticated facade of yours, the truth is you like a brawl better than I do."

"You taking up for Barnette?" Logan demanded.

Russ dropped his long length onto the mushroom-colored leather sectional sofa. "Hell, no. The man's slime. Charming in his own way, of course, but I wouldn't trust him as far as I can throw him. But I think you're wasting your time."

"Dad doesn't."

"Yeah, well, Jack doesn't know everything," Russ muttered. His glance sharpened. "And speaking of that, he's not going to be pleased when he finds out you've been messin' with Bliss."

Logan's hands clenched. "Just what are you saying?"

"I'm saying I want to know what the hell's going on between you two."

"That's none of your damn business."

Russ surged to his feet, belligerence in the assertive thrust of his jaw. "The hell it's not!"

"You staking a claim?" Logan asked angrily, his voice rising. God, he hated it when he lost it, but the subject of Bliss Abernathy made him insane. He drew a deep breath, fighting for control.

Russ scowled. "Of course not. No one hog-ties Bliss. She roams free, always has, always will. But the last thing she needs is a spoiled playboy trifling with her affections."

Logan's bark of laughter was bitterly sardonic. "What a load of Victorian bull. She can take care of herself."

Russ bristled with a show of pure male protectiveness, a possessiveness that set Logan's teeth on edge. "She's not as tough as she likes to pretend sometimes."

"And you should know," Logan sneered. "What's

the matter, Russ? You object to someone else crossing into your territory?"

Fists raised, Russ took a step toward him. "Why, you—"

"That's enough, boys!" Valerie stood in the open doorway of her room, wrapped in a velour robe, her face wan but determined. "Haven't we got enough to deal with without your constant bickering?"

Instantly chastened, Logan shot Russ a final warning look, then went to escort Valerie into the room. "Sorry, Mother. Things are just a little...tense. Can I pour your coffee?"

Valerie watched Russ turn and stare out the wide windows, noted the cessation of hostilities, then nodded. "Please. Then we all need to get to the hospital. I want you both to donate blood for your father this morning."

That snapped them to attention. "Why, what's happened?" Logan demanded.

"I've been on the phone with the doctor," Valerie said, a tremor of fear in her voice. "He's talking about bypass surgery." She swallowed hard. "And it has to be soon."

Chapter Ten

"You worried your mama pretty bad, boy."

Surrounded by medical monitors and IV equipment, Jack Campbell's craggy face was a bit more haggard than usual, maybe his mustache a trifle grayer, but otherwise there didn't appear to be so much as a crack in his abrasive, domineering attitude. Standing at his father's bedside, Logan twisted his mouth wryly as he admitted frankly, "I had a couple of anxious moments myself."

"Not me." Jack plucked at the sheet and his checked hospital gown. Hot Texas morning sunlight poured through a wide window on the far side of the room. "Knew you two kids would be okay. Raised you up to tough out the critical situations. Didn't let us down, either."

Logan could almost have laughed. This was pure Black Jack, refusing to acknowledge anything in the world that didn't suit his own plans. He flexed his arm, testing the small bandage covering the site from which he'd donated blood earlier that morning. If pure bull-headedness would serve, then he knew he didn't have to be anxious about his father's condition or the possibility of major cardiac surgery.

"I'm glad your faith in us was warranted," Logan said.

"Well, accidents happen. I'll never forget that Odessa Blowout. But it's going to be a mess getting the insurance straight on that plane. And Bliss was especially fond of that aircraft, picked it out herself and all."

"She'll get over it."

Jack's gaze narrowed in speculation. "You get anything settled with her?"

"Not yet. I'm working on it."

"Maybe I should have a talk with her."

Somehow, having Jack and Bliss teaming up didn't seem like a good idea, Logan thought. No, he'd deal with Bliss in his own way, just as soon as he figured out how. "Why don't you stop being a busybody and concentrate on getting well? I'll tend to Bliss while you work on getting your sorry butt out of this place."

Jack grinned. "You can't talk to your daddy like that."

"Gotta keep you honest somehow, old man." Unable to resist the impulse, Logan squeezed Jack's hand hard, then released it. It was as much affection as they could show, but it was enough. Neither wanted to mention the threat of impending surgery. They both cleared their throats.

"Damn nurses," Jack muttered. "Took away my cigarettes. You don't think—"

"Don't press it, Dad." Logan laughed. "Besides, I'm

not about to risk Mom's fury if she caught me aiding and abetting.''

''Yeah, she's still a slave driver, that woman.'' Jack's dark eyes softened with affection and respect. ''Of all my regrets...'' He shook his head. ''Well, enough of that. You just take care of her. She's been through quite a round with me and you kids.''

''Count on it, Dad.'' Logan looked around, then drew up a chair. ''By the way, thought you'd want to know I heard from Tom Barnette.''

''The hell you say!''

Back on more familiar and comfortable ground, Logan recounted Tom's visit to the suite.

''That snake,'' Jack said, his mouth set in a determined line. ''You must have him worried bad to come to you direct.''

''That's what I think. But even if we can prove he cheated you and Ben, there's not a great chance we'll recover much of our investment.''

Jack made a negligent gesture. ''That kind of loss we can take. But he made fools of us, and Ben Lattimer, too, and that I will not tolerate from any man.''

''I know. Incidentally, Ben called. He's planning to drop by later to see you. Feel up to it?''

Jack shrugged. ''Got nothing better to do until they spring me.''

''Except calculate Tom's fall from grace,'' Logan suggested.

''Sure. Someday, somehow, we've got to see that that slick shyster pays. And if he's got his heart set on a political career, I think it's our civic duty to put a spoke in his wheel, don't you?''

''Oh, yeah, this is for the good of mankind,'' Logan replied, a sardonic twist curling the corner of his mouth.

"Your motives are altruistic, right? Pure as the driven snow."

"Hell, no. I want to get the bastard where he lives—in his ego." Jack's eyes glinted with cold humor. "And I'm counting on you to do it. Don't let me down, Logan."

It was a charge Logan could do nothing but accept. "You can bet on it. After all, I'm something of a slick shyster myself."

"Knew that fancy law degree would be good for something."

"Glad to know I'm appreciated."

There was a soft knock at the door. "Anybody home?"

Jack perked up at the sight of Bliss's fair head poking into the room. "There's my girl."

Logan felt the breath go out of him as if someone had kicked him in the gut. Hair falling free down her back, dressed in a crisp scarlet shirt, oversize gold hoop earrings and a narrow denim skirt that skimmed her slender curves like a lover's caress, she was stunning, a totally feminine creation fully at home in her wonderful skin. To look at her, no one would ever guess what a grueling experience she'd so recently endured. No one would guess that she'd needed Logan in the desert, depended on him. No one would imagine that mere hours ago she'd been clinging to him, making him feel things no woman had ever been able to evoke before.

Her composure scared him, challenged him. And made him mad as hell.

Bliss sauntered to the bedside, flicking a quick glance in Logan's direction, then planted a kiss on Jack's weathered jaw. "Howdy, Jack. They treating you all right around here?"

"Bunch of jackals and vampires." He caught her upper arm, holding her still for his inspection. "You don't look the worse for wear, baby. You're really okay?"

"Right as rain." There was another darting glance at Logan from those incredible, inscrutable sapphire eyes. "Believe it or not, your city boy son is a fair hand at that wilderness stuff."

"I just don't want either of you pulling that kind of stunt again," Jack said gruffly. "Is that clear?"

"Believe me, as educational and edifying as it was, neither Logan nor I want to repeat the experience," Bliss replied firmly.

The certainty in her tone stabbed at Logan. It was one thing for him to understand her affections lay elsewhere. It was something totally different to have his nose rubbed in it, however obliquely. The muscle in his jaw tensed as he fought for control.

So what had happened between them meant nothing to her. What else had he expected? He forcibly squashed the astonishing sense of loss and devastation that churned his innards. What was the matter with him? Dammit, if she could be cool as the proverbial cucumber, then so could he.

"Yeah, the next time we go down in flames together, I'm seeing to it we land someplace civilized—like Palm Springs or Monte Carlo," he drawled. "I nearly perished without room service."

"Softy," Jack chuckled. "That does it. I'm getting Russ to haul your rear end out to the next drilling site for a refresher course. Señor Garcia's leases should pan out and you can get your hands dirty like a real Campbell."

"Thanks, but no thanks," Logan answered. "Where is Russ, anyway?"

"Who knows?" Jack dismissed the whereabouts of his other son as unimportant. "He hates hospitals, and he's had his fill lately."

"He should be here."

"Cut him some slack, Logan," Bliss interjected. "He's around someplace."

That she'd take up for Russ for what Logan considered a clear dereliction of familial duty ticked him off. But his father's hospital room wasn't the place to take either of them to task. He stood abruptly.

"You look a little tired, Dad, and since you've got Bliss to keep you company, I think I'll take off. Business waits for no man, and I've got a few things I need to see to."

"Is your mother coming by?" Jack asked.

"I'm sure she is."

"She's a brick, that woman."

Logan smiled. "I'll tell her you said so."

"You'll be back later?" Something totally unexpected flickered behind Jack's dark eyes—anxiety, uncertainty, fear? Not from his stalwart father, Logan thought fiercely, then realized that even Black Jack Campbell was having to come to grips with certain realities.

"I'll be back, Dad," he said quietly. "Whatever the next step is, we'll take it together."

"All of us, Jack," Bliss added, taking his hand in hers.

The anxiousness disappeared from Jack's face, replaced by satisfaction. "I've got great kids. The best," he said, his mouth lifting under his mustache. He pointed a finger at Logan. "Now get out of here, you outlaw. And bring me back Tom Barnette's ugly carcass strapped over your saddle."

"Laura!"

At the sound of her name, Laura Ramirez paused at the entrance to the hospital cafeteria, juggling two cups of coffee on a paper tray. It was the three o'clock shift change and it took her a moment to identify Shelby Lattimer waving her down amid the crush of people coming and going along the wide polished corridor.

As Shelby elbowed her way toward Laura, Laura realized she was leading an entourage that included her husband, Jake, her silver-haired father-in-law, Ben Lattimer, and a weary-looking Logan Campbell. Laura hesitated, searching with a vague sense of alarm for another face among the group, but there was no one else with them. Her involuntary sigh of relief annoyed her, and she set her tired shoulders under her casual denim dress and forced a smile as they found a quiet place out of the stream of traffic to talk.

"Hi, Shelby." She nodded to the men, who returned her greeting with murmured hellos.

"I thought that was you." In jeans and crisp white shirt, Shelby tilted her fair head in concern as she inspected Laura. "You look beat. What's going on? Rufio's not sick again?"

"Oh, no. But we've been going through tests all day. Precautionary, the doctor says, but have you ever tried to keep a five-year-old occupied?"

"With all the waiting in a hospital? I can imagine the challenge," Shelby said, instantly sympathetic.

Laura laughed ruefully. "My sister, Inez, is sitting with Rufio in the pediatric clinic while I take a coffee break, and let me tell you, I need it."

"The hospital routine can really wear you out," Ben agreed.

Laura glanced at Logan. Cleaned up and rested, he looked a lot better than he had when he and Bliss Abernathy had arrived at the airport yesterday, but there were lines of tension in his face that clearly showed the stress he was under. Of course, there'd been some underlying strain between the two crash survivors that Laura's reporter's antennae had immediately picked up, but, curious as she was, she hadn't been able to put it down to an exact cause other than their general ordeal.

"That was your article in this morning's paper, wasn't it, Laura?" Logan asked. She nodded, and he continued, "I appreciate your not making it more sensational than it had to be. My mother was upset by the whole situation, as you might expect."

"I was just doing my job. Your story was certainly newsworthy, especially considering Campbell Drilling's ties to the area and Jake's part in the search, but I'm not into tabloid journalism. Is your mother here?"

"Bliss took her back to the hotel to rest for a while."

Again, her instincts went into overdrive as she observed how he said Bliss's name. *Curiouser and curiouser.* "How's your father today?"

"Not out of the woods yet." His jaw worked. "His doctor will make a decision on open-heart surgery today or tomorrow."

Now it was Laura's turn to feel sympathetic. She remembered Black Jack Campbell—J.R.'s grandfather, she reminded herself—as a larger-than-life figure, maybe someone she'd have liked her son to have gotten to know under different circumstances. A guilt she didn't want to examine too closely stabbed at her tender heart. "I'm sorry to hear that. Is there anything I can do?"

Logan half smiled. "Thanks, but I don't think so. Not unless you can rustle up a few friends to donate blood. We're taking directed donations, just in case. Neither Russ nor I are compatible types, as it turns out."

Laura's heart jumped at the mention of Russ.

"But I am," Jake interjected, fingering the Band-Aid in the crook of his arm. "Can you beat that?"

"The blood bank will cross match, but it never hurts to have plenty of units on hand," Ben said with a shrug.

"I don't mind making a few calls," Laura said with an encouraging smile. "It's the least I can do."

"Thanks. Russ went out to the drilling office to do the same."

Laura felt a sense of relief, knowing Russ wouldn't come sauntering around the corner any time soon. Then she berated herself for her feeling of cowardice. She wouldn't go out of her way to dodge Russ Campbell—she was made of sterner stuff—but there was an old adage about letting sleeping dogs lie....

"He's useless around doctors and hospitals anyway," Logan finished. "Been that way since he was a kid."

"They're not my favorite place in the world, either," Jake said, his expression reminding everyone of the bullet he'd taken protecting Shelby from criminal Gus Salvatore's ambush.

"They have their uses, cowboy," Shelby said, sliding her arm around her husband's waist. The look she slanted him brought to Laura's mind the first time she'd seen Jake and Shelby together, spitting and fighting like cats and dogs.

That's it. Comprehension clicked into place. Logan and Bliss had the same look about them when Laura saw them together at the airport interview. Warily circling each other, fascinated, challenging, in lust if not in love. Laura knew with a certainty borne of her instincts that more than mere survival had taken place out there in the desert between the two of them. Maybe it wasn't any of her business, but she'd give her eyeteeth to know what, and what might come of it in the aftermath.

Though she liked Logan and would like to know Bliss better, Laura put on her professional hat and reluctantly set that particular issue of the heart aside. She had other more important concerns to pursue with Logan Campbell.

"I know this isn't the time or place, Logan," she said, "but as soon as you're able, I'd like to get together about that Barnette thing. Maybe while you're still here in the city?"

He nodded. "I'll make a point of it. As it happens, I heard from our illustrious candidate today. We're making him very nervous about the whole situation."

Ben Lattimer frowned. "You think you've dug something up on the old scoundrel?"

"I'm almost certain of it."

"Revenge is a two-edged sword, son."

"It's justice we're after, Ben," Logan returned. "And truth. Dad's already told me he doesn't care about the money, but if Tom is as crooked as I think he is, well, we'll be doing the taxpayers a favor to expose him for what he really is. And Laura's going to help."

"I wouldn't mind breaking the top story of the whole campaign," she agreed. Laura was ambitious enough to know a coup like that might just land her the network reporting job she hoped was coming her way. "Just as long as we have our facts down cold."

"Then we'll dig a little deeper."

She pursed her mouth thoughtfully. "If Barnette had shady dealings with you, it probably wasn't the first time. And insurance might not have been his only scam." She turned to Jake. "When I interviewed him about your adoption, I had a feeling he wasn't leveling with me. It might pay to take another look into his connection to that home for unwed mothers."

"I think you're barking up the wrong tree there," Ben said. "Everything I knew about that was strictly on the up and up. Why, Tom even told me once he'd referred the teenager who was baby-sitting his own girls to that home when she got herself in the family way. That shows a certain level of confidence, I reckon. Surely he wouldn't have even told me that if he was trying to hide something."

"All that's old news. It's Aegean Insurance that'll be his downfall," Logan said. He glanced at his watch. "Look, I've got to go, and your coffee's getting cold. We'll get back on this soon, Laura, all right?"

She nodded. "Take care, and good luck with your dad. I'll be in touch."

They parted and Laura hurried toward the bank of elevators, sure that Inez would think she'd taken off for parts unknown by now. But her brain was spinning with ideas and questions. Just as soon as she got Rufio's tests behind her and could pin Logan and perhaps Valerie Gaspard Campbell down for a few more details, she would be hot on the trail to perhaps the biggest story of her career. Two stories, really, intertwined—Tom Barnette, candidate, and Tom Barnette, adoption attorney. Her Adoption Then and Now piece would be all the juicier for a prime political connection. It was just a question of tracking down the facts.

Truth. Yes, sir. That was a journalist's primary mission, and this story had the promise of a big payoff.

Despite Ben Lattimer's feelings about Tom's innocence in connection to Jake's adoption, the place Laura intended to start was with the retired nurse who'd been in charge of the Brownsboro unwed mother's home, Lillian Hampstead.

"We've got to talk."

Wary, Bliss held the door of the travel trailer halfway open while Gusher yipped his objection to Logan's presence on her steps. It was late, the Campbell Drilling yards were deserted under their floodlights, and her freezer turkey pot pie sat half-eaten on the narrow kitchen table. She tugged the sash of her pink cotton robe a bit tighter and tilted her chin, struggling to squash the sudden surge of hope that rose mutinously within her.

"About what?" she demanded, trying to make her tone haughty, fearing it trembled instead.

"Things." Despite the fact that they'd both spent the better part of the day and evening at the hospital, Logan had the audacity to appear unrumpled in dress shirt and slacks, except for an inviting shadow of sandy late-day stubble on his jaw. Without waiting for an invitation, he brushed by her, carrying a butter-soft leather briefcase. "Would you call off that mutt?"

"Gusher, down." Whether she was prepared or not, it seemed Logan was determined to have his say. With an efficient motion, she clipped the twisted hank of her hair to the back of her head, then snapped her fingers at the dog. "Go lie down."

Whining, Gusher looked dubiously at Logan, gave what could only be considered a disdainful canine sniff, then trotted off through the open door of Russ's bedroom at the other end of the trailer and planted himself in the middle of the striped spread.

"That's got to be the ugliest animal I've ever seen," Logan said.

She slammed the door shut. "Did you come here to insult my taste in pets, or was there something on your mind?"

"Where's Russ?"

Shrugging, Bliss sat on the banquette and picked up her fork, stirring the glutinous mixture of overcooked vegetables and tofu turkey. "Still at the hospital, I suppose."

"That'd be a switch." He gave the shabby interior of the trailer a once-over, then dismissed it as inferior, just as she'd known he would.

She dropped the fork and glared at him. "Darn it, Logan! Give your brother a break. He's the one who's taken the brunt of Jack's care while we were out of pocket, and he's done a heck of a job in spite of his aversion to doctors."

Logan slid the briefcase onto the countertop and shoved a hand through his hair, mussing it like a little boy so that she longed to reach out and smooth it down. He seemed to fill the narrow confines of the trailer, broad shoulders and tanned skin, urbane and confident. She looked at him hungrily, finding the weariness in his features, so handsome and familiar and utterly appealing her heart ached.

"I didn't come here to discuss Russ's phobias," Logan said.

Her throat clogged on a mixture of trepidation and hope. "Then what do you want?"

Logan unbuckled the briefcase and slid a sheaf of papers across the table to her. "Here."

Almost as if it were a bomb, Bliss gingerly examined the document. As she scanned the pages, her fingers went numb and cold, and something died within her.

"I think you'll find it's an equitable arrangement." Logan leaned against the counter opposite the table, his hands shoved into his front pockets, his ankles crossed negligently, as if the fact that he was shattering what was left of her illusions was no more than a minor matter.

"We're prepared to offer a lump sum to start," he continued, "then annual payments until your inheritance is paid off. Further, we'll guarantee a line of credit so you can finance whatever planes, equipment and real estate you decide on."

"You seem to have it all figured out," she said slowly.

"This way Campbell Drilling will only be minimally impacted, but you'll still get the settlement you want." His tone was brisk, businesslike. "Equitable for all parties, as I said."

She flicked the pages. "You've been a busy little bee today."

Logan frowned. "Wasn't this what you wanted?"

"Why the hurry all of a sudden?" Hurt rushed to the surface, heated her face, made her want to lash out. Her words became a taunt. "Feeling guilty, amigo? Trying to buy me off?"

He stiffened. "That's not it. As usual, you've misinterpreted everything."

"Have I?" She rose unsteadily to her feet, feeling buffeted and bruised.

He didn't want her, and he didn't want her cluttering

up his tidy life. So uncomfortable. So inappropriate. No world-weary wench in Logan Campbell's ordered existence, no, sir! She just hadn't been prepared for the lengths he'd go to usher her firmly and swiftly out of his orbit. It appeared no price was too high to pay. But she wouldn't let him run her off without at least an explanation.

"Tell me, Logan," she said carefully, "do you care for me at all?"

He might have turned away but for the narrowness of the aisle. "Dammit, Bliss, what kind of question is that?"

"A fair one, after what happened, I think."

Ruddy color stained his tanned cheeks and he sucked in a breath, muttering. "Things got...out of hand."

She hadn't known she could be hurt any further. She'd been wrong. "That's all it meant to you? The great Logan Campbell let slip some of his world-famous self-discipline and now you're willing to give me what I want as a sort of—what? Damage control?"

He muttered something obscene. "Look, I can see what's in front of my face. And I'm not one to butt in where I don't belong. You and Russ—"

"Russ?" Astonishment made her stare. "You think Russ and I— Are you stupid or just delusional?"

A muscle jumped in his jaw. "At least I'm not a liar."

Fury clenched her fists. "No, just so full of yourself you think you know it all! Russ and I never...he's like my brother, for God's sake."

"And I'm not?"

Embarrassment stained her face. "Obviously not, considering. Though I wish to hell I'd had better sense than to get involved with you again! Get out. Now."

Logan tapped the papers with a fingertip. "Not until we get this settled."

"Settle this!" Bliss ripped the document in half and threw it at him. The pieces of paper fluttered to the worn linoleum like birds with broken wings.

He crossed his arms over his chest, his jaw turning stubborn. "You're being unreasonable, as usual."

"Don't you dare presume to call me unreasonable." Bliss knew her voice was shrill, but she was so shamed, so angry, for once she couldn't summon her own brand of coolness. "I gave myself to you, and you want to reduce it to a business deal! How dare you hide behind some corporate mumbo-jumbo? You felt something, I know you did, only you're too cowardly to face it. Now, I said get out!"

Incensed, she shoved him hard on the chest. It was like trying to move a brick wall. He caught her hands, glowering into her flushed face.

"Why make more of it than it was? I'm just another in a long line for you."

She was past discretion. "Much you know," she sneered. "Fancy-pants playboy. Mr. Sophistication. I'd think a guy with your experience would know when it's a girl's first time."

"What?" Dumbfounded, his hands tightened on hers, hauling her closer in the confined space between the table and kitchen cabinet. "What did you say?"

"Forget it." Chagrin at her foolhardiness filled her, and she struggled frantically to free herself. "Let me go, Logan."

"You were a *virgin?*"

His incredulity enraged her anew. "Don't look so shocked. It is possible, you know." She tossed her head in defiance, and bitterness tinged her laugh. "A thirty-year-old virgin, isn't that a hoot?"

"I was your first lover?"

"If that's what you want to call it." Her chin wobbled and she clamped down hard on raw feeling. She'd totally revealed herself to a man who didn't care.

Confusion and regret etched his features with strain. He flattened her palms against his chest, and she could feel the hard thump of his heart against her skin. "I didn't know...why didn't you say?"

"What's the difference? I knew what you thought of me, and idiot that I am, I still wanted you."

"No." Logan bent his head, brushing her mouth with his, murmuring. "I'm the idiot. I must have hurt you. I'll make it up to you, I swear."

"Stop it." Tears smarted behind her eyes, and she turned her head, straining against his grip. Anger she could deal with, but tenderness destroyed her. "Damn you, Logan. Don't do this to me again."

He shifted, one arm going around her waist, locking her in the V of his thighs, the other hand catching her jaw to tilt her face to meet his descending mouth. His lips were warm, masculinely hard and persuasive, and though there was a fierceness in his kiss that stirred her to her depths, his mouth moved gently on hers, seducing her, dragging her under again to that place where she was mindless with need and love. Too stunned to resist for the first bewitching moments, she moaned her distress, then, dredging up the last ounce of her strength, she thrust free of his arms, gasping as she floundered backward against the paneled door leading to her tiny bedroom.

"Go away." She hated the desperation, the weakness in her voice.

He followed her, flattening his hands on the wood beside her head, trapping her within the circle of his arms, then buried his face in the curve of her neck. "God help me, I can't."

Logan transferred his kisses to her chin, her cheekbone, the corner of her tremulous mouth. Somehow his hand was inside her robe, warm on her naked skin, caressing the fullness of her breast and curve of her hip.

Bliss shivered uncontrollably, melting at the moist brush of his breath, his tongue against her skin. "Oh, you're good at this, aren't you?" she asked bitterly. "The conquering hero claiming the maiden. Now that you know, suddenly I'm good enough for you, is that it?"

"It doesn't have to be so difficult."

Ragged breaths cut her words into bites. "My purity or lack of it making a difference to you now only proves what I've always known—you're a snob who never thought of me as anything but trash beneath your heels."

He pulled back, a muscle ticking in his jaw, his tawny eyes glimmering with passion and an infuriating tenderness. "Unreasonable woman. You don't know how wrong you are."

"Let me go." Her gasps were nearly sobs. "I want you to go. And go to hell while you're at it. I hate you."

"I've been there more years than you know." His fingers found the snap on her hair clip, and her hair spilled over her shoulders. Burying his fingers in the shining mass, he caught the sides of her head, latching his mouth onto hers for a blistering kiss that turned her inside out. When he raised his head, they both sucked in unsteady breaths, and Logan's voice was as husky as if he'd gulped mountain moonshine.

"You've fascinated me since the day you tackled me in that crummy trailer in Tulsa and pistol-whipped me with a fruit basket. Then you turned into a woman before my eyes, but we were both so damned young. But it's our time now, can't you see?" He slid a possessive hand down her breastbone, across her belly to cup her womanhood, evoking a shuddering gasp. "And you don't hate me."

She didn't know what she felt. Love, hate—two sides of the same coin, as the old saws told it, and she feared they were right. Their time, Logan said, and her heart cried. *For how long?* But it was too late. She was reaching for him, searching for his lips, too needy at this moment to be strong when all she wanted was to feel him again.

With a murmur of satisfaction, he took her mouth, plumbing the depths of her sweetness with his tongue. There was a tenderness, a gentle protectiveness that had never been there before, and it undermined her completely, made her his in ways she couldn't fathom. She tore at the buttons on his shirt, needing to touch him, desperate to feel his skin against hers once more.

Somehow they were through her door, Logan kicking it closed behind them, falling with her onto the violet-sprigged bedspread that was her only concession to feminine style and comfort in this tiny pseudo-home. He slipped her robe from her shoulders and tore out of his own clothes, coming to her with a power that took her breath away, his hands and mouth everywhere, driving her mindless.

When he entered her, she was slick and wet and ready, and they both shuddered at the goodness of the joining, teetering on the edge of perfection. Holding her close, kissing her with a passion that tore her heart in twain and then mended it, Logan rolled so that she was above him, letting her set the pace. His consideration touched her, but she was strong, as strong as this man who held her so intimately, and she pushed them both past tenderness to ecstasy. And when the release came they cried out in unison, joined and bound and pleasured in ways that transcended the merely physical.

But with nothing settled or changed, Bliss thought afterward, draped bonelessly over Logan's heaving chest. She fought back tears, her cheek pressed to his shoulder, her legs still tangled with his. Was she strong enough to accept only what he could give? So weak she'd stay until it was over? Would passion be enough, or would her desire for roots and family eventually push her into bitterness that would destroy what they did have together? She fought within herself, wondering how happiness and despair could be so intermingled, then pressed her lips against his sweat-salty chest, determined to take what she'd been given and be satisfied—at least for now.

Logan shivered at the touch of her lips, and his arms tightened around her. "Oh, Bliss—"

Outside the room, the front entrance door slammed open and Gusher exploded in a frenzy of yapping. Logan was already on his feet and halfway into his pants when the fist pounded on the thin bedroom door.

"Bliss!" Russ's bellow from the other side was strangely choked. "For God's sake, wake up!"

Mussed and rumpled, her hair in a wild tangle, Bliss dragged the spread over herself as Logan threw open the door. Russ's stupefied expression said it all as he took in Logan's half-dressed state and Bliss's damning position in her bed. Then his jaw and eyes grew hard.

Logan didn't back down an inch, his expression just as challenging. "What do you want?"

"It's Dad," Russ said harshly. His gaze darted to Bliss, then away, and fiery embarrassment flooded her. "He's taken a bad turn. You'd better come. Both of you."

Black Jack Campbell died three hours later.

Chapter Eleven

Laura Ramirez checked the address on her scribbled note, then turned her modest sedan down a tree-lined street in one of Dallas's older sections. The rangy ranch-style homes were from another era and not very elaborate, but it seemed that this was all that oilman Black Jack Campbell had required.

Making another turn, she instantly picked out the house from the cars lined up on both sides of the neighborhood street. The guests who'd come to the home for the wake after Black Jack's interment had arrived in everything from a white stretch limo to the shabbiest wildcatter's pickup, complete with gumbo mud still clotting its oversize wheels. She drove slowly past the house, looking for a parking place, then made a U-turn and eased up on a neighbor's sidewalk between a Jeep and a Lincoln.

Killing the engine, Laura drew a deep breath and

watched an elderly couple entering the house. Without the air conditioner, the late September heat made her perspire under her sedate navy coat dress, but it wasn't the temperature alone that made her nervous. Was Russ inside? She couldn't tell who greeted the visitors. Jack Campbell's unexpected death three days earlier had sent shock waves through the petroleum industry, but it was here that his true friends would appear. Laura had no doubt that there would be plenty of ribald tales and lots of liquor—a proper send-off for a man who'd carved destiny out of Texas dirt and then conquered the world on his own terms.

She hadn't summoned the courage to attend the funeral service, though she knew it had been jammed. But considering Jack had been Rufio's grandfather, decided a brief visit to the home was mandatory. Offering her condolences to Valerie, who, it was rumored, was taking her ex-husband's passing especially hard, was the least Laura could do. Still, she drummed her fingers against the steering wheel, hesitating.

Determinedly, she reached for the door handle, then gave a little moan of despair and dropped her forehead to the steering wheel.

I can't do it.

There. She admitted it to herself. Even if it was the right and appropriate thing to do, facing Russ Campbell for the first time in six years was more than she could ask of herself, even under these circumstances.

Facing Russ would open up a proverbial Pandora's box. She was already playing with fire. She never forgot that through her connection to Logan, there was a chance Russ would hear her name and somehow learn that J.R. was his son. It might be far-fetched, paranoid even, but there it was. She couldn't take that chance.

Straightening, she cranked the car and pulled away from the curb. She'd continue her investigations with Logan and discuss the old hospital where the twins had been born with Valerie at a later date. She'd write her story and sever all ties to the Campbells. The sooner the better.

Satisfied with her decision—or at least relieved—Laura drove out of the neighborhood toward the main thoroughfare. She'd taken the afternoon off and felt at loose ends. Not enough time to return to work, too early to pick Rufio up from Inez's. Her brain clicked over with an idea. There *was* something she could do that might eventually help solve the mystery of Jake and Zach's separation.

Thirty minutes later, Laura pulled up in front of Lillian Hampstead's Tudor town home. Even before she rang the bell, she knew the place was deserted. Evidently, the former nurse was still on her extended vacation. Frustration filled Laura as she returned to her car.

Forgetful or not, there were questions only Lillian could answer about Zach and Jake's separation and about Tom Barnette's involvement in the adoption, and Laura was determined to get to the bottom of things. She and Zach Rawlings went back a long way, to the time she was just a cub reporter and he was a beat cop, and if she could help uncover how he and his brother had come to be separated at birth, then it was the least she could do for an old friend.

Obviously, since neither Jake nor Zach had physical problems, Lillian's recollections about an infant with a heart ailment had been in error, but as the old woman had said, she had seen a lot of babies during her years of service. Maybe with a little more careful probing,

Lillian might remember something useful. Besides, curiosity was a powerful motivator, and Laura certainly had her share of it.

If I could only locate the old lady!

Deciding it was worth a try, Laura drove to the town home complex manager's office.

"Yes, sir, Mr.—" Laura glanced at the nameplate on the rotund, fiftyish man's desk "—Galloway. I'm very anxious to get in touch with Miss Hampstead. Did she happen to indicate to you when she was returning from her trip?"

"Well, now, let me see." Galloway pushed his half-glasses down his nose and thumbed through a messy box of index cards. "No, ma'am, I don't have a record of it, and that sure is queer. Usually we know to the day when our tenants are returning. Have to get the yards in order and that sort of thing. I'd guess she'd be back in a couple of weeks, though. You know how these elderly ladies like their own beds." He scratched his nose. "Howsoever, seems I recollect her saying something about a cruise after that bus tour to the northwest. Maybe Alaska?"

Laura barely contained her groan of impatience. "That's no good. Um, look, if I could even reach her by phone that would be a big help. Do you happen to have her nephew's phone number? Maybe he has her itinerary, and I could contact him."

Mr. Galloway frowned. "Nephew? Miss Lillian hasn't got a nephew that I know of."

Laura blinked in surprise. "Are you sure? I'm positive she told me it was her nephew who insisted she move into this complex—for security reasons, she said. In fact, I had a hard time tracking her down in the first place because there was no forwarding address from her last location.''

''I'm very sure,'' Galloway said firmly. ''We've talked. Poor lady. Except for a couple of distant cousins, she's all alone in the world, got no one at all. It's really sad to be that old and all by yourself, don't you think?''

This fabricated nephew of Lillian's couldn't be chalked up to vagueness or slip of the memory.

Lillian Hampstead had deliberately lied to her. Why?

Bliss had never guessed that grief could be so clarifying.

Muted conversations swirled through Jack Campbell's home, punctuated by an occasional burst of laughter from the corner of the living room where Russ was holding court, drinking and reminiscing with some oil field buddies about his dad's hoariest adventures. In the opening leading to the dining room where neighbors and friends had set out a buffet for visitors after the funeral service, Logan conversed in a more sedate fashion with an assortment of conservative business acquaintances come to express their condolences. In the sunroom at the rear of the house, Valerie, ultra-chic in black linen but with dark circles under her eyes, sat in a wicker chair surrounded by female friends while Ben Lattimer hovered protectively in the background.

Bliss glanced into the black brew in her coffee cup and felt the knot of loss swell in her chest. Despite outward appearances, none of them were dealing very well with losing Jack. With a murmur of distress, Bliss walked through the crush into the tiled kitchen to deposit her cup in the sink. Plates and glasses were stacked haphazardly on the counters. Unmindful of her blue silk sheath, she began to run water in the sink, welcoming the task—any task—that would take her mind off the pain of her loss.

Of course, it was impossible. Up to her elbows in suds, she still knew that Jack—her foster father for so long—was really gone. She'd cried until the tears wouldn't come any longer, wondering how she'd ever get along without his blustering and fussing and loving. She supposed she'd endure, just as others who'd lost a parent had endured, but oh, it was hard!

The only benefit to her grief was a certainty that had come to her in the midst of her shock and disbelief. She had been given a clearness of thought that made her understand that no matter what had happened between her and Logan up to this point, it wasn't going to work. And to hope for more, to hold on to illusions, was only to prolong an even greater agony.

It added a new layer of pain to her grief to realize this, yet at the same time, Bliss felt a sense of relief at the understanding and her decision. It was time to go. She had the rest of her life to think about, and she was certain that Logan Campbell would not play a part in it. They were oil and water, fire and ice, and their worlds would never connect except on the most basic level.

And she knew in her deepest soul that it wasn't enough for her. To continue anything with him, hoping against hope that he could give her what she needed, would only bring bitterness and disappointment and more pain. As hard as it was, finishing with Logan once and for all was the only reasonable solution for a woman who was going to do her best to survive.

Though neither one of them had time or inclination to talk in depth since Jack's death, to his credit, Logan had made one or two faltering attempts to raise the subject of their affair. She'd avoided him on all accounts and cut him off ruthlessly, afraid of her weakness where he was concerned. Perhaps he assumed grief accounted for her coldness. But if he decided that she was reverting to the type of woman he'd always thought her to be, so much the better. She wasn't going to have him assuming any guilt or responsibility simply because she'd been fool enough to admit to him he'd been the first man to take her to the limits of sensuality and physical love, not even if her heart was breaking.

Bliss rinsed a glass and set it in the dish drainer, glad the kitchen was deserted. She was tough. Hadn't Jack raised her to be self-reliant, adaptable, able to take on the world? As difficult as it was, she'd survive without Logan, too.

She blinked back a tear. It was just going to be so damned *hard.*

"You shouldn't be doing this." Valerie drifted to Bliss's side, setting her cup and saucer on the cabinet. She looked beautiful, as usual, but terribly weary, and her dark eyes held shadows instead of their usual sparkle. Bliss wondered how long those shadows would last. "Someone else can see to this."

"It helps to keep my hands busy," Bliss said, stacking the last plate in the drainer and reaching for a tattered dish towel.

How like a man to hang on to something comfortable instead of replacing it, she thought as she dried her hands. Not for the first time, she wondered why neither Jack nor Valerie had remarried. With a shrug, she decided some matters of the heart were simply imponderable.

"I understand," Valerie murmured. She gave the

kitchen a distracted look. "I'd be cleaning out cabinets if I thought I could get away with it."

"Are you all right? Can I get you anything?"

Valerie eased onto a kitchen stool at the center island and gave Bliss a wobbly smile. "Thank you, *chére*, but all I want is a little breathing room. Ben just left, and I've had all the sympathetic chitchat I can stand for a while."

"Maybe I should take you to the hotel."

Valerie shook her head. "No, we'll both do our duty, won't we? It's the least we can do for Jack. God, I'm going to miss that man."

The sudden crystalline sparkle in Valerie's eyes had Bliss tearing off a paper towel and passing it to her, then grabbing one to blot her own moist eyes. "Yeah, me, too."

Crumpling the towel, Valerie caught Bliss's hand, squeezed it hard and released it. "In case I never get a chance to say this again, I just want you to know that I think Jack did a hell of a job with you. You do him proud."

Bliss blinked, taken aback. "Thank you."

"I know we never had a chance to be very close, but I admire you more than I can say. You've got spunk and talent and a certain...freedom about you that I've always envied."

"Me?" Surprise brought color to Bliss's pale cheeks. "Oh, Val, how can you say that? I've always thought if I could only be more like you, so chic and charming and grounded, with roots and a real sense of place in the world."

"Ah, *chére*," Valerie said with a soft, sad laugh, "why do we always wish for what we don't have? Like

Jack and me. You know I never stopped loving him, not even for a minute."

"Then why..." Bliss shook her head. "No, that's none of my business."

"Why weren't we together? Because sometimes people are fools." Valerie sighed. "We just couldn't live together for long without tearing it apart again. Too stubborn or stupid to give enough, I guess, and that's something I'll regret to *my* dying day."

"We all make mistakes," Bliss said, knowing the banality was awkward and inept. To cover her discomposure, she went to the empty coffeepot, reaching for filters and coffee to replenish the brew. Not all the guests would want Russ's offering of bourbon and branch water.

"That we do," Valerie agreed. Her gaze narrowed. "So you'll have to forgive an interfering mother when she asks what's going on with you and Logan."

Bliss nearly dropped the carafe. "Nothing. At least nothing but our usual cat and dog routine. Don't worry about it."

"You might lie to someone else and get away with it, *chére*, but not me," Valerie said firmly. "You're in love with him, aren't you?"

Coffee grounds scattered over the countertop. Swallowing, Bliss scooped together a pile and threw it into the filter basket, then snapped on the machine.

Valerie refused to take her silence for an answer. "Well, aren't you?"

How could she deny it? She turned and faced Valerie defiantly. "Yes, but it doesn't matter."

"Not matter? What else could be more important? Of course it matters."

"Not if we take after you and Jack." Bliss closed

her eyes and drew a deep breath. "It's an impossible situation."

"But you could make him very happy, and yourself while you're at it."

Bliss shook her head. "Val, it's no good. Please, leave it alone."

"I know Logan's not an easy man. In many ways, he's just like his father. Separating the boys the way we did..." Valerie's expression grew sorrowful. "It seemed best at the time, for several reasons, but now, looking back, I see how Logan always felt he had something to prove to Jack. He's always taken his responsibilities far too seriously, making demands on himself I never asked. He didn't have to take control of Gaspard Enterprises, or take on the legal aspects of Campbell Drilling, but it isn't in his nature to shirk what he feels are his obligations. I see now he somehow thought that would make his father love him more."

On an instinctual level, Bliss had always known this, but to hear it put into words brought a staggering sorrow for the burdens Logan had accepted even from a young age. "Oh, Val..."

"Logan has to accept that he never lost Jack's love in the first place, that there's nothing to prove and never was. Jack loved both of his boys with his whole heart. It was just circumstances that created those doubts in Logan, and Jack and I will both have to answer for that." The coffeepot had finished its cycle, and Valerie joined Bliss at the counter to pour herself a fresh cup. "You could help Logan figure that out, Bliss."

Pain seared Bliss's heart. "It wouldn't work. We're from two completely different worlds. I'm just not what Logan needs, and he's made that abundantly clear."

Valerie uttered a completely unladylike expletive that

told Bliss exactly what she thought of that sentiment. "You're exactly what he needs to keep him out of that rut he's heading for. If you truly love him, *chére*, isn't he worth fighting for?"

Bliss buried her face in her hands, overwhelmed. "You don't understand."

Valerie set down her cup and gently pried Bliss's hands away so she could see into her eyes. "I understand all too well. But don't give up like I did, Bliss. Don't settle for less than everything you can have, that you deserve. A mother's instincts seldom lie, and I know you and Logan could be very happy together if you'll work at it. And if it's one thing I can do for Jack Campbell, it's try to see that our boys are happy, and you, too."

"I wish I could tell you I'll try," Bliss said, her throat thick. "But I can't, Val. I—I've already made my decision. When I leave here today, I'm going home to pack."

Alarm widened Valerie's eyes. "But where are you going?"

"I'm making a clean break with Campbell Drilling. I've got time now while Logan attends to the paperwork to settle the estate, so I'm going to look around the country for a while, find a place to set up my charter service."

"But—"

Gently, Bliss slipped her hands free. "It's what I want, Valerie."

"What you want, or what you're willing to settle for?"

"At this point," Bliss answered, her tone bleak, "there's no difference."

"Is everything all right in here?" Frowning, Logan

stood in the doorway watching the two women. In his dark suit, he looked impeccably handsome, wonderfully heart-stopping and totally unattainable. Bliss knew that she was doing the right—the only—thing.

"We're fine," she said, then turned and gave Valerie a hug and a whispered, "I'm sorry."

She left the kitchen, passing Logan with a composed expression as he took a solicitous step toward his mother. Without pausing, Bliss wended her way through the crowd of visitors, caught Russ's eye for a brief wave, then retrieved her purse from the hall table and went outside to her car.

It was time to go. Her mind was set. And her heart would mend. Someday.

Driving his truck through the late afternoon traffic congestion toward the airport, Russ glanced at his mother's pale features in concern. The wake the day before had left Russ with a mild hangover and a sense of emptiness. With Jack's passing he'd lost not only his father, but also his best friend. It was going to take some time to get over that.

"Are you sure you're up to the flight, Mom?" he asked. "That was a pretty rough headache you had last night."

Valerie straightened her shoulders under her ivory knit tunic and gave him a wan smile. "It's better. And I'm ready to have my own things about me again. Home is the best medicine I can think of."

"I'm sure you're right. But I'm going to miss you."

She patted his hand on the seat beside her. "I'm as close as a phone call. Besides, you and Logan will have a lot to do, getting the business settled and deciding about the house."

Russ turned onto an access road leading to a parking lot. "It'll all get done, and in double-quick time, if I know my brother. And a thousand times better than if I'm standing around in the way. Still, it's going to be quiet around here with both you and Bliss gone."

Valerie's arched brows drew together in a worried frown. "She's already left town? I had hoped she might change her mind."

"Hightailed it for parts unknown," Russ quipped, but his mouth flattened in a stern line. "I hope she goes off and has a high old time with that François fellow. Best thing for her."

"Why do you say that?"

He hesitated, then said baldly, "Because Logan's been messin' with her, Mom."

"Well, of course he has, *chér*," Valerie returned in a calm tone. "And about time. He's been totally head over heels for the lady for years."

"What?" Gritting his teeth, Russ slid the vehicle into a parking space, killed the engine, then turned to look askance at his mother. "Mom, the last thing Bliss needs is a heartbreaking playboy like Logan toying with her affections. She may act tough, but she's soft as a marshmallow inside."

"All the more reason for her to depend on someone strong like Logan."

"I can't believe this." Staring at his unflappable mother, Russ felt his cheeks go hot, then cold. "You can't believe that Bliss and Logan, that the two of them... Not together. Why, Dad's probably rattling the pearly gates this very minute at the very idea."

Valerie's soft laugh was a surprising grace note to his outburst. "Russell, it's the very thing your father wanted for those two."

Dumbfounded, he shook his head. "I don't believe it."

With a show of impatience, Valerie began to gather her purse and check her plane ticket. "Really, Russ, sometimes I swear you see only what you want to. When Bliss decided she wanted her inheritance, why do you think Jack sent her directly to Logan?"

"Because...because he's always handled Campbell Drilling's legal affairs."

She gave a negligent wave. "But to have her confront him face-to-face? There were a thousand easier ways to work things out. But the last time your father and I were together in Acapulco, we agreed that by forcing them to work together, they might both realize how much they've always cared for each other and work things out. Of course, we had no idea that there'd be a plane crash, and then Jack..."

She broke off, digging in her bag for a lace-edged handkerchief to dab at the moisture that appeared in the corner of her eye. "But now I don't know what's happened between them. Maybe when things settle down again..." Biting her lip, she gave a helpless shrug. "Children can be so difficult sometimes."

Totally astounded, Russ dragged a hand along the nape of his neck. "I can't believe what I'm hearing, Mom! Logan's a user. He'll just hurt Bliss, if he hasn't already. If you think I'm going to let that shyster—"

"She may be your little sister, but they're both adults now, Russ, and they don't need your permission or mine. It's not like when they were kids down in Mexico."

He gulped. "You know about that?"

"Certainly." Valerie's lips compressed in indignation. "I'm not totally blind where my children are con-

cerned, you know. And it's not your place to come between them if they can find a way to solve their
differences, is that clear?''

"I won't let him hurt her," he growled, jerking his
keys out of the ignition.

"Since Bliss is gone, I suppose that question is moot
for the moment."

"At least there's something to be thankful for. Shows
she still has some sense left." Russ's grumbling ground
to a halt as sudden realization hit him in the gut.
"Did...did you say you were with Dad in Acapulco?"

Valerie's smile was bittersweet. "Yes."

Reeling, he tried to take in the implications. "You
and Dad?"

She nodded. "Twice a year for the past twenty-five
years. More, if we could make it." Her smile grew
sweeter, memories rushing in to help heal the grief.
"Oh, the times we had. Jack Campbell could always
make my blood pound."

"*You* were the hot number he gallivanted off to
see?"

Her expression was just the teeniest bit exasperated,
her feminine pride tweaked at his astonishment. "Don't
look so flabbergasted, Russ. Even parents are entitled
to a little romance occasionally. And just because your
father and I couldn't live together didn't mean we ever
stopped loving each other."

Russ was red-faced. His mind spun as he sought to
assimilate this very different picture of two people he
thought he'd known so well. "I see."

Valerie patted his hand again. "No, I doubt if you
do, and you won't until you find the right woman yourself and settle down."

"As much trouble as it causes, I'm not looking, that's for sure!"

She eyed him narrowly. "You never told me, but I know there was someone special once. It'll happen again, and this time, I hope you won't blow it."

Somehow his mother was seeing too much, her words touching places deep within him he'd boarded over and ignored like an abandoned house for a long time.

"I guess I'll just have to take my chances, but don't count on any grandchildren from me," he said gruffly.

Valerie shook her head impatiently. "I won't say any more, but you and Logan both have a lot to learn about matters of the heart. That's why I don't want you interfering with him and Bliss. They'll have to find their own way."

"I can't make any promises about that."

"You'll have to accept it if it's their choice, Russell."

"I think Bliss's leaving has made it clear what her choice is," Russ said with some relief.

"Unfortunately, you may be right." Disappointment and regret clouded Valerie's eyes. She glanced at her watch. "We'd better go or I'll miss my flight."

Russ came around to open her door and retrieved her luggage from the back seat. They hurried across the hot pavement toward the sliding glass doors leading into the terminal. Russ gave the baggage to the skycap, then draped an arm around his mother's shoulders.

"All this has me floored, Mom, but I'm glad we talked."

"I am, too. We don't get to do enough of it." Valerie brushed his hair from his forehead as she had when he was a little boy, then said impulsively. "Why don't you come home with me for a few days? It'll do us both good.''

He'd grown up rough and ready with Jack and never regretted a moment of it, but there had been times when he'd missed his mother desperately. He was tempted, not so much for the chance to visit and decompress, but for the opportunity to get to know the woman she'd just revealed to him—a woman who'd loved his father and made a life that wasn't the norm, that wasn't at all what was expected of the belle of New Orleans society.

"Well," he said, "Logan—"

"Can cope perfectly well on his own for a while. Staying busy here will help him get over…things.''

Things like Jack's death and Bliss's leaving? Russ wondered. She could be right, though he had his doubts about whether Logan was capable of caring enough about any woman to even notice that Bliss was gone. Damn him. No doubt that was the real reason she'd taken off, rather than her cockamamie tale of scouting out charter service sites. The urge to plant a fist in his brother's handsome face was fast, intense.

"We could probably all use a little breathing space," he said slowly.

"Then you'll come?"

Russ couldn't resist the suddenly hopeful light in his mother's eyes. If he could be a help to her during this time, even a little, how could he refuse?

"Yeah. But I'm bringing the trailer over so I can have my own space.''

Valerie shrugged. "Fine.''

The suite was empty. Silent. Alone. Like his soul.

Logan dropped his suit coat onto the leather sofa, gazed out the wide windows at the lights blazing in downtown Dallas and listened to nothing. He couldn't even hear the hum of the air-conditioning.

His mother had gone back to New Orleans. Russ, damn him, had bailed out of his responsibilities and gone with her. And Bliss was nowhere to be found.

With an angry snort, he grabbed up the room service menu and began to thumb through it. Well, to hell with them. He didn't need any of them. Or anybody.

A sudden surge of weariness made Logan's shoulders feel as though they weighed a ton. Despite his growling belly, he dropped the menu back onto the tabletop and slumped to the sofa. Jack's death, the funeral and the thought of all the work ahead of him was finally taking its toll. His head lolled on the rolled edge of the couch. After all, even the strongest man could keep up appearances only so long before he cracked.

Not that he was close to that. No, sir. Not the golden boy. He was made of sterner stuff. Just because a woman had twisted him inside out then left him stewing in his own juices didn't mean he wasn't capable of adjusting. After all, he'd never expected more from Bliss Abernathy than what he'd gotten.

But it rankled that he'd allowed himself to be blindsided by passion even for a moment. So they'd enjoyed each other for a brief time, so what? They were both adults, capable of a no-frills fling, even if the startling revelation of her virgin state had caught him off-guard and aroused a basic male possessiveness. She'd made her choices, as had he.

It didn't surprise him at all that she'd reverted to type, leaving town without so much as a goodbye. Flighty and impulsive and totally outrageous and inappropriate, that was Bliss to the core. At least when he'd broken off a liaison, he'd had the good breeding to send flowers.

Well, so be it.

Logan grabbed up the TV remote control and began flipping through the channels, trying to fill the silence rumbling through his brain. He and Bliss had been caught in a pressure cooker, and things had gotten out of hand. They'd been off balance from the start, but now things would get back to normal.

Yes, that was it. They'd finally satisfied the itch that had haunted them both for years, answered a few questions, settled some old scores. It was finished. Even if—when—they saw each other again, there would never be that urgent need to investigate a chemistry that had bubbled between them for far too long. Hell, it might even improve their relationship. They might even get to be friends eventually.

Yeah, right.

Logan placed a hand over his chest, wondering why his heart felt like an empty hole.

A familiar voice sounded from the TV and Logan straightened abruptly, his finger stilling on the remote. What he saw made him scowl.

Tom Barnette, clad in a plaid good ol' country boy shirt, sat on a grassy lawn surrounded by his family, talking about the good he would do the state of Texas. Vignettes flashed in rapid succession, showing the competent, compassionate lawyer at work, the eager candidate shaking hands, the loving grandfather fishing with his two grown daughters' young sandy-haired sons while Tom's svelte and elegant wife served lemonade.

Here was something Logan could focus on. Hadn't he promised Jack to bring Tom Barnette down? Well, he hadn't forgotten, and it was just the job he needed, along with settling the probate on Campbell Drilling and paying Bliss off to get the damned woman out of his head once and for all.

The scent of the hunt excited him, made him forget his fatigue, his sadness, his losses. He began making a mental list. When all else failed, there was always work.

Chapter Twelve

Laura Ramirez picked up the phone in her tiny reporter's cubical, hesitated, then punched in the New Orleans number Logan Campbell's secretary had just given her. The clatter of word processors and urgent conversations swirled through the newspaper's busy city room, but she tuned out the noise, intent on passing on the information she'd just managed to pry out of Zach Rawlings.

The housekeeper who answered the phone at Gaspard House didn't have anything encouraging to say. "No, ma'am, I'm not exactly sure where Mr. Logan Campbell can be found today. He's been in and out of town over the past ten days a good half a dozen times. Settling up his father's affairs and all, you know. However, Mr. Russell's just come in—"

"No, that's all right," Laura interrupted hastily. "Er, but perhaps if Mrs. Campbell is available I could have a word with her?"

Valerie Gaspard Campbell's voice was warm when she came on the line. "Laura, how lovely to hear from you. What can I do for you today?"

Laura swiveled her padded office chair and curled the phone cord around a finger. "I've been meaning to call to offer my condolences, Valerie, and I'm looking for Logan. Would you happen to know where I can find him?"

"Thank you, dear, that's kind of you. Actually, Logan's schedule has been frantic, working on Jack's estate and trying to hold the fort down here, as well. You'll probably be able to catch him at Campbell Drilling here in town at some point. Russell is headed that way this afternoon, too, and he could give him a message. Is it something important?"

"Perhaps. I don't know how much you know about Logan's interest in Tom Barnette...."

"Enough." Through the telephone, Valerie's tone was suddenly acid with disapproval. "I'm not sure my son's vendetta against the man is justified."

"Well, as they say, where there's smoke, there's fire," Laura said. "And I just got unofficial word that the state attorney general is planning a full-fledged investigation of the complaints against Aegean Insurance. It seems the Campbells aren't the only ones with a beef against the candidate."

"Unofficial?"

"From a very reliable source."

"Ah," Valerie guessed, "Zach."

Laura smiled at the other woman's astuteness. "You never heard it from me."

"I suppose we'll see where this leads," Valerie said with a sigh. "I'll try to pass on your message."

"Thanks, and I'll keep trying to catch Logan at the Campbell Drilling office." Laura picked up a pen and tapped it against her notebook. "One other thing, if it's not too much trouble?"

"Of course."

"I'm still trying to find out more about the night Zach and Jake were born."

Valerie laughed. "It was a wild night. Stranded in that tiny little town, the storm knocking out the lights, no doctor—and double duty. It wasn't the anesthetic that made me cuss like a sailor that night!"

"Do you recall the nurse on duty?"

"Let's see—Hampton? Hampshire?"

"Lillian Hampstead. She was also running a home for unwed mothers at the time."

"I remember she was certainly no-nonsense. Not a comforting word from her to me or any of the other mothers-to-be, that's for sure. Of course, everyone was rather frazzled, but I remember thinking she was a cold-hearted witch—probably the drugs talking. Why, is something wrong?"

Laura chewed her lip. "Just a few things she's said don't quite add up."

"You mean she's still alive? Why, she must be close to eighty."

"Well, she was a little vague when I interviewed her. I suppose age has caught up with her. Do you recall anything about Abby—Zach's and Jake's mother? Evidently, she was in labor the same time you were. Was there anyone there with her? Family members or boyfriend?"

"I wasn't paying much attention," Valerie admitted ruefully. "Until all this came out about Jake and Zach, I had no idea there was another set of—"

A young male journalism intern tapped on Laura's cubical and shoved a sheaf of faxed sheets concerning a story due before day's end into her hand. She grimaced, nodded her thanks and forced her mind back to what Valerie Campbell was saying.

"—twins born then. Jack was in such a hurry to get us all to Lubbock that he whisked us out of there barely a day later, against the doctor's orders. We paid the price later for that foolishness, spent some time in the hospital in Lubbock, all of us. Russell had an especially hard time of it. He still hates hospitals. You can be sure I never let Jack forget it, either.

"That's how we met Ben and Retha Lattimer, you know, and I've always had rather a soft spot for Jake, the little rapscallion."

The same young journalist who'd given her the fax papers poked his head around the corner and held up a piece of paper that said the managing editor wanted to see her ASAP.

"Mrs. Campbell, I've got to run," she said, "but I'd really like to help Zach and Jake figure out what happened, so if you remember anything else, anything at all, no matter how small, could you give me a call?"

"Certainly, my dear. I'm sorry I went on so."

Assuring the other woman that she hadn't gone on, and with another round of thanks, Laura hung up, the faxed documents hanging forgotten in her hand as she stared into space.

There were a lot of pieces floating around in her head, all parts of the same puzzle. When would she get that one piece of information that would make them all come together with a clear picture of what had happened that night?

Bars of light from the six o'clock setting sun pierced the slatted blinds in Campbell Drilling's spartan offices. Plain metal desks and ancient typewriters, overflowing file cabinets, a coffeepot crusted with a decade's worth of crud, hard hats and work gloves, a water dispenser topped by a large plastic bottle, copy machines and phones—an oilman's paradise. Outside, the work yards were empty except for Gusher prowling his territory. Parked in a corner of the yard, Bliss's and Russ's trailer was dark and deserted.

Inside, the secretaries had gratefully packed up and gone home after another grueling day under Logan's direction. He'd been doing his best to pull Campbell Drilling's fat out of the proverbial fire, getting the probate settled so that business could continue as usual, mollifying investors, coming up with plans to salvage the company. In a minute he would get up and adjust the blinds to cut the glare out of his eyes, but right now he planted his hands on the piles of paper cluttering his dad's desk and smiled a grim smile of satisfaction.

Laura Ramirez's phone call about the attorney general's investigation into Aegean Insurance was the first domino in a line that was finally going to fall his way, and down with it would come Tom Barnette, just as he'd promised his father. In the past week and a half, good news like this had been scarce indeed, so he latched on to it with the desperation of a drowning man. It didn't go a long way toward filling the emptiness inside, but it was a start.

"What's got you looking like the cat who swallowed the canary?"

Squinting against the light, Logan scowled as his brother materialized at the office's front door. Russ wore his usual Campbell Drilling shirt and jeans, as opposed to Logan's dress shirt and tie.

Logan shoved a stack of papers into a more secure position on the desk and rose. "About time you showed up."

Russ tossed a flight bag carelessly into a chair. "You didn't answer my question."

"We've got the SOB."

"Who?"

"Haven't you been paying attention? Barnette, of course." Logan's expression took on a feral quality. He felt the excitement and the urgency building, a distraction he welcomed so he wouldn't have to think about other things. "I've got a source who assures me the attorney general's opening up an investigation. Now's the time to move. I've arranged a meeting in Austin tomorrow with the witness my PI located and the chief investigator. She'll testify she saw Barnette destroying documents related to Aegean Insurance."

Russ stuck his hands in his pockets and rocked back on his heels. "So?"

Logan's irritation increased. Couldn't his brother see beyond the next oil rig or latest sweet thing in a short skirt? "So the odds are it'll lead to an indictment. The timing couldn't be more perfect. It'll be a death blow for Barnette's political ambitions, cost him time, money, humiliation."

"I guess you've got it all figured out."

Logan stiffened at Russ's tone. "Somebody had to, since you conveniently bowed out of the decision-making process around here. You know this place isn't going to run itself now that Jack's gone. And it seems you've been too busy to tend to business."

"Don't start in on me, Logan," Russ warned. "I wanted some time with Mom. You're the one who's obsessed with this Barnette business. And things will work out. They always do."

"Easy for you to say, since I'm doing all the work."

Russ shrugged. "Your choice." His tawny eyes met his brother's in challenge. "Seems as though you're running so hard eventually you're liable to catch your own tail, and that isn't healthy.''

"Maybe you're just feeling a little left out." Logan took a document from the desktop and shoved it at Russ. "Here. Take a little responsibility for once and have a look at this. It'll need your approval now, too."

Russ took the papers, scanned them, tossed them onto the desk. "Bliss's settlement. You're in an all-fired hurry to pay her off."

Logan circled the desk, avoiding Russ's eyes, aware that he'd echoed Bliss's accusation. Making the settlement was going to put the business into an even greater financial pinch, but it was one decision he was going to see went through, rational or not. Damned if he wouldn't put an end to things once and for all. As if a few pieces of paper could end what was between them.

He went to the coffee table, found there was no more than an inch of sludge in the bottom of the pot and set it down with a sound of disgust. "That's what she said she wants."

"Great. So let's give it to her. Where do I sign?"

Logan felt the heat rise in his neck, turned and shot a sharp glance at his brother. "What do you mean by that?"

Russ's face grew stony. "That the sooner she's got what she needs and gets the hell away from you, the better I'm going to like it."

Anger bubbled in the pit of Logan's belly. What was between him and Bliss had nothing to do with what Russ liked or didn't like. With an effort, Logan kept his voice low, but the menace in it was clear. "I was wondering when you'd get around to that."

Russ shoved a hand across the nape of his neck, color rising beneath his tan. "Yeah, well, finding the two of you in bed didn't exactly make my day."

"It's none of your business."

"The hell it's not!" Russ took a step forward, his fists clenching. "Mom said to butt out, but I can't. Not when Bliss's happiness is on the line. We both know you're her worst nightmare, right on a par with that slime bag Barnette."

"Now you're getting personal, brother," Logan growled. "Especially if you ran and tattled to Mother about something you had no business to."

"I didn't have to tell her anything. She's got some lamebrained notion about you and Bliss getting together and living happily ever after." Russ poked Logan hard in the chest. "But get this. Bliss deserves better than a roll in the hay with a spoiled playboy, and that's all you can offer."

Logan gritted his teeth as fury seethed within him. Russ's condemnation pricked him in all his most vulnerable places. What did he have to offer Bliss? She was a magnificent woman, worthy of the deepest devotion, of family and commitment and time, and he'd never shown her anything but hostility and contempt and disappointment, despite the hottest sex he'd ever experienced. Small wonder she'd decided to cut her losses where he was concerned. After all, she was the smartest, most courageous woman he'd ever known, not one to suffer fools gladly, and Logan was beginning to think he'd been nothing but a fool where she was concerned. But knowing that didn't make the bitter pill Russ was trying to force down his throat any more palatable.

"I'm warning you, Russ, don't push it."

Russ's laughter came out a derisive bark. "I know you, Logan, and I'm telling you right now that to get to Bliss again you're going to have to go through me."

Logan's temper exploded. "That can be arranged."

Instead of merely pushing Russ's hand away as he'd intended, the blow Logan landed on his brother's solar plexus sent him spinning backward over a desk. Papers and folders and pens went flying. Russ surfaced with a roar, catapulting over the desktop in a flying tackle that brought Logan to the floor in a flurry of punches.

Rolling, wrestling, chairs toppled and the water dispenser crashed to the floor, the tall bottle gurgling out its contents. Russ slammed a fist into Logan's nose, crunching cartilage so hard he saw stars. Logan retaliated with a blow that split Russ's lip. Slopping around on the wet floor, they tussled to a draw, hands twisted in the other's clothing, breath coming hard and fast, neither one willing to cry uncle, but both realizing almost simultaneously that they were too evenly matched for either one to claim victory.

Blood smearing his chin, Russ pinned one of Logan's shoulders to the sopping tile. One eye already beginning to swell, Logan grappled with Russ's collar, immobilizing him in a stranglehold.

"You get out and stay out of Baby Sister's life." Russ grunted the order.

Logan wheezed against the pain in his battered ribs. The back of his shirt was soaked from the still-gushing water bottle, and Russ's hair was plastered against his forehead. "That's between me and Bliss."

"You don't want her."

"The hell I don't!" Logan, so calm, so collected in every other venue, was shouting his lungs out. Over the past days he'd pretended that Bliss's going was what he'd wanted, the best thing for everyone, that it hadn't hurt. He was not only a fool, he was a liar.

"You only say that because she was smart enough to get the hell out of Dodge and you're used to having everything your own way." Looming over his brother,

Russ panted out his accusations. "Well, Bliss rates better than the likes of you, *Golden Boy.*"

Infuriated, Logan twisted under Russ's hold, reversing their positions with a surprising burst of power. "Don't you think I know it?"

Russ glared into his brother's identical tawny eyes. "Then why won't you leave her alone?"

"Because I need her, dammit!"

"*You* need? You selfish bastard." Russ reared back a fist.

Logan caught his twin's hand in mid-flight, but he might as well have taken the blow for the force of the impact that hit him—hard, implacable, undeniable, and eternal. "I love her, Russ. I love her!" The words held conviction, disbelief, wonder.

Russ relaxed against Logan's grip, and a faint smile quirked his puffy lip. "It's about damned time you realized it."

Overwhelmed by his admission, Logan rolled off his brother into a sitting position, ignoring the water saturating his slacks.

He had never felt so miserable, so useless. He'd fought everything that Bliss evoked in him, all the passion and tenderness and life, and had driven her away. And when she'd gone, she'd taken the best part of him, the part that made him human, not some high-toned working machine whose emotions were simply switched on or off at his convenience. The future without her loomed empty and futile.

Burying both hands in his hair, he groaned. "God, I've made a mess of things."

Russ came up on an elbow, cautiously checking for damage, then sat in a way that mirrored his twin. "So go fix them. Isn't that what you do best?"

"She'll take one look at me and kick me in the teeth," Logan said.

"More than likely," Russ agreed, gingerly fingering his lip. "But if she feels the same way you do?"

"I don't know."

"You too chicken to find out?"

Logan raised his head to glare at Russ. "You want another smack?"

"Well, are you?"

"I guess I'll find out." Determination firmed his sore jaw as he levered himself from the floor, then extended a hand to Russ. "I've got nothing left to lose."

Taking his brother's hand, Russ vaulted to his feet, then raised an eyebrow. "Yeah? What about all this urgent business stuff, Campbell Drilling on hold, the Tom Barnette thing tomorrow?"

Logan didn't even have to think. Everything he'd been working for was absolutely meaningless unless he had Bliss at his side. He only hoped he wasn't too late.

He looked around the tumbled office, realizing how unimportant his agenda had been in the big scheme of things. "Screw it. Let it all go bankrupt. And Barnette, well—Dad's revenge will have to wait. I've got more important things to do."

Russ's expression was astounded. "You can't just walk away."

"Watch me."

"But—"

"If you're so worried about it, you handle it," Logan snapped. "I'm out of here."

"So you mean to go after her?"

"Damn straight."

Russ's eyes narrowed. "You'd better be talking marriage here, or I'm going to have to lay into you again."

"You and what army?"

Russ bristled. "Logan—"

He knew his sudden smile was crooked as he hooked an affectionate arm around Russ's neck. "Yeah. Marriage it is, if she'll have me."

"All right. Then you have my blessing, for what it's worth, just as long as you make her happy."

This charge made Logan gulp. Could he make Bliss happy? He didn't know much about happy marriages, only that there were no guarantees. Would she be willing to risk her heart on a man who'd known too little of what giving and caring really meant? She could teach him, he knew that, and he also knew that he desperately wanted to learn everything about what loving this woman could mean, now and for the rest of their lives.

His voice grew suddenly thick with emotion. "I'll do my best, I promise."

Russ grinned. "I don't envy you, brother. Baby Sister can be damned stubborn."

Releasing his twin, a portion of Logan's euphoria evaporated into worry tainted with desperation. "Yeah, that's what I'm afraid of."

"Then you'd better get busy." Russ flicked Logan's blood-speckled shirt with a fingertip. "After you get cleaned up, of course. Where'd you learn to fight like that?"

"I'm not a Campbell for nothing." Logan gave a critical eye to the both of them, sodden and bloodstained and bruised, then chuckled. "I expect Dad's laughing his butt off right about now."

"You can bet on it." Russ shook his head. "He and Mom—well, I'll tell you about that later. Anyway, good luck with Bliss. Now get your can in gear."

"Right." Logan nodded, plans unfolding in his brain already. He hadn't become a powerful and successful businessman without learning some skills, and he knew

Bliss wasn't indifferent to him. With a little luck, a little charm... He broke off that chain of thought with a grunt of disgust. Who was he trying to kid? He'd eat crow, go down on bended knee, anything to get Bliss to listen to him, to have her hear him when he said he loved her and wanted her in his life forever.

He glanced at Russ. "So, where'd she run off to, anyway?"

Russ blinked in surprise. "You think I know?"

"You mean you don't?" A fission of alarm raced down Logan's spine.

"Haven't heard from her since the funeral."

"She could be anywhere."

Russ nodded, concern etching his features. "With anyone."

A thousand pictures rushed to fill Logan's head, none of them to his liking. "Oh, *hell.*"

"You're a sweet little thing."

"And you're a smooth talker."

"It's been grand. Hadn't had anyone make me feel this special in I don't know how long."

Bliss smiled and squeezed Mittie Powell's gnarled fingers. "The pleasure was all mine, Miss Mittie. I hope we can do it again real soon."

They stood outside a small deli-bakery on Alpine's sunny main street, full of a lunch of hearty brisket sandwiches and cheesecake.

"Anytime you want, honey," Mittie said with a chuckle, moving to where a brand-new shiny blue stepside pickup truck with heavy-duty shocks sat parked beside the curb. "Thanks to that feller of yours, I can get into town a whole lot easier these days. Yes, sir, hated to retire Old Betsy, but I sure do get a lot of envious looks from the teenage boys when I'm driving around in this snazzy contraption.''

"I know Logan will be pleased you like it," Bliss said with a wry twist of her lips. She didn't correct Mittie's assumption about "her feller."

Despite three weeks and the scouting trips to Taos, Memphis, Chapel Hill and Denver that had packed every moment of her time, thinking about Logan was still too painful. She'd thought planning her next move, finding the perfect place to set up a charter service would be the ideal panacea for heartache, but although she'd found several attractive markets that would do very well, nothing felt like home. Her restlessness had driven her here to Alpine on a whim to see Mittie, and she was glad she'd come, even though once she said goodbye to the old lady she wasn't sure where she'd be headed. Not that it mattered much.

But leave it to Mr. Organized to say thanks in a spectacular way. She had to admit, the gesture of a new truck—something the old lady obviously needed—was quite touching, even though it made the basket of feminine goodies—lotions, soaps, bubble baths—that she'd brought Mittie seem paltry by comparison. She hefted the large basket into the passenger door for the old woman.

Mittie settled her battered straw cowboy hat on her grizzled curls and jingled her new set of keys. "Tell you the truth, I'm just as tickled with all these female gewgaws and our little woman talk. Working the land, sometimes I forget what fun it is to be a gal. You look great in them earrings, by the way." She winked. "My new truck ain't the only thing that's getting the once-over around here."

Bliss laughed, setting the silver drops at her ears swinging and her hair flying loose about her shoulders.

A matching silver chain nestled in the V of her sleeveless denim vest, and she'd donned her favorite jeans with the split in the knee. "That settles it. I'm coming to visit on a regular basis. You're definitely good for my ego."

"You'll always be welcome, you and that young man of yours, too." Surprising Bliss, the old lady laid a quick peck on her cheek. "I got to go if'n I want to get the stock watered by sundown. You be happy, now, you hear?"

Waving as Mittie drove away, Bliss fought the sudden lump in her throat. True happiness seemed as far removed from her life as the next solar system. Oh, she could cope. She was hell-on-wheels Bliss Abernathy, wasn't she? But what kind of price was she going to pay for loving a man like Logan Campbell?

Bliss made her way up the sidewalk toward the historic Holland Hotel. Alpine was small, but it had its own Texas charm. Maybe she'd stay a few days before she flew out again to—where? As she entered the hotel's foyer and made her way past the restaurant to her room, she realized the destination didn't matter when all you were doing was running.

Bliss came up short in front of her door, her fingers clenching so tightly around the room key she'd dug from her jeans pocket it cut into her fingers. Determination firmed her jaw. Since when had she run from anything in her life? Jack Campbell had taught her better. She always tackled her problems head on. And Valerie's words echoed in her brain.

"If you truly love him, chére, isn't he worth fighting for?"

Bliss thought about Logan, his tenderness, the vulnerability and doubt that lay underneath all that masculine machismo, the strength of character that made him who he was. Yes, he was worth fighting for! And she could be the complement that completed him, loving him for the man he was, the man he could become with her help. He *needed* her, her exuberance, her joie de vivre, or else he was liable to turn into a driven, bitter old man with no one who really cared about him to draw him up short when he got too big for his britches.

And it wasn't a one-way street. Logan possessed the balance and steadiness that would keep her from leaping before she looked, that would give her the solidity and roots she so desperately wanted. They'd fight like cats and dogs on occasion, of course, but hadn't they always? And now that she knew what making up would be like, how could she be so cowardly as to give up the chance of happiness without so much as a whimper? Why, she hadn't even told him she loved him!

Maybe it wouldn't work. Maybe he was too stubborn to see their potential, but she knew in that moment that she couldn't give up just yet, not without knowing for sure. She could pack, get to the Alpine airport and fly into New Orleans before suppertime if she hurried. Then, by golly, she'd make him listen, and even propose, because she wanted it all with that man. Pride be damned. All he could say was no, and that couldn't hurt any worse than things already did. At least she'd have the satisfaction of knowing she'd given it her best shot.

Taking a deep breath, Bliss inserted the key, opened the door, then froze. Her gaze swept the figure sprawled on her bed, from the scuffed boots, up the faded, form-fitting denims, across the blue Campbell Drilling shirt. But it wasn't Russ propped against the pillows, ankles crossed negligently, but a sandy-haired figment of her imagination with a faint bruise around one eye, evidence that he'd been in—a brawl?

"Lady, you are one hard bird to track down," Logan said.

The air whooshed from her lungs as the door swung shut behind her. It was as if her thoughts had conjured him, and she struggled to form coherent words. "How did you get in here?"

Logan tossed the magazine he'd been reading onto the bedspread and shrugged. "Everybody in this town thinks I'm your fiancé, remember?"

All she really wanted to do was fling herself into his arms, but caution made her hesitate and habit made her retreat into familiar patterns. "Yeah, well, looks can be deceiving, can't they?"

Logan came up off the bed in one fluid movement. "Dammit, Bliss! Don't start. Don't you even want to know why I'm here?"

"It's most likely business." She bit down hard on her lower lip to keep it from wobbling.

Logan cursed and ran a hand through his hair. "I guess I deserved that. And yes, it is business, probably the most important of my life."

So he'd come about her settlement, found her in the back of beyond just to clear up unfinished business and close one more door between them. She felt hope die, but lifted her chin valiantly. "All right, just show me where to sign, but before I do, I've got a few things to say to you, Logan Campbell."

"Like what, *querida?*"

"You are the most stubborn, infuriating man I've ever known, and someone should have kicked your spoiled playboy butt a long time ago."

"Yeah?"

She nodded. "Absolutely. And here's the bottom line, Mr. Businessman. I'm the woman for the job. I can keep you honest."

Something softened behind his eyes, warmed them to molten caramel. He walked to her, stroking her arms so that she shivered, and his voice was silky. "You think so? Why?"

"Because I'm in love with you, damn you." She blinked hard, fighting the prickle of tears. "And I really think we ought to get married."

"Actually, you're not the first woman to say that to me," he murmured.

Pride could only carry her so far. "Well, just forget it then!"

His hands tightened on her when she would have jerked away. "But you're the only woman on earth who'd make me take such a proposal seriously."

"I—I am?"

He brushed her lips in the briefest of kisses. "Only you. I know you're a free spirit, and I'm stuck with my feet on the ground, but I think I've been in love with you all my life. We've already made our mistakes, *querida*. Do you think we can take a chance on getting it right from now on?"

"I—" She gulped, quivering, her hands pressed to his wide chest. Here was the miracle she'd prayed for. She took the leap of faith—and love—without hesitation. "I'm willing to risk it if you are, amigo."

A tension she hadn't realized he'd been containing vanished from him, leaving behind a dazzling smile and a flash of dimples, proving to her endearingly that he hadn't been certain of her, either. He dug in his pocket and opened his palm. "Just to prove to you that great minds work alike, I brought this, hoping, praying..."

Bliss's eyes widened at the sapphire and diamond ring in its antique setting. "Oh, Logan."

"It was Great-grandmother Gaspard's. If you could

wear it for me as my wife, you'll make me the happiest man on the planet."

"Well, I certainly wouldn't want to take the responsibility of making the golden boy unhappy," she said, her voice shaking with a bubbling laughter and the heady euphoria of love.

He slid the ring onto her finger, its perfect fit like a portentous omen of their future. "Brat. Will you ever curb that sassy mouth of yours?"

"Never."

"Thank God." His lips covered hers, and their kiss was tender, possessive, undeniably passionate. Breathing hard, hearts pounding, he pulled her down on the bed. "I guess this officially makes me your fiancé. Forgive me for breaking in?"

She reared up in surprise. "Logan, you didn't!"

He grinned. "Had to pick the lock."

Bliss threw back her head and laughed, rolling onto Logan's chest in delight. "Maybe there's hope for you yet!"

He settled her between his thighs, letting her feel his need as he grasped double handfuls of her hair and set about ravaging her mouth. "You won't be sorry, I promise."

"I'm sure I will, a dozen times a day. And I'll be glad twice as often," she replied. "Hope you can live with chaos."

"I can live with you. And maybe a couple of little ankle biters?"

Her breath caught. "Oh, yes, I want your babies."

"And you can run your charter service out of New Orleans. It won't be all work for me anymore, I swear. Not with you to keep me balanced. Hell, I'll even learn to barbecue."

Her heart melted. "Oh, Logan…"

"Is that all you can say?"

The things his hands were doing to her took her breath, her words, and made her nod soundlessly, a foolish smile on her lips.

Logan chuckled. "Well, that's a first. While I've got you in a weakened condition, what's say we find a justice of the peace? I'm sure there's one around here someplace."

"Oh, no. Valerie would never forgive either of us."

He groaned. "Oh, no, is right. You're not really going to make us go through the orange blossom routine, are you?"

Bliss twined her arms around his neck and gave him a smile that brought a simmering heat to his tawny eyes. "Logan, I want it *all* with you."

He pulled her closer, love tempering his expression with a tenderness that ensnared her heart forever. "*Querida,* you've got it."

Epilogue

A condition. Of the heart.

Dazed, Laura Ramirez made her way through the
lobby of Southwestern Hospital, then looked around un-
certainly. She was supposed to be doing something...
Oh, yes, her car. She needed to get to her car. But she
couldn't remember where she'd parked it.

Fists clenched, white-knuckled on her briefcase, she
stumbled toward an upholstered chair in a secluded al-
cove behind a potted palm. She barely made it before
her knees collapsed. Fear and nausea clogged her throat,
and her breath came in shallow gasps.

J.R. Rufio. Her baby. Oh, God, her baby!

The doctor in the pediatric consulting room she'd just
left had been kind but clear. Rufio's lethargy, his gastric
upsets, his bouts of seemingly unrelated symptoms were
all due to a cardiac condition that could, under the worst
scenario, be life-threatening. There were treatments, and

sometimes, if luck and miracles played a part, the child could even outgrow the malady.

"These things tend to run in families, Ms. Ramirez," the doctor had said. "The more information you can give us, the better."

She'd shaken her head. "No one in my family has ever..."

"What about Rufio's father?"

She'd had to admit she didn't know. "He...he hasn't been in my life since before my son was born."

The doctor's expression was stern. "We can't afford excessive sentimentality here, Ms. Ramirez. Any familial history could be vital to Rufio's well-being."

She understood. Sitting in the lounge chair, plucking at her tailored suit, Laura understood all too well.

But how was she going to tell Russ Campbell that he had a son? That their blazing six-week affair had borne fruit of the most tender kind? And how was she going to explain why she'd kept that secret from him for five long years?

She gulped, battling the wave of fear again—for Rufio, for herself, for a man who'd undoubtedly feel she'd betrayed him. But Rufio had a heart condition, something that couldn't be ignored or denied, no matter what the personal cost.

Tends to run in families...

Like a dash of ice water, a sudden burst of clarity and instinctive comprehension washed over her, making her gasp anew. From somewhere deep in her mind came the memory of her last conversation with Valerie. Russ's mother had said that something was wrong with Russ when he was born. Something about having had a hard time and still hating hospitals. Could it have been a heart condition? She didn't remember. She did recall being interrupted. Maybe she'd missed something important that Valerie had said.

Laura rummaged in her purse for the little notebook that held important phone numbers. She punched in the number of the Gaspard home in New Orleans with a trembling hand. Luckily, Valerie was in—but barely. She was going out the door to a garden club meeting.

"Hello, Laura, how are you?" she asked warmly.

"Fine, Mrs. Campbell," she said, struggling to hold on to her control. The last thing she needed was to give away her feelings to Russ's mom—or to tell her about J.R. She wasn't ready for that yet. "I need to ask you a couple of questions."

"Surely."

"When we spoke the other day, you said Russ had a hard time after he was born, but you didn't say what his problem was."

"I didn't?"

"No."

"He had a hole in his heart."

Laura felt the room dip. Russ had had a heart problem.

"He outgrew the condition," Valerie was saying. "It closed on its own, but it caused us a lot of worry for a few of his early years, let me tell you."

"I imagine it did," Laura said, trying to hide her shock.

"We were just thankful that Logan didn't have one, too."

Laura frowned.

"The doctors said that sometimes both twins would have the condition."

"Twins?" Laura said. "What twins?"

"Why, Logan and Russ of course," Valerie said. She laughed. "Don't tell me you didn't know?"

"No," Laura said in a faint voice, "I didn't."

"Well, they are twins, even though they don't look much alike. Or act alike, for that matter."

Laura's heart pounded in her chest. Her head felt light, as if she were going to pass out.

"I don't want to keep you, Mrs. Campbell," she said, wanting nothing more than to get off the phone and try to put what she'd just heard into some sort of perspective. "But thanks for taking time to talk to me."

"Have you found out something, Laura?" Valerie asked.

"I'm not sure," she said. "I'll let you know."

She and Valerie said their goodbyes and Laura hung up. She covered her face with her hands, not wanting to admit what her heart whispered to her. Dear God! She should have known!

Lillian Hampstead had told her that one of Abby Pickett's twins had a heart condition, which is why she'd decided to let a wealthy family who could afford the medical care adopt the child. But Jake had never had a heart problem, and neither had Zach.

Russ did—or had. Rufio had just been diagnosed with a heart problem—an inherited heart problem.

And Russ and Logan are twins, Laura. Twins. Which means one thing...

Laura pressed her cold hands to her mouth. Could it be true? Had Abby Pickett's and Valerie Campbell's babies been switched at birth? If so, so many things would begin to make sense. Why hadn't she seen it? Why, the elder Campbells' dark coloring hardly matched their sons' fairness, and from all accounts, Abby Pickett had been a lovely blonde whose sons were as brunette as they came. She suddenly remembered something else. The Campbell twins' blood type had been incompatible with Black Jack's. It wasn't clear evidence, but the clues had been right before her eyes the whole time!

Another thing struck her. Had the mix-up been an accident or deliberate?

As a journalist Laura was obligated to find out the truth. All the men involved in this massive mix-up—if that's what it was—deserved to know it, to understand how their lives had been shaped by a set of bizarre circumstances. The implications were life-altering. Laura shuddered. The thought of facing Russ Campbell again, of telling him what she'd done, made her white with trepidation. But this was Rufio's *life* she was dealing with!

Oh, God, what was she going to do?

*   *   *   *   *

Take 4 bestselling love stories FREE

Plus get a FREE surprise gift!

Special Limited-time Offer

Mail to Silhouette Reader Service™

3010 Walden Avenue
P.O. Box 1867
Buffalo, N.Y. 14240-1867

YES! Please send me 4 free Silhouette Special Edition® novels and my free surprise gift. Then send me 6 brand-new novels every month, which I will receive months before they appear in bookstores. Bill me at the low price of $3.34 each plus 25¢ delivery and applicable sales tax, if any.* That's the complete price and a savings of over 10% off the cover prices—quite a bargain! I understand that accepting the books and gift places me under no obligation ever to buy any books. I can always return a shipment and cancel at any time. Even if I never buy another book from Silhouette, the 4 free books and the surprise gift are mine to keep forever.

235 BPA A3UV

Name	(PLEASE PRINT)
Address	Apt. No.
City	State	Zip

This offer is limited to one order per household and not valid to present Silhouette Special Edition® subscribers. *Terms and prices are subject to change without notice. Sales tax applicable in N.Y.

USPED-696

©1990 Harlequin Enterprises Limited

SILHOUETTE WOMEN KNOW ROMANCE WHEN THEY SEE IT.

And they'll see it on **ROMANCE CLASSICS**, the new 24-hour TV channel devoted to romantic movies and original programs like the special **Romantically Speaking—Harlequin™ Goes Prime Time**.

Romantically Speaking—Harlequin™ Goes Prime Time introduces you to many of your favorite romance authors in a program developed exclusively for Harlequin® and Silhouette® readers.

Watch for **Romantically Speaking—Harlequin™ Goes Prime Time** beginning in the summer of 1997.

If you're not receiving ROMANCE CLASSICS, call your local cable operator or satellite provider and ask for it today!

ROMANCE CLASSICS

Escape to the network of your dreams.

See Ingrid Bergman and Gregory Peck in *Spellbound* on Romance Classics.

As seen on TV!
Free Gift Offer

With a Free Gift proof-of-purchase from any Silhouette® book,
you can receive a beautiful cubic zirconia pendant.

This gorgeous marquise-shaped stone is a genuine cubic
zirconia—accented by an 18" gold tone necklace.

(Approximate retail value $19.95)

Send for yours today...
compliments of ▼ *Silhouette*®

To receive your free gift, a cubic zirconia pendant, send us one original proof-of-
purchase, photocopies not accepted, from the back of any Silhouette Romance™,
Silhouette Desire®, Silhouette Special Edition®, Silhouette Intimate Moments®
or Silhouette Yours Truly™ title available at your favorite retail outlet, together with
the Free Gift Certificate, plus a check or money order for $1.65 U.S./$2.15 CAN. (do
not send cash) to cover postage and handling, payable to Silhouette Free Gift Offer. We
will send you the specified gift. Allow 6 to 8 weeks for delivery. Offer good until
March 31, 1998, or while quantities last. Offer valid in the U.S. and Canada only.

Free Gift Certificate

Name: _____

Address: _____

City: _____ State/Province: _____ Zip/Postal Code: _____

Mail this certificate, one proof-of-purchase and a check or money order for postage
and handling to: SILHOUETTE FREE GIFT OFFER 1998. In the U.S.: 3010 Walden
Avenue, P.O. Box 9077, Buffalo, NY 14269-9077. In Canada: P.O. Box 613, Fort Erie,
Ontario L2Z 5X3.

FREE GIFT OFFER
084-KFD

ONE PROOF-OF-PURCHASE
To collect your fabulous FREE GIFT, a cubic zirconia pendant, you must include this
original proof-of-purchase for each gift with the properly completed Free Gift Certificate.

084-KFDR2